D0397316

ALSO BY TATYANA TOLSTAYA

On the Golden Porch

Sleepwalker in a Fog

Pushkin's Children: Writings on Russia and Russians

The Slynx

White Walls: Collected Stories

AETHERIAL
WORLDS

Aetherial Worlds

STORIES

Tatyana Tolstaya

*Translated from the Russian
by Anya Migdal*

Alfred A. Knopf *New York* 2018

THIS IS A BORZOI BOOK
PUBLISHED BY ALFRED A. KNOPF

Compilation copyright © 2018 by Tatyana Tolstaya
English translation copyright © 2018 by Anya Migdal
Original Russian text copyright © Tatyana Tolstaya

www.aaknopf.com

Knopf, Borzoi Books, and the colophon are registered
trademarks of Penguin Random House LLC.

Several stories first appeared in the following publications: *Iowa
Review:* "Smoke and Shadows" (2015). *The New Yorker:* "Aspic" (2016),
"Father" (2015), "See the Reverse" originally appeared in different form
as "See the Other Side" (2007), and "The Square" (2015). *Zoetrope
All-Story:* "Nowhere" and "A Young Lady in Bloom" (2015).

Library of Congress Cataloging-in-Publication Data
Names: Tolstaia, Tatiana, [date]- author. | Migdal, Anya, translator.
Title: Aetherial worlds : stories / Tatyana Tolstaya ;
translated from the Russian by Anya Migdal.
Description: New York : Alfred A. Knopf, 2018. | "Borzoi book."
Identifiers: LCCN 2017032042 | ISBN 9781524732776 (hardcover)
ISBN 9781524732783 (ebook)
Subjects: LCSH: Short stories, Russian—20th century—
Translations into English.
Classification: LCC PG3489.O476 A2 2018 | DDC 891.73/44—dc23
LC record available at https://lccn.loc.gov/2017032042

Jacket photograph: *Touch* by Johan Lilja. Private collection / Bridgeman Images
Jacket design by Stephanie Ross

Manufactured in the United States of America
First Edition

For my father

Contents

Aetherial
Worlds

20/20

My grandfather Aleksey Tolstoy, a famous Russian writer, attended the Saint Petersburg Technological Institute in his youth, starting in 1901, thinking he would like to become an engineer. But he never became one. He described to my father how difficult it was for him studying there.

Here is his professor by the blackboard, addressing the students: "Let's picture a cigarlike object. . . ." And that's it! My young grandpa is in a trance. He is picturing something cigarlike . . . he sees a cigar. . . . You need to clip the end of it before you can smoke it. . . . Golden cutters carefully trim away the dry brown leaves—what wonderful aroma wafts from quality Havana tobacco! . . . Out of nowhere appears a balloon-shaped brandy snifter full of heavy, red-brown cognac, casting golden reflections. . . . Oh, to grasp the glass in your palm, warming it . . . the undulating golden flickers . . . the bluish smoke . . . you inhale it, you tap the cigar to break off the ash. It's dusk, the heavy drapes drawn back. Outside, through the window, there is a crepuscular early evening on snowy Saint Petersburg streets; a sleigh pulled by a courser silently whooshes by—who's rushing, and where? To the theater? To a romantic rendezvous?

Suddenly reality interrupts this waking dream. Chairs thunder, the professor erases the blackboard, wiping away formulas interesting and useful to any engineer—"See you next time, gentlemen!"

Grandfather never finished his studies at the Institute; he committed himself wholly to literature, becoming famous for, among other things, his historical novels. Writers who knew him personally described his imagination in the later years as clairvoyant: he was able to improvise, creating on the fly the most complicated dialogues, keeping them psychologically astute and peppering them with convincing historical specifics. He saw the past in great detail: every button on a jacket, every wrinkle in a dress.

This ability to daydream was passed on to me, although not to the same extent. I didn't start out a writer, and had no plans of becoming one. Although I happily swam in imaginary expanses, I had no words to describe them.

Then one fine day, when I was thirty-two years old, I decided to correct my myopia by undergoing surgery in the famous eye clinic of Professor Fedorov. This was in 1983, before they used lasers for the procedure, as they do now, but instead made corneal incisions by hand, with a regular razor blade. The incisions took three long months to heal. All this time, while the eyes recuperated, you could see things only poorly, approximately, through tears that constantly streamed like rain on the windowpane. And after it was over, one day you'd literally wake up with perfect vision, 20/20.

But before that happened, you had to sit in complete darkness; such were the idiosyncrasies of the process that any light caused insufferable eye pain. At first, for three or four days, the agony was so great that no analgesics, no sleeping pills brought any relief. Then it subsided a bit. Nonetheless, even at dusk my eyes were ablaze, and the temporary respite of night was interrupted by accidental glances at the stars, their light burning like

4

fiery needles. Finally it was all I could do to sit at home wearing dark sunglasses, the black drapes closed, living by touch. Not a single word—neither handwritten nor typed—did my eyes take in during that prison sentence; only music, invisible in its essence, saved me from this existential desert. All that was left of the world was music and pain.

Gradually, something unfamiliar began to happen to my mind. The blindness was still near-total. I didn't yet dare take off my sunglasses to peer outside, but in my mind's eye I began to see bright visions from my past. They were not simply visions as before, similar to dreams—no, these were words, phrases, pages of text, plotlines; it was as if someone awoke in my head, a second me, one who had been slumbering until now. Visual experiences now came with a narrative; in fact, they were inseparable from it. If the wording wasn't exact, then the imagery it conjured seemed obscured by dust or fog, and only the right words cleared it away.

I was remembering—no, I was seeing—my childhood. Our neighbor who lived on the other side of the fence and whom I had long forgotten: I was six when he was sixty—never before could he have been interesting to me. And why him, specifically? No matter: suddenly I saw him, I understood his life, I felt his anxiety and his joy; suddenly his house, his garden, his beautiful but not-so-young tsarina of a wife appeared before me, and with these images words emerged, words that could describe them; a plotline materialized and filled up with meaning. Unexpectedly, the subtext and hidden significance of this yet-to-be-written story appeared—the eternal metaphor of banishment from paradise.

My external eyes were still awaiting the sunrise, while my internal ones were looking around, seeking out details. Here is one. Here is another. Here is a whole bunch. As soon as I was able to emerge from my room into the dim light of the table lamp, I typed up my first-ever short story in great haste. I knew just how to do it—what to write, what not to write—and I understood that what remains unwritten possesses a special kind of power, a certain gravity by absence, similar to a magnetic force that can both attract and repel, a force we can't see but that is nonetheless there.

This heretofore invisible, hidden world was now within my reach. I could enter it at any point, but it had particular doors—with keys of sound, with lock picks of intonation. The doors could be opened with love. Or with tears.

One day, all of a sudden, my sliced-up eyes could see again; my vision returned completely and immediately, 20/20, as promised. And this was bliss! Meanwhile, I found that the second world, having first appeared to me in darkness, was here to stay; it turned out to be a multifaceted underside of so-called reality, a dungeon full of treasure, an aetherial world through the looking glass, a mysterious box with passcodes to all enigmas, an address book with the exact coordinates of those who never existed.

I don't know its geography, its mountains, or its seas; it's so vast, it must be limitless. Or perhaps it's not simply one world—perhaps there are many. They are unpredictable; they can show themselves to you, or not. Some days they may not let you inside: Sorry, the doors are locked, we're on holiday. But to the patient and the devoted, they will in the end always yield. The doors will open, and you won't know what you will come across until you enter.

Aspic

Truth be told, I've always been afraid of it, since childhood. It's prepared not casually, or whenever the fancy strikes you, but most often for New Year's Eve, in the heart of winter, in the shortest and most brutal days of December.

Darkness comes early. There is a damp frost; you can see spiky halos around the streetlamps. You have to breathe through your mittens. Your forehead aches from the cold, and your cheeks are numb. But, wouldn't you know it, you still have to boil and chill the aspic—the name of the dish itself makes the temperature of your soul drop, and no thick gray goat-hair shawl will save you. It's a special kind of religion, making the aspic. It's a yearly sacrifice, though we don't know to whom or for what. And what would happen if you didn't make it is also a question mark.

But, for some reason, it must be done.

You must walk in the cold to the market—it's always dim there, never warm there. Past the tubs with pickled things; past the cream and the crème fraîche, redolent of girlish innocence; past the artillery depot of potatoes, radishes, and cabbages; past the hills of fruit; past the signal lights of clementines—to the farthest corner. That's where the chopping block is; that's where the blood and the ax are. "Call Russia to the Ax." To this one right here, digging its blade into a wooden stump. Russia is here, Russia is picking out a piece of meat.

"Igor, chop up the legs for the lady." Igor lifts his ax: *hack!* Lays out the white cow knees, cleaves the shanks. Some buy pieces of the muzzle: lips and nostrils. And those who like pork broth—they get little pig feet, with baby hooves. Holding one of those, touching its yellow skin, is creepy—what if it suddenly shook your hand in return?

None of them are really dead: that's the conundrum. There is no death. They are hacked apart, mutilated; they won't be walking anywhere, or even crawling; they've been killed but they are not dead. They know that you've come for them.

Next it's time to buy something dry and clean: onions, garlic, roots, and herbs. And back home through the snow you go: *crunch, crunch.* The frosty building entryway. The lightbulb has been stolen again. You fumble in the dark for the elevator button; its red eye lights up. First the intestines appear in the elevator's wrought-iron cage, then the cabin itself. Our ancient Saint Petersburg elevators are slow; they click as they pass each floor, testing our patience. The chopped-up legs in the shopping bag are pulling your arm down, and it seems as if at the very last moment they'll refuse to get into the elevator. They'll twitch, break free, and run away, clacking across the ceramic tile: *clippity-clop, clippity-clop, clippity-clop.* Maybe that would be for the best? No. It's too late.

At home, you wash them and throw them into the pot. You set the burner on high. Now it's boiling, raging. Now the surface is coated with gray, dirty ripples: all that's bad, all that's weighty, all that's fearful, all that suffered, darted, and tried to break loose, oinked and mooed, couldn't understand, resisted, and gasped for breath—all of it turns to muck. All the pain

8

and all the death are gone, congealed into repugnant fluffy felt. *Finito.* Placidity, forgiveness.

Then it's time to dump this death water, to thoroughly rinse the sedated pieces under a running faucet, and to put them back into a clean pot filled with fresh water. It's simply meat, simply food; all that was fearsome is gone. A calm blue flower of propane, just a little bit of heat. Let it simmer quietly; this is a five- to six-hour undertaking.

While it cooks, you can take your time preparing the herbs and the onions. You'll be adding them to the pot in two batches. First, two hours before the broth is done cooking, and then, again, an hour later. Don't forget to stir in plenty of salt. And your labor is done. By the end of the cooking cycle, there will have been a complete transfiguration of flesh: the pot will be a lake of gold with fragrant meat, and nothing, nothing will remind us of Igor.

The kids are here; unafraid, they are looking at the pot. It's safe to show them this soup—they won't ask any tough questions.

Strain the broth, pull the meat apart, slice it with a sharp knife, as they did in the olden days, in the age of the tsar, and the other tsar, and the third tsar, before the advent of the meat grinder, before Vasily the Blind, and Ivan Kalita, and the Cumans, and Rurik, and Sineus and Truvor, who, as it turns out, never even existed.

Set up the bowls and the plates and place some fresh-pressed garlic in each one. Add the chopped-up meat. Use the ladle to pour over it some thick, golden, gelatinous broth. And that's that. Your job is done; the rest is up to the frost. Carefully take the bowls and plates out to the balcony, cover the coffins with lids, stretch some plastic wrap over them, and wait.

Might as well stay out on the balcony, bundled up in your shawl. Smoke a cigarette and look up at the winter stars, unable to identify a single one. Think about tomorrow's guests, remind yourself that you need to iron the tablecloth, to add sour cream to the horseradish, to warm the wine and chill the vodka, to grate some cold butter, to place the sauerkraut in a dish, to slice some bread. To wash your hair, to dress up, to do your makeup—foundation, mascara, lipstick.

And if you feel like senselessly crying, do it now, while nobody can see you. Do it violently, about nothing and for no reason, sobbing, wiping away your tears with your sleeve, stubbing out your cigarette against the railing of the balcony, not finding it there, and burning your fingers. Because how to reach this *there* and where this *there* is—no one knows.

Smoke and Shadows

It's December, 4:00 p.m., and getting dark. I am sitting in the student cafeteria. The space is enormous; its ceiling disappears into the dim light and cigarette smoke somewhere around the third floor. It's the mid-1990s and they haven't yet prohibited smoking in American public places, but they soon will. In the halls and in the classrooms, it is, of course, already forbidden. The professors' lounge has also been sterilized. But in this dingy student cafeteria it's still allowed, and so all the professors— the ones who haven't yet signed on to a healthy lifestyle—eat, smoke, and conduct their student conferences right here.

"Life is but smoke and shadows," as the sign over a gate that shall remain nameless proclaims. Smoke and shadows.

The food, of course, is god-awful. One popular dish is a chunky pasta we call "little horns" in my faraway, snowy home-land. It's drowned in a yellow sauce, but not of egg—I'm scared to dwell on its provenance. They serve pale turkey meat, but it's taken from parts nowhere near the bird's bosom: if you poke around with a fork, you might find the trachea, which looks like a little tube; also some bits resembling knees, or skin with hair. Hopefully that's just the comb, which doesn't rest on the turkey's head but hangs from its nose down to the neck. Lord, that is what You decided on the fifth day of Creation, and I am no judge of You. Here they serve, in all seriousness, canned

11

pureed corn. Not to mention the tepid brown water they call "coffee," although if you add some soy creamer it's not that bad—quite potable, actually. I'm used to it.

At a table across the room from me is Eric. He's an American. We're having an affair.

I can't say anything particularly good about Eric: he's not all that handsome, his main virtues being his teeth and his height. I also like his rimless glasses and his fingers, lanky like those of an imaginary pianist. Alas, he's no good at the piano, and all that he can extract from the instrument is "Chopsticks."

I couldn't even say whether he's smart. I don't have enough to go on. How can I gauge someone's intellect if he doesn't speak a lick of my mother tongue, which is Russian, and out of my country's entire literary canon he has heard only of *Uncle Vanya*? Not that I would claim to understand the first thing about what Eric does. He's an anthropologist, specializing in the Pu Pèo people of Vietnam, an ethnic minority of just four hundred members. The Pu Pèo are part of a larger group called the Yi; well, not that large—eight million, living mostly in China. Out of China's entire population it's a pitifully small handful. The Yi people speak a number of different languages, including Nousu, Nisu, and Nasu. Just to keep things interesting. Yet Eric specializes not in the language but in the everyday life of this distant minority-within-a-minority. He's traveled to their part of the world and brought back their national costume, their headdress (which resembles an overnight train window with the drapes drawn back), wooden bowls, and an exotic grain: buckwheat!

A few months ago he hosted a small get-together for some colleagues from our department: standing buffet, wine in plastic cups, smoking outside only, in the chill, autumnal air of the backyard—"Please close the storm door, not just the screen door: it reeks of smoke in here, yuck, yuck." Crudités and spreads—"Dip the celery sticks in the hummus and the carrot sticks in the guacamole."

With triumphant false modesty, Eric's wife brought out a dish filled with hot buckwheat; the guests—the bravest, anyway—reached for it with plastic forks. Exclamations of multiculturalism and feigned delight. I tried some, too: they forgot to add salt to the kasha. It was inedible.

It was necessary to explain some things that may have escaped Eric and his colleagues, to lower the flame of exoticism down to a common, grocery store fact: this rare pinkish grain can be obtained under the name Wolff's Kasha at any American supermarket. Yes, it'll be expensive, and yes, outrageously so. Cheaper buckwheat, of the dreaded Polish variety, can be obtained in any Russian store in Brighton Beach or beyond. The quality will be awful, and so will the taste; it is under-roasted and upon boiling it swells to mush, but at least there is no need to travel to Vietnam. We Russians can eat kasha for breakfast, lunch, and dinner. Doctors prescribe it for diabetes. There is even an old Russian saying—"Buckwheat compliments itself"—meaning it's so naturally delicious, there is no need to compliment the cook. You could fry it in a pan; you could slow-cook it in a cast-iron pot inside a Russian masonry stove if you had cast-iron pots and Russian masonry stoves, but you don't; and you can never add too much butter to kasha. Oh, and if you add mushrooms! . . . and onions! Actually, why don't I just show you!

I took the kasha from his wife and quickly refried it properly. Her heart filled with hate. And Eric's with love. Or something like it. It's hard to tell. When I see Eric, my heart swells. But what swells in him—I just don't know.

§

13

Our affair proceeds with some complications, and, frankly, it'd be better if it weren't happening at all. The clock points to December, and when it's over, I'll be leaving here never to come back. I'll return to Russia; I'll visit New York occasionally—that bolted, splendid, acicular, cast-iron, windy anthill that never sleeps; I'll visit my friends in San Francisco, where it's always spring and where, as the song goes, "a lilac coatroom man will hand you your manteau"—maybe he'll hand me my coat, too, a belted cashmere one with a shawl collar, if I buy it in time. I'll rent one of those really wide jeeps; buy myself some embossed-leather cowgirl boots with pointy toes, a cowboy hat and aviator sunglasses; stock up on water and beef jerky; and, cigarette a-danglin', I'll zoom through California, Nevada, and Arizona, across rocky deserts—brown and pink, lavender and purple—their mirages trembling over salty and waterless lakes. Where to? No idea. Why? No reason, just because: there is nothing better out there than the desert. The fresh, dry air through an open window, the smell of rocks, the smell of emptiness, loneliness, freedom—the right kind of smell.

But to this tiny, ornate, gingerbread town covered with the purest of snow, I will never come back. So what do I need this love for? As I keep telling myself: I'd be better off without it. Or maybe it just seems that way.

In the Yi language, "snow" is *vo*.

Every day I keep repeating to myself that Eric is limited, poorly educated, and generally not that smart. Or if he is smart, it's not readily apparent. And not even that attractive—teeth, shmeeth. And we have nothing to talk about. I mean, we can't keep talking about the Pu Pèo, can we? But every time we meet, be it in that smoky student cafeteria, or in the chichi little bagel shop (and there, progressive bagels "with everything" for intellectuals and also cranberry scones, rare coffee varietals, and a free copy of the latest *New Yorker* for quick browsing—this could be Paris!), or at the post office—accidentally on purpose—or quite unexpectedly in the boundless campus parking lot, every time he's back to chewing my ear off about the Pu Pèo, and every time, to my dismay, I find myself listening to his mumbling as if it's a chorus of angels. With every passing day I get more and more stuck in this love like it's glue.

In the Yi language buckwheat is *nge*. At least that's how I hear it. *Nge*.

I'm a steadfast tin soldier: nothing gets to me—even love can't get to me—but, dear God, when I see that lanky four-eyes; when I watch him climb out of his car like a daddy longlegs; when I suddenly recognize him, absurd in his long coat, as he materializes out of the whirling snowflakes, turning his face from the wind, covering his eyes against the blizzard, all my inner towers, bastions, and barricades melt, crumble, and disintegrate in slow motion, as in a lousy, drowsy cartoon. Tell me, dear God: Why him, specifically? Aren't there other absurd and inarticulate bespectacled gents? Why him? I don't understand You, Lord. Please reveal Your plans to me!

Whenever confusion stirs within my soul, instead of going to the student cafeteria to dine on turkey corpses, I drive to that progressive bagel shop, buy myself the biggest cup of real coffee they sell and a cranberry scone, and sit by the window with the local paper. Turn it inside out and then fold it over twice to read about the latest goings-on. Pretty standard stuff: Two sedans collided on the highway with a van that was transporting dry ice—four casualties. A house was robbed: the owner stepped out for a bit and didn't lock the front door, pinning his hopes on the storm door—hopes dashed, computer stolen. Two people fell into an ice hole on the lake and couldn't get out. Once again campus police have detained J. Alvarez, a homeless man who for the sixth time had ignored warnings about loitering around the university. He was taken to the local precinct, where the situation was explained to him yet again, to no avail. Alvarez likes the campus; it's spacious and pretty, and with its tree-lined paths it's equally beautiful in the winter and summer. The female students are pretty, too, and so Alvarez comes to check out the ladies, who, in turn, complain to the administration.

"What do you want from me, Eric?"

"Tell me something surprising about your alphabet. The Russian alphabet."

"In Russian we have the letter Ъ. The 'hard sign.'"

"What does it sound like?"

"Like nothing."

"At all?"

"At all."

"Then why do you have it?"

"It's a certain type of silence, Eric. Our alphabet has elements of silence."

Of course I could easily explain to him the reason for using the letter Ъ, its derivation, as well as its modern and historical contexts—but why? He's not planning to learn Russian, and he really has no need to know. It's a waste of time. And besides, it's already December, and I'll soon be leaving, never to come back. I look out at the bluish evening, the town all lit up and covered with beads and tinsel—it's close to Christmas, and here the shops have started selling gifts, sparkles, candles, and flickering well in advance. Right around Thanksgiving they start. This is a northern town, as far north as they get. Farther than that, where the earth curves, there are only simple little settlements with savage Poles and detached-from-reality Canadian-Ukrainians, cliffs and snow, giant stadium-sized supermarkets selling only canned goods to the local population that consumes no fresh greens for historical reasons, and then again cliffs and snow, snow and cliffs.

Up there, up north, is the boundary of the habitable world, and beyond that the kingdom of darkness; from there the Arctic air comes down in massive blocks and hangs in the dark above our uncovered, or perhaps bundled-up, heads, while stars piercingly shine down through an icy lens, prickling our eyes.

Americans don't seem to wear hats—perhaps they are waiting for their ears to fall off from the cold? I've seen them wear gloves, scarves, sure, but not hats. Perhaps they feel that it looks weak to wear them, unless, maybe, one has gone to Moscow's Red Square and bought one of those Chinese-made polyester *ushanka*s with earflaps and a red star; then they expect all Russian hearts to melt at the sight of them. Eric is no exception: in order to get closer to my heart, unreadable by means of his cultural codes, he tried wearing an Uzbek *doppa*—a square, pointed hat—only his was embroidered with beads and pink paillettes. This reminded me of Maksim Gorky when he was terminally ill. I banned it.

Me, I swaddle my head in a warm scarf to ward off meningitis, arachnoiditis, and trigeminal neuralgia; I've forbidden Eric to call this scarf a "babushka" with the erroneous stress on the *u*. I've already weaned him off saying "borscht" instead of "borsch" and likewise explained to him that in Russian, as opposed to Yiddish, there are no "blintzes" but only "blinis," no "schav" but only green "shchi," also known as sorrel soup. I know I'm disseminating useless knowledge. I'll leave, and he'll go back to his erring ways, his linguistic and cultural poverty. He'll go back to adding cumin and star anise to buckwheat, to making salad with cold farfalle pasta, red caviar, and sesame oil. Driven by his unbridled imagination, he'll make a heap of something awful and ridiculous from mushrooms or beef.

Rice, I'd bet, he could do well. Rice is rice, a basic, simple thing, no need to invent anything. Some things should be simple and clear. You don't need to add anything to it—let it stay pure and unchanged, as it's been for thousands of years.

"Eric, how do the Pu Pèo say 'rice'?"

"*Tsa.*"

§

This town, to which I'll never return, is small, so everyone sees everything. Even if you don't know someone, they know you. Students are the majority here, and of course they know their instructors' faces. There is virtually no place where Eric and I can be alone. Sometimes, when we manage to see each other in some coffee shop while his wife, Emma, is teaching, we don't even get to talk: too many acquaintances around. I know how watchful they are of other people's affairs—I myself have gossiped with them about this one and those two. Eric is scared of Emma. And so he sits in a far corner, looking past me staring at the wall or at his cup. I respond in kind. I get heart palpitations. Don't know what he gets.

Emma is a beautiful, high-strung woman with long hair and anxious eyes stretching back to her temples. She teaches something artsy and can make anything and everything imaginable with her hands. She sews complex blue quilts covered with the delirious stars of otherworldly skies, weaves beaded shawls, and knits thick, puffy white coats resembling snowy hills. She hand-makes lemon and vanilla soap and other such things, conjuring up acute jealousy in women and fear and bewilderment in men. She orders emerald- and tree-bark-hued cowhides from special designer catalogs and from them makes little boxes with silver inserts—I bought one myself at a local shop, not knowing that it was made by Emma.

She's a real woman, unlike me; she's a goddess of the hearth and a protector of all arts and crafts, not to mention that she volunteers at the student theater, designing and painting sets for plays that her students produce. She suspects that while she's painting those sets Eric isn't sitting around his office but circling the town trying to run into me—accidentally, inadvertently, unintentionally. Emma is a witch and she wishes me ill. Or maybe it just seems that way to me.

Due to the fact that we are often unable to speak, Eric and I have developed an ability to read each other's thoughts. It's not terribly difficult, but of course it results in many mistakes, and our limited vocabulary comes down mostly to the nitty-gritty:

Later. Yes. Not now. Me too. No. I'll get in the car and drive—follow me.

We tried meeting in another town, fifteen miles away from ours, where, at the edge of human settlement, we scouted a quiet inn surrounded by snowbanks but at the last minute, almost on the threshold, we ran away in fear: through a lit window and its little lace curtains we spotted two professors from our college, two married ladies—who would have thunk it?—kissing and embracing quite unambiguously over a cup of coffee in the cozy bar draped with premature Christmas lights.

Sure, we could have wandered in saucily from the cold and resolved our mutual awkwardness with a jovial cackle: Ha-ha-ha! You too? But Eric is timid and considerate. Me, not so much, but he's the one who lives here and I'm leaving and never coming back.

I couldn't have brought him back to my place: I lived at the campus hotel for homeless professors. It was cheap, but splendid and mysterious, like a haunted house. Back in the 1930s, some wealthy patron of the college donated this house when she inexplicably found she had no more use for it. The building was surrounded by the world's fluffiest snowbanks; the rooms were so overheated that everyone kept their windows open regardless of the weather; and the beds were so narrow that one would fall off of them without fail, even while sleeping on one's back and at attention, like a soldier in formation, there being no other godly way to sleep on them. The rooms also had odious little low armchairs, with legs like a dachshund's. There was no smoking allowed, but of course everyone smoked while hanging out the window. No, this was wholly unsuitable for a clandestine rendezvous.

Theoretically, we could have risked meeting at Eric's place while Emma was teaching or set-designing, but I feared it wouldn't end well: there have been times in my life when I was scared to death—or conversely, to laughter—and when it was necessary to urgently hide in the closet or under the bed. Emma may have been a mind reader, too; I could see it in her eyes. Having caught us, she would have given chase, pursuing us through the snow, over the treetops, through the dark blue night, leaving her students behind.

Emma, you see, had a third eye, clearly visible when she was lit from the side, when it pulsated under her thin skin. When she would turn her head in alarm, it picked up my thoughts, like a radar detector. I felt it whenever she and Eric hosted one of their get-togethers for colleagues, which had become a weekly thing. I kept attending these by default. Not coming would certainly have aroused her suspicions. At these parties Emma would read my thoughts, watching me with her subcutaneous, still-unhatched third eye, as she filled with hate.

To ward off this evil eye, I bought an amulet at a local antique shop. In our little town there were many such shops with all kinds of delightful thingamajigs, from old license plates to empty glass perfume bottles. Tin watering cans; porcelain kitties; dishes, washbowls, and chests of drawers. Lifeless corsets, for women with small breasts and unimaginably tiny waists; hopelessly rumpled lace parasols, for a sun that had set and stopped shining long ago. Faded enamel jewelry, old magazines, and patterned ice trays.

The charm jumped out at me right away from where it lay, between a silver jewelry box and a Victorian lorgnette. It was a small *mano fico,* a real amulet, a thing of power—it was unclear how it had got there and why no one had purchased it yet. The shop owner hadn't picked up on its value and meaning, and so, luckily, it didn't cost me that much. I took it to a jewelry store to have a little loop soldered to it, and I also bought a silver chain for it.

"Do you want to have it engraved, perhaps?" asked the saleswoman. "Usually these things get engraved with a name. Or a word. You know, like an incantation."

I looked out the window at the swirling flakes and the snowdrifts. Pure and endless. I'll leave and they'll stay. They'll melt into water, and then it'll snow again.

"Okay, engrave it with *vo. V-o.*"

"Good choice!" exclaimed the saleswoman, with not a clue what I was talking about. An excellent professional reaction.

I started wearing the amulet under my clothes. I kept it on at night. Emma panicked and twitched, but she was powerless against it.

Love is a strange thing; it has a thousand faces. You can love anything and anyone. I once loved a bracelet from a shop window, but it was too expensive and I couldn't afford it: I had a family, I had children. I worked hard, burning out my brain, so I could pay for our apartment and the kids' college tuition, so I had something to set aside for illness, for old age, for my mother's hospital bills, for unexpected emergencies. I couldn't buy that bracelet, and I didn't, but I did love it. I thought about it while falling asleep, I pined for it and shed tears for it.

Then the spell passed. It unclasped its jaws from my heart and mercifully let me go. What difference does it make who or what it was? It could have been a person, an animal, a thing, a cloud in the sky, a book, a strophe in somebody else's poem, the southern wind tearing at grass on the steppe, an episode from my own dream, an unexplored street making a turn in the honey glow of a setting sun, a smile from a stranger, a ship's sail upon a blue wave, a springtime evening, a pear tree, a few notes of music from an incidental window.

I, for one, have never been in love with waterfalls, or high-heeled shoes, or a woman, or dancing, or inscriptions, or coins, but I know those who have been and were blinded by their love, and I understand them. Maybe one day I'll fall in love with something from that list—who's to know? It happens suddenly, without warning, and it envelops you immediately and completely.

In this way, Eric was the object of my obsessive and inexplicable love. I had to rid myself of it somehow. Overcome it, somehow.

I'm sitting in a bagel shop (the one that feels like Paris), looking out at the blue night, the snowy scene like a stage set. *We'll take Route 50, just follow me, then we'll make a turn at the fork,* Eric telepathically communicates. I drop my magazine, steal a bunch of napkins to wrap up my cranberry scone, bus my table, bundle myself up in my scarf—I'm warm, my blood is red-hot, my palms and my heels are like boiling water; I don't know about you, but I could burn holes in the ice; yes, I'm the only one like this in your gingerbread town—and walk out onto the street, which is spruced up with swaying garlands of sparkling lights. I drive down Route 50, make a turn at the fork, and pull over. Cars are whizzing past me in a hurry to get home. Or away from home. Who's to say?

Eric stops his car, gets into mine.

"I have an idea," he says. "We should go to Lake George."

"What's there?"

"A motel. It's beautiful there. We can go this weekend. She'll be visiting her mother in Boston."

"And what's happening in Boston?"

"Uh . . . her mother has some sort of anniversary coming up. She can't miss it."

"Why aren't you going?"

"I have an urgent deadline and an inflammation of the gallbladder."

"I wouldn't buy that."

"Neither will she. It's just an excuse."

I look into his sad, gray, sincere eyes.

"In our culture," he says, "the most important thing about an excuse is that it be plausible."

"Oh, really?"

"Yes."

"So any kind of a lie is okay? Even an outrageous one?"

"Yes. As long as there is plausible deniability."

"You know, we're big on lying, too. I doubt you're the world leaders there."

"We respect other people; we try to lie credibly."

"Okay. Good thing I'm leaving soon and never coming back."

"You can't leave!"

"Sure I can."

"What if I killed her?"

"What for? She didn't do anything."

"No, I think I'll kill her. It'll make things easier for me."

"But not for me."

We both just sit there, sulking. Then Eric asks, "Did you know that buckwheat, sorrel, and rhubarb are related?"

"I didn't. What stunning news."

"There are two types of buckwheat: bitter and sweet."

"There is also a Polish type, a special varietal called 'Crappy.'"

"You'll leave and fall out of love with me."

"Yes. I'll leave, fall out of love, and forget you."

Eric's feelings are hurt. "Women shouldn't say such things! They should say: 'I'll never, ever forget you! I'll never, ever stop loving you!'"

"That's women lying plausibly out of respect for other people. Of course they'll forget. Everything is forgettable. In that lies salvation."

"I'd like to break your heart," says Eric vengefully.

"Only solid things break. I am water. I'll run off and seep through somewhere else."

"Yes!" he says, with sudden anger. "Women are water! That's why they cry all the time!"

We sit in silence for a long time, as our car is swept by a fine, dry, rustling snowstorm.

"It's coming down like rice," says Eric, "like *tsu*."

It's as if he's reading my mind. It's hard to stop loving Eric. I have to pull myself together. I have to turn my heart into ice.

But then wouldn't that mean it could break?

§

It's the second half of December, only a week till Christmas. The central street of our town, that ubiquitous "Main Street," is ablaze with gold, green, and crimson shop windows, strings of lights stretched from pole to shining pole. There are so many Christmas lights that the snow, as it blows through the street, appears multicolored: multicolored sparkling *vo* that sounds like *tsa*. "Jingle Bells" creeps and seeps ad nauseam from under every door, drilling holes in your brain and turning it into a sieve; by the umpteenth store you want to run up swinging a baseball bat, and—*whack! whack! whack!*—smash the crap out of the mirrored glass. But, of course, one has to contain oneself.

I'm picking out some gifts for myself: an embroidered tablecloth, scented candles, and striped pillowcases. I don't need any of it, but that's no reason not to buy it. Back in the day, the Magi also brought strange gifts: gold, frankincense, and myrrh. It's unclear what they meant by it, what they were hinting at, and where those gifts wound up, although all kinds of beautiful explanations were later proposed: gold for kingship on earth, myrrh for mortality, frankincense for burning, believing, and praying. Legend has it that the gold was stolen by two thieves, and that thirty-three years later those two very thieves were crucified, one to the left and one to the right of our Savior. Jesus promised that if they would believe in Him, they would be with Him in heaven that day. Since they all went back to nursery days, as it were. Here, truly, was a case of someone benefitting both from Christ's birth and His death.

I also really like this beautiful, soft purse with silver inserts, but something about it perturbs me. Who is the artisan? What if it's Emma? The saleswoman doesn't know, and the owner of the shop isn't here. An inner voice, perhaps it's the amulet, tells me: Don't buy it. Don't buy anything; put back the tablecloth, and return the candles to where you found them. Nothing here is yours; it's all Emma's. All of it.

"Thanks, I changed my mind. No, I don't need the pillowcases, either."

Eric is hosting a Christmas party, his last gathering of the year. He sends me a wordless invitation—we have fine-tuned our communication technique: *Come by tonight, I'll make* nge *prop-*

erly. Don't you want nge? Oh, for God's sake, Eric, I only want one thing—for someone to erase you from my eyes, from my heart, from my memory. To forget everything, to be free. "No dreams, no recollections, and no sounds," surrounded only by a dark sky in a snowy blizzard, and nothing else, just as on the second day of Creation. So I can purify myself of you and begin anew. I need to begin anew, for I won't be coming back here again.

Lights are shimmering; Christmas songs are seeping out of everywhere, making their way inside your brain. In a few days the baby Jesus will be born. Does this mean He's not among us now, absent, just as before Easter? Does this mean that He's abandoned us during the darkest, gloomiest, most commercialized and hopeless week of the year? And does this mean there is no one to turn to inside your heart, no one to ask what to do? Figure it out yourself, is that it? Not far from town there is a Russian monastery. The monks there are sullen hobgoblins, of the standard sort, but perhaps it's worth a visit for some advice? What if among them is one with a strange, all-seeing heart? I could ask him: Is it a sin to kill and trample love within yourself?

Alas, the blizzard has swept over the back roads, and there is no way of getting to the monastery in this weather. There is no Russian Orthodox church in town. I can't go to the Evangelicals, or whatever—those aren't churches, they're community centers where they encourage bright-eyed honesty and where you're greeted by a ruddy man in a blazer—"Hello, sister! Jesus Christ has a wonderful plan for your salvation!" Somehow that plan will entail loving thy neighbor and immediately sitting down to gift-wrap donations with youthful, undertreated drug addicts from broken homes. Or coming together for a sing-along with tambourine accompaniment. Or listening to a sister-in-Christ speak: some lady in a nubby cardigan, in the manic stage of a bipolar episode, who insists it's because of her relationship with our Lord and Savior that her chocolate chip cookies always come out so well. Always.

Well, I don't want to love my neighbor. I'd like to stop loving him, actually.

The Catholics have a much better setup. Their church is more mysterious, but now is not the time to be there: it's too bright, too festive, too joyful, full of too many happy expectations, and I just can't; I don't want joy, I just want to sit in a dark room full of vile and bitter people so I can turn my heart into ice. Because life is but smoke and shadows.

I drive to visit the hexadactyls: there is a small town nearby where almost everybody has six fingers. They are all related, from one big family. Way back, one of their forefathers happened to have a sixth finger, and the deformity was passed on to subsequent generations. Now they are everywhere: at the gas station, in the bank, at the local stores. At the pharmacy window. At the bar. At the café. Full of bitterness and spite.

It feels good here, it feels right. A bitter waitress brings me my coffee; she knows that I'm looking at her hand, and I bet she has already spat in my cup as a preemptive measure: cappuccinos are well designed for this. Okay, lady, I feel you. A spiteful hexadactyl bartender is wiping down glasses, and a sullen young man sits on a barstool talking to him; it's so strange to see which fingers he's using to hold his cigarette. Is there a name for this extra digit? And do the local six-fingered grannies knit special gloves for their six-fingered grandkids?

They cast unwelcoming side-glances at me, knowing full well I'm here to gawk at them. They instantly sniff out us nosy scum, the normal, regular-looking strangers, who out of boredom or schadenfreude, to lift our own spirits and have a cheap thrill, come to seek out those for whom having more is no cause for joy.

One could also spit into seltzer with great pleasure. Or into Diet Dr Pepper, the cherry-flavored one with fewer calories. Me—I'm water. Spit at me, you ugly and miserable people, for I am planning a murder.

The Nativity is only a day away—just twenty-four hours left without our Lord. Eric is right: it's time for decisive action— time to get rid of her. She's a witch: she's sewn all the clothes in town, made all the quilts so I couldn't hide under them with Eric, knitted all the scarves and the shawls to strangle me with, stitched all the boots to hobble my feet so I couldn't escape, baked all the bagels and scones so I would choke on their crumbs. She poisons food, cuts up bird tracheas into the pale sauce, boils cartilage and skin to put a curse on me, to turn me into a turkey with a comb for a nose. She picks cranberries in a swamp, ones that smell like a crow's armpit. She paints sets. Once she's finished, it'll be too late. If not now, then when?

I arrive at Eric and Emma's. The screen door has been removed for the winter, the wooden one is wide open, and through the storm door you can see the flames dancing in the fireplace. The guests—campus colleagues that I'm, quite frankly, already fed up with—stand around the buffet, twirling wineglasses filled with cheap wine. Eric has made *nge;* he's proudly admiring the pinkish heap of buckwheat, as if it contains a secret meaning of some kind.

But there is none.

It's crappy food.

He bought that Polish muck again.

A lovely Mozart recording is playing in the background. Emma's third eye has finally hatched: blue and bloodshot, without eyelashes, it's covered with a translucent extra eyelid, like a bird's. But what good can it do her now? It's useless.

Eric, Eric, get ready. Don't drink any wine—you have to drive. We'll go to Lake George and drown her there.

Telepathy is a wonderful and truly convenient means of communication. It's indispensable in social situations.

Why Lake George, specifically?

I don't know any other lakes around here. It was your idea.

The guests disperse early to get ready for tomorrow's festivities, to wrap presents in sparkly paper. As for us, we get into the car: Eric and Emma in front, and me in the back. Emma is using two eyes to look ahead at the snowstorm and her third eye to look into my heart, that piece of wicked, black ice; thanks to my silver amulet she can't see what's in store for her.

It's pitch-dark at the lake, but Eric has brought a flashlight. We walk along a fisherman's path—seems we are not the only ice-fishing enthusiasts in the area. Today, however, the others are all at home, warm and cozy, by their decked-out trees.

The ice hole is covered with a thin layer of frost.

"What are we doing here?" Emma wants to know.

"That's what!"

We push Emma into the ice hole. Black water splashes my feet. Emma struggles, trying to grab on to the sharp, icy edges. Eric pushes her, using an ice pick for good measure—wait, where did the ice pick come from? Doesn't matter. *Bloop.* Done. They won't find her till spring.

"My hands are freezing," Eric complains.

"So are my feet. Let's have a drink."

"You brought booze?"

"And meat pirozhki. They are still warm: I wrapped them in foil."

And right there on the ice, we drink Popov vodka out of a flask—awful swill, truth be told. We eat meat pies. We finally kiss as free people—relieved to know that no one will see us, or stop us. Freedom is precious, as every American understands. I toss the flask and our leftovers into the water. Take off the silver amulet and throw it in there, too: it's served me well but I don't need it anymore.

We slowly walk back toward the shore.

The ice cracks under Eric's feet, and he falls up to his armpits into a snowed-over ice hole.

"*Ahh!* Give me your hand!"

I step away from the ice hole's edge.

"No, Eric. Farewell!"

"What do you mean, 'farewell'?! What the—What do you mean? Why 'farewell'?"

Yes, farewell. Don't grab at me, don't call after me, just forget me. Well, you won't remember, will you, because you don't exist, you're an invention; you don't exist and never did. I don't know you, I never talked to you, and I have no idea what your name is, tall stranger, sitting at a table across the room from me in a dingy student cafeteria, enveloped by darkness and smoke, in your rimless glasses, holding a cigarette with your lanky fingers, like those of an imaginary pianist.

I finish my last cigarette—it's easy to get lost in thought and absentmindedly go through an entire pack. Wrapping myself up in a warm shawl, I leave without looking back, walking from the shadows and smoke into a blinding December snowstorm.

Passing Through

Things, as we know, disappear— —often under strange circumstances—and they don't come back. That which happens with
socks and the washing machine is known to all. It's a universal
mystery, and some even refer to the washing machine as a "sock
eater."

Of course, there are rational explanations for this strange
and selective disappearance phenomenon. Basically, three of
them:

1. The washing machine sucks the socks in through the
   holes in the drum during the spin cycle.

This explanation is ignorant and ridiculous.

2. Socks get entangled in the other laundry, perhaps
   slipping into the corners of duvet covers and staying
   there quietly, like flattened mice.

This isn't actually so much an explanation as it is an attempt
at avoiding one—every experienced doer of laundry, furious
at yet another disappearance, shakes and turns all bed linens
inside out. And besides, duvet covers must be ironed—there is
no place to hide.

3. You're imagining things.

Nope, not imagining. I spent almost a decade in an apartment I absolutely loved, but all good things must come to an end, and I had to move out. The apartment was stripped bare to the wallpaper, and I ended up taking that down, too, by way of revenge on the new tenant, a young communist-turned-priest, who pulled some political strings to evict me unfairly, just as the rain did to the itsy-bitsy spider. Not only did I strip off the wallpaper, I also removed all the doors. So with everything open to view, in the corners, under the ghosts of beds and sofas, a few socks were recovered. Four socks, to be exact, unmatched.

I had long suspected that my washing machine was up to no good, so I developed a system: any unpaired sock that was extracted from it, instead of getting thrown out, was carefully stored in a special box. Times were tough—Soviet tough—good socks didn't grow on trees, and I had two boys and my husband to think of: that's six feet total! But I wasn't saving these socks out of poverty or thrift, but rather out of spite. The machine's name was Oka. She was semiautomatic. I hated her.

And so, after recovering those four single socks and finding their pairs in my sock box, I counted the rest: there were forty-seven single socks. Forty-seven! That's what my "Oka" had swallowed in eight years. So no, I'm not imagining. Not at all.

Other things dear to one's heart also tend to disappear: they were just here, and now they're nowhere to be found, but no one could have taken them, and there is no explanation for this. That little jar—it was just on this shelf! Where is it? Where did it go?

But never does it come to pass that you open up your closet

and *wham*—there is an extra jar, out of nowhere. Or that a third boot suddenly appears next to an existing pair.

So this means that the universe in not symmetrical! Someday I'll write a story about its creation and describe the structure according to which it was built, as it presents itself to me. But not now. Right now, I'd like to say the following: If things disappear into "who knows where," there must be a "there," some unknown location where all this stuff is just sitting, piled high or neatly placed on shelves—we don't know. Maybe that world is exactly like ours but in miniature; maybe it can all fit in a nutshell. Maybe all the missing things are stretched out lengthwise there. Or maybe they're rolled up.

I have an apartment in Saint Petersburg. I don't get to spend much time there. It's like a dream—everything is in its proper place, nothing gets moved or changed. Sometimes my friends or my siblings spend the night there, but, out of politeness and tact, they don't move furniture around and don't scatter their stuff, but rather glide through the still air, pulling up their legs so as not to touch the parquet floor. All they might leave behind is a package of smoked salmon in the freezer, as a pleasant surprise for when I return.

But lately someone has taken up residence in this apartment. He's small. This year, when I went there, I found a tiny—no more than an inch or so—dagger, dirk, or something, I'm not sure. A black-and-gold naval one. I asked everyone who could have passed through the apartment, but no one knew a thing. They were all just as perplexed.

Then a little crystal ball with a short chain was found—also about an inch in length. What is it? I said to myself, full of dread from that sensation of a draft blowing in from another dimension. What is this ball? Multifaceted, the size of a big cranberry or an underdeveloped cherry.

Something transpired here while I was gone. Inhabitants from other worlds, parallel to our own or perhaps even perpendicular—Lobachevsky is dead and no one is left to calmly and kindly enlighten me—the inhabitants of these worlds were up to something in my apartment. They chose it as . . . what? A battlefield? And for what—sacrifices? Or romantic rendezvous?

The latter appeals the most to my imagination. A male and a female, both small—ten inches in height, no more—arranged to meet here for a date, a romantic evening. He had a sword, she had a sparkly ball. Don't ask me what that ball is for in their invisible, secret dimension, but clearly it belongs to the female—all you have to do is look at it. They met, were delighted, they talked, they loved—that much is clear. He unbuckled his sword, she cast aside her ball. And then someone spooked them, they made a run for it, they climbed over the fence, or over the prickly bushes, he held out his hand to her, she gathered up the hem of her skirt, and their hearts were pounding, their cheeks aflame. But they made it. Nothing else was left behind.

I took their belongings, set them out on a blue, filigreed saucer—I have one that dates back to an olden world that was drowned a hundred years ago. I put the saucer on top of the bedroom dresser, by the mirror; the reflection doubled their possessions. Let them come, let those looking-glass lovers return, I've saved all their stuff, they can retrieve it whenever they want.

I know that one day I'll walk into the bedroom and the saucer will be empty. Except, perhaps, for a long, squiggly scratch made with an unknown object.

A Young Lady in Bloom

While I was a sophomore at university, I lost my monthly stipend. I needed money—you know, coffee, taxis, cigarettes—so I got a job at the post office delivering telegrams.

It was June. Evenings were as bright as day, not at all menacing, but rather quite beautiful: Leningrad, deserted for the summer; magical streets of Petrogradsky Island. On the building walls and above the entryways, mascarons of cats and mermaids, triangular female faces of resounding beauty: downcast eyes, luscious hair, daydreams. Alleyways bathed in crepuscular light, purple-hued lilac trees in the parks and gardens, and in the distance, beyond the Neva River, the spire of the Admiralty building.

The post office branch was on Kronverksky Avenue. They were happy to have me—not many people wanted to work there in the summer, the pay being poor and the weather sublime. The boss—a woman inflamed with governmental concerns and the weight of financial responsibility—broke down the effortful job of the telegram delivery person.

There is route number one, to the left, and route number two, to the right. The postman comes to the post office branch, picks up the newly arrived telegrams, and walks first this way and then that way, in turn. Officially, the telegrams are sealed,

37

but the postman will definitely peek inside—there is no privacy in correspondence, you can forget about that. This is because the postman is not some dumb robot but a keen psychologist.

What does psychology have to do with it, you ask? Well, for one thing, it's summer. People are apt to drown in lakes and rivers, you see. Every month at least one telegram announcing that Nikolai drowned is sure to arrive. So just imagine: You bring said telegram and hand it over to a lovely woman who is, perhaps, brushing away a strand of hair with the back of her hand, or maybe wiping her palms on her apron—women, as we know, are forever cooking something. And there you stand, at the threshold of a communal apartment, and this woman is smiling at you as the sun floods the landing, as if shining through water, via the miraculously well preserved stained-glass windows dating back to prerevolutionary days. Nice and clean.

And if you, unaware of the contents of the telegram, should also find yourself smiling, enjoying life, commenting on the beautiful weather or other silly nonsense just as she unfolds that paper only to read "Nikolai drowned"—well, that is quite a blow, quite treacherous, really. It might even cause a heart attack.

No. One needs, whenever possible, to be eased into grief. Bad news is easier to cope with when it's delivered by a mean person. Thus you must assume a disagreeable, vicious-looking scowl. When the door opens, you have to boorishly blurt out: "Telegram!" No smiling; look away, down at the floor. Shove the receipt toward her—"Sign here." Once she signs, thrust the telegram into her hands and run like the wind down the stairs. Reaching the landing below, you can catch your breath by the wall, close your eyes, grit your teeth, and tilt your head back, unable to banish the image of this unsuspecting stranger's sweet face—a face that was just happy for the last time, there, upstairs. On the shore.

Stand there. Try to forget. And back down the delivery route you go.

Contrariwise, suppose one is bearing an arrival telegram— for instance, "Arriving on 15th, train 256, car 8," a quiet, happy bit of news—but then it's an old granny who opens the door. That's who stays home in the daytime for the most part, old grannies. And this granny—we are talking about the early 1970s, mind you —this old lady still remembers the war, still hasn't quite recovered from it, and God knows how many death notices she's held in her hands! Therefore, as soon as she sees the telegram, she starts backing away with fear in her eyes, her palms raised to push back the impending news, mumbling, "No, no, no . . ." To prevent this, one must, preemptively, from outside the door, assume a carelessly happy visage and right away, without crossing the threshold, wave the telegram, crooning: "Everything is okay, here is a nice and happy message for you, they are on their way, start baking those pies!" Blather like that.

The pay for a successfully delivered telegram was seven kopeks; for a failed attempt they paid three kopeks each. That is, if nobody was home, you'd write out a little slip that read "You've got a telegram, it's at the post office, feel free to call," and you'd pop that into the mailbox. That didn't mean, however, that you wouldn't attempt to redeliver. No, you'd duly bring it back in an hour, and again in two, but everyone would still be at work, you see, still nobody would be home. . . . The particulars of this profiteering scheme are clear, yes?

Therefore, the morning shift brought in more bacon. Three

unsuccessful delivery attempts and one successful—that's sixteen kopeks per telegram for you. Many made a living that way. The fixed monthly income of a salaried postman was thirty-two rubles, if memory serves. Now, if you chose to be a free agent, so to speak, it came out to about the same, a ruble a day— six of one, half dozen of the other—but it left the door open to pilfering the government budget for sixteen kopeks, and I wouldn't cast a stone at such a pilferer. Not every thief deserves to rot in jail, as far as I'm concerned.

Another source of enrichment was other people's grief. Wakes, specifically. One time I got lucky. I delivered a sympathy telegram: "Please accept my deepest condolences. My heart goes out to you." The door was opened by a grieving widow; behind her, the well-to-do apartment of an intellectual. Blue wallpaper, French Empire–style furniture, portraits in oval frames. Assuming an appropriately somber countenance, I handed her the telegram. The widow signed the receipt and gave me a twenty-kopek tip.

Wowza! This was my very first tip. What a peculiar feeling! I walked out and sat down on a park bench to have a smoke and a think. This was a lot of dough. I contemplated: Are tips degrading to a human being? Nah, they are not. They bring only joy—apologies to the widow and the stiff. Your time to fade, my time to bloom. I was eighteen years old, and I fully intended to bloom. With flying magenta colors.

I finished my cigarette and walked back to the post office— another sympathy telegram. I promptly delivered it to the widow. She accepted it, but a shadow made its way across her face—a specter not of the grave but of the impending expenditure: she rewarded me with fifteen kopeks. All right, I could see where this was going. "Quit coming here begging me for handouts" was written all over her tear-stained face, though I never said a word—solemnly handing her the delivery receipt, my ballpoint pen hanging from its burlap cord, before silently disappearing into the malodorous darkness. Her apartment was on the first floor, off the back courtyard. There were radiators—ice-cold in the summer—with oakum poking out. Earth-brown walls. An empty light socket. The third telegram got me ten kopeks, and all subsequent ones—nothing. The widow simply tore the telegrams out of my hands with unadulterated hatred in her eyes and slammed the felt-padded door with a dull thud. Sayonara.

The courtyard system in Saint Pete is fascinating and convoluted. Apartments are numbered in unpredictable ways. In a particular building there could be apartments numbered 14, 15, 15a, 3, 78, 90, 16, 24, 18, and—on the very top floor— apartment number 1. Numbers 7 and 8 would be skipped and the entrance to apartment number 6 would be from another building. Or maybe from the alleyway. Some doors had no numbers at all, and the landings had no light, and so you'd stand there on the back staircase, the faint smell of garbage permeating the darkness, your hands probing the outer padding of the doors, while you'd try to make out the indistinct voices behind them. Or, more often than not, you'd stand in deafening silence, disoriented, as if under water. Many precious hours were wasted in trying to find the right apartment.

Toward the end of my post office days I befriended a disabled postman who'd made a little book with clear diagrams of all the front and back entrances along route one and route two—what a joy to behold! He was a full-time employee for thirty-two rubles, and he had respect for his work: he took his time, walked at a moderate pace, knew the dangerous and the friendly apartments and the one where the psycho resided—the one who would grab your hand and drag you inside his hot, balmy abode reeking of sweet cologne—knew where the twin girls lived, knew who was bedridden and who spent weeks away from home. He was a strange man, more cuckoo than a clock factory, off his trolley and out to lunch. He had only one interest: delivering telegrams.

It was as if he were a proud soldier of some Postal State, a humorless Government Agent in awe of Postal Work as if it were some lustrous Project, or a System that—like the lymphatic or nervous—was responsible for the smooth operation of the body politic. And for us—the temporary and the carefree—he, to say the least, lacked respect. Perhaps he imagined himself some Old World official, circa 1808, in the newly designed livery of His Majesty the Tsar's Royal Post Office: a dark-green kaftan with a black collar and black cuffs, buttons adorned with a crossed anchor and ax. That's how I perceived him, anyway, and upon spotting him from afar in the sparse summer crowds—thin, back straight, walking his route—I would think: There, through the careless and laughing masses, comes the Government itself, advancing sternly and with measured step, smelling of sealing wax, burlap cords, ink, and rubber stamps.

He showed me his diagrams without quite sharing them, never letting them out of his hands—If you need 'em, pound the pavement and make your own—as if he were privy to State Secrets, schematics of railroads, blueprints of underground factories, floor plans of strategic granaries. He would not surrender them to either a friend or the Enemy. If a bullet or death claimed him, he'd quickly chew up and swallow his little book, the ink from its pages dripping into his stiffening larynx.

Petrogradsky Island had many beautiful buildings not yet

entirely lifeless despite it all: the blockade, Soviet poverty, the specters of those who were unjustly arrested and dragged away, on wobbly legs down battered steps. One building had a fireplace in the lobby; it had just sat there neglected and cold since prerevolutionary days. There must have been a time when the fireplace was lit—a time when there was a carpet lining the staircase, at least up to the second or third floor; when the entryway smelled of coffee and vanilla; when the building was warm, and there was a mustachioed concierge; when the elevator was a box of light in the filigreed wrought-iron shaft. Now the fireplace was but a grave pit covered in green paint, like the rest of the lobby—green oil paint right over the old marble.

Most of the apartments were, of course, communal, every front door studded with a cluster of doorbells, some dating back to the turn of the century—a flat brass knob the size and shape of half a butterfly, with a sign encircling it that read "Please Turn." Those were mechanical doorbells, not electric. I knew how they worked—our friends had one at their apartment. From that half butterfly a wire ran up to the ceiling, where a brass strip with a little bell attached to it stuck out from the wall. If you turned the butterfly, the bell would ring. (When people found out that brass contains copper—a valuable material—all those sweet "Please Turn" signs were ripped out by their roots and sold for scrap metal; the brass doorknobs were unscrewed from the doors but were too good for scrap— they filled up antique shops. What beautiful doorknobs they made in 1914! Lilies and water plants—not just plain old handles.)

One door had a particularly remarkable doorbell: a glass box with the owner's name underneath it, and when you rang, a light went on inside the box, illuminating a sign that read "Heard It. Coming." They can hear me! They're coming! What lovely people! And if there was no one there, it would read "Sorry. Not Home." I asked the young lady who opened the door: "How do the signs switch?" Apparently they were connected to a lock cylinder on her door inside the communal apartment. Upon leaving she'd turn the key and, presto chango: "Sorry. Not Home." How splendid!

You deliver a telegram to the end of the route—a kilometer there and a kilometer back—and there is a new one waiting for you at the post office. Got to return the same way. I was eighteen: I wanted to bring rationality and order to the postal system, if not to the entire world. I wanted to be useful. I'd say to my boss: "Why should I rush to deliver this arrival telegram when this person isn't actually arriving for another week? And everybody is at work during the daytime anyway. Let me accumulate, say, ten telegrams, and walk the route in a few hours. It'll be more fun for me, and the post office will save money!" But she'd fearfully reply: "No, no, we can't; the instructions are to deliver immediately." She was a jittery and anxious woman.

One sunny and beautiful June morning—dewy, filled with birdsong and lilac trees—I saw her hurriedly walking to work, hunched over, eyeglasses pointed forward, not seeing anything beyond her governmental concerns, arms dangling limp like ropes in front of her. She had trouble sleeping; mornings did not bring her joy: To hell with morning dew, birds be damned, lilacs be burned. There are instructions, and people keep trying to deviate from them. How does one keep track? How does one restore order? You can't check up on everyone! You can't follow them down route one and route two simultaneously! And there is also a secret organization to deal with: SIGMA! Coded governmental communiqués arrive via the telegraph wire. Painful though it is, one is forced to entrust these ultrasecret telegrams to a frivolous coquette. What if the enemy, you know, does something or other? Maybe it's best to wait half an hour for the cripple from route two and entrust the Government Secret to him. He's a soldier! He wears a uniform! But waiting is forbidden! The instructions say IMMEDIATELY! Ay, there's the rub.

The boss lady would hand me a carefully sealed telegram for SIGMA, and I was to march straight to the checkpoint at the gates, deliver this Government Secret wordlessly to a watchman with a rank of no less than colonel, and likewise without a word accept a countersigned receipt, before marching straight back. She'd squeeze my hands in her icy grip, looking deep into my eyes with apprehension and distrust: Will you deliver? You won't let me down, will you? Can I trust you?

She'd watch me go, her teeth chattering anxiously, but never did it come to pass that I crossed over to the enemy lines through an underground passage, taking secret ciphers and codes with me.

Meanwhile, all the locals, as is often the case, knew perfectly well what lurked behind those unmarked walls—the Institute of Applied Chemistry, where poisonous liquids and explosives were developed, polluting the water and soil of one of the most beautiful parts of town for decades to come. For those of you unfamiliar with our topography: here, right in the city center, is the Pushkin House (also known as the Institute of Russian Literature), and there—just across the river—metal barrels filled with sarin and soman or whatever, some type of mustard gas. Unmistakably Soviet city planning.

First time I went there, I got lost: What do you do when there is no sign and no address? "Do you happen to know where SIGMA is?" I asked the first person I came across. "Oh, the Institute of Applied Chemistry? Just cross over there and walk along the fence—that's where the checkpoint is!" It goes without saying that I'd fold over a corner of the telegram, peek behind the safety seal, and read the secrets sent from Central Command via such insecure channels. Anybody would have done the same. Alas, it contained nothing of interest.

Luckily, on the other side of Kronverksky Avenue there was a zoo, peaceful and overflowing with white and purple lilac trees, and occasionally I would deliver there, too. First, some men had caught a bear cub in the Altai Mountains and wanted to see if the zoo had any need for it. Then, for some reason, a telegram arrived declaring that sixty blankets had been stolen. What blankets? Who could have stolen them? And from where? What did this have to do with the zoo? These were bits and pieces of other people's stories, a scattered mosaic, a peek into other people's lives—a little cloud of music drifting from a window, laughter coming from an open door, a corner of a room glimpsed through a slit in the drapes. Somewhere in the vicinity lived my most mysterious addressee, a certain Konkordia Drozhzheyedkina. How old was she? What had her parents been thinking with that name? Was she happy? Did she see from her window the white night outside, the alleyways covered with transparent haze and twilight-colored bushes? Whom does she love? Who loves her? And me, whom do I love?

As a post office employee, I was able to get into the zoo for free. I would wander to the farthest corners, toward the water, toward the Neva River, where only the birds were, where no one else would go: people want to look at elephants, at polar bears, at giraffes, to visit the nursery where you can pet baby tigers while they're still harmless, but they don't go to look at the birds. I decided to pluck a feather from a peacock and to wear it in my hair, or something; I hadn't yet figured it out. I just really wanted a peacock feather and that was that. It occurred to me to lure the bird with some bread, and when it approached the fence, to grab it by its tail—perhaps the feather would simply fall out. Strewn over there, just out of reach, were a bunch of feathers shed by other peacocks. The enclosure was a dense chain-link fence, and the peacock, untempted by my offering, was eyeing me belligerently, when loud, mocking laughter suddenly filled the air: clearly I'd been discovered by the zookeepers.

I lurched away from the crime scene, hurriedly getting up from all fours, pretending that nothing was going on, brushing the dirt off my knees and assuming an expression of detachment: Who, me? I'm not doing anything, just bent down to read the sign—I can't see very well. But there was nobody around me, not a soul to be seen in the alleys, while that snide, high-pitched female laughter, loud and derisive, hung in the warm air like an umbrella, like a dome or a semisphere of summer sky—Ha-ha-ha-ha! It hovered above me, above my plans to mug the peacock, above my cheapskate calculations— a kopek saved is a kopek earned—above my plans to bloom and my plans to live. It was as if the Creator had suddenly taken notice of me: So you like to spy on others, do you, you pitiful gnat? I can see right through you! Ha-ha-ha-ha!

It was a moment of truth, albeit an indistinct one: when someone is laughing at you but you can't see who, unforeseen horizons open up, walls move, lights switch on, a vastness is revealed. I stood there, my feet rooted to the sandy walkway, overcome by a vaguely existential shame. So that's how it will be at Judgment Day. Ha-ha-ha-ha! The woman—or was it God?—was beginning her third round of denunciatory laughter when I spotted her: light of color, with gray wings and skinny, long legs, beak open and head tilted back, she was laughing inside her enclosure—a Caspian gull, or *Larus cachinnans*. Go to hell, stupid bird. You scared me shitless.

"Please send bedpan and enema." I went to deliver the telegram: no one was home—delivery slip in the mailbox—back to the post office. "Bedpan and enema no longer needed." So do they need it or not? What's happening over there? I asked the boss—she never slept, she just sat there, staring with red, puffy eyes at the uncontrollable world around her—Should I deliver these telegrams or not? They cancel each other out, and there is nobody home! Perhaps they are boating on the Neva? Maybe, to hell with them?

"Deliver both! Instructions are to deliver! Who knows? They might check up on us!"

I attempted to deliver these mutually exclusive requests once, and then again, and then for a third time, to the mysterious owners of the colonic irrigator. I walked back and forth well into the night, but the apartment was silent: nobody ever opened the door, nobody called the post office; nobody was home the next day, or the one after that.

And then I got tired of it all, and I quit.

The cripple watched me go with disapproval: he knew, he just knew I'd make a lousy soldier of the Post Office. The boss lady was already nervously contemplating her next recruit—fresh out of prison, he was as white as a drowned man; he was being led around by the hand by his beautiful young wife, who wore an enormous, puffy gold bracelet. "Do you think I can trust him?" the boss lady asked me, without bothering to wait for an answer, as she was talking to herself.

I left, taking home a whopping thirty-five rubles, the equivalent of an honor student's monthly stipend. I feasted on black currant ice cream with syrup and then went to my parents' dacha: July promised to be just as lovely as June had been. And indeed, it was. Only it seemed to me for a long time afterward that the world had changed imperceptibly. As if the noise and the interference had quieted down somehow. Or perhaps I'd simply gone deaf.

Nowhere

N. has died.

He and I had something akin to a flirtation, bordering on—but never quite materializing into—an affair. He was hopeful, and I, for some reason, kept leading him on. Being nineteen, it all seemed oh so fun, but not without its dangers: What if he latches on and won't let go?

Me, personally, I was interested in the Real Thing, in Grand Emotions. But someone else's feelings? Eh, not so much.

Perhaps he had suspected me of treachery, of playing a dirty game, but nonetheless persisted in his gentle yet tenacious wooing. He invited me to his country house, which was at the farthest end of the railway line, an hour from Leningrad. I was torn: the invitation implied a romantic liaison, and I didn't want one. Yet one can't just go around discarding admirers, right? You never know. And so I promised to come, thinking I'd just figure it all out when I got there.

It was the end of May, warm. I boarded the train and rode for a long time, and then walked for a long time to reach his small, wooden dacha. All the while, I was plagued with doubts—Why am I doing this? Is it the right thing to do? Perhaps it's best to turn around? It was as if some dour, unpleasantly moralistic being had materialized from thin air to give me reproachful looks: Turn around, girl; this isn't right, this isn't right. It wasn't the first time that I'd felt the presence of this moralizer, this third wheel, and he pissed me off. "What's it to you?" I replied into the ether. "What? I'm curious. I do what I want. So buzz off!" That's what they used to say back in the days of my youth—"Buzz off!"

A light was on in the window. I carefully made my way through the wet, versperal grass and peered in. There was a brief moment of darkness during this white night in May. He was sitting at a table—kitchen? dining room?—reading a book propped against a teakettle and nibbling on a piece of something hanging off his fork. His face was slack and purposeless, as is often the case when someone is reading. I took in his—let's be honest—handsome profile, his chin, his neck, his hands. I didn't love him. My heart didn't beat any faster, my breathing was unaffected, my eyes didn't brim with tears. Silly, pompous words—the kinds that are embarrassing to remember later—didn't bubble up in my brain. Grandiose, impossible plans didn't crowd my imagination.

N. was having tea and waiting for me. I stood beneath his window, surrounded by stinging nettle; he didn't sense my presence. I quietly moved through the underbrush and walked away—back to the station. As luck would have it, the last train for the night had already departed, and the next one wasn't due until six in the morning. Dangerous-looking drunkards were milling about—staying here was out of the question.

I walked back to N.'s dacha but decided not to knock. In the garden I spotted a large shed, and I gingerly climbed into its loft. There was some hay there—or what was left of it, anyway—gathered at an unknown time and for unknown purposes. In the corner there sat a pile of old newspapers dating back to the 1940s, probably from when the dacha was built. I lay down in the hay, lining it with the newspapers, and bundled myself up in my sweater. My legs remained uncovered, and they were feasted upon by mosquitoes. The temperature dropped; I was shaking from the cold. Never before had I slept in the loft of a shed; I was a good little homegrown city girl. My parents were probably at their own dacha and they surely presumed that I was home in the city, getting ready for my exams. My Big Unrequited Love, too, had no idea of my misadventures. Not a soul, including N., knew of my whereabouts. I was nowhere.

It's the most important place in the world—*nowhere*. Everyone should spend time there. It's scary, empty, and cold; it's sad beyond all bearing; it's where all human communication is lost, where all your sins, all your shortcomings, all lies and half-truths and double-dealings emerge from the dusk to look you in the eye with neither disapproval nor empathy, but simply and matter-of-factly. Here we are. Here you are. "And filled with revulsion, you read the story of your life." And you make decisions.

From all corners of the garden, nightingales chirped and whistled. I'd never heard them before, and always assumed their song sounded more operatic—*aaah, aaah, aaah, aaah.* But still I recognized them. From time to time I'd crawl to peek through the cracks in the loft walls: N. stayed up reading for a long while, then the lights went out. I tossed and turned and languished till morning. At five I got up, disheveled, my hair full of hay, my neck itching from dust, reports of Soviet witch-hunt trials imprinted on my thighs and calves. Wrinkled and unwashed, with confusion in my heart, I dragged myself to the train station, to the rattling train, away from here.

Nothing happened afterward; I didn't explain anything to him. What was there to say? And now a lifetime has passed, and he's dead.

I thought of him late last night, while waiting for a trolley at a filthy, noisy intersection in the center of Moscow. At a construction site right next to it, quite improbably, a tree was still growing, all in white bloom—hard to tell in the dark exactly what kind of tree it was.

And in the midst of this urban stink, these dangerous drunkards, the cops nearby, and all this nonsense and hopelessness, a flock of nightingales were singing from within the white flowers.

Have they no shame? Singing as if there were no tomorrow.

Father

Father has a new habit of turning up in a rabbit *ushanka* and a coarse black wool coat; a hint of his torn and scratchy red-checkered scarf can be made out from under the top button. Or perhaps there is no scarf. Then it must be his prewar silk shirt, periwinkle with white stripes. They had an amusing way of sewing shirts then: in the back, between the shoulder blades, they'd pleat the fabric so one could move one's arms more freely. The shirt would billow out like a sail—clearly a slim silhouette wasn't the goal.

I found this shirt recently while going through old suitcases—you know, the kind with leather patches on the corners, the ones that are heavy even when completely empty, just by themselves. There were wonderful things inside, simply wonderful: pants with wide cuffs made from lovely tweed, clearly not of Soviet fabrication. Their outward color was gray, but, tweed being tweed, if you look carefully, bring it close to your eyes, then you see not only gray but also some green thread, some red dots, and something sandlike; you sense the creaking of the oars, the oily sheen on the river Thames, the sound of splashing water, and the runny, flickering glow of a streetlamp on a wave; the air is damp, and the mold on the logs of the dock is silky to the touch. But I digress.

So. Pants made from scratchy wool, and the faint, lingering

smell of a mothball. Nowadays, moths wouldn't be bothered by such nonsense, they'd simply feast on the pants and have the mothball for dessert. Moths these days are impudent and pushy, their stare watchful and harsh. But back in the years when these pants were packed away in the suitcase and the suitcase was shoved into the attic, there lived a different kind of moth—clean and tidy, meticulous, with old-fashioned manners and self-respect, and, one would surmise, concerned about the health of its young: Don't go there, children, there's naphthalene there! Let's go look for another suitcase!

So, pants; and then pantaloons—hilarious stuff. With ribbons, with ties! In the front—cross my heart—three white horn buttons, cracked and chipped. A boy's blazer—poorly sewn, with a half belt in the back—also of tweed, but less fancy. Somebody's eight-panel red wool skirt. Two shirts: one periwinkle striped, the other coffee colored, also striped.

I fell in love with the periwinkle one, although the coffee one was just as good. I fell in love with the blue, and that's why he keeps turning up in it, I bet. Although I can't be sure; he never takes off his coat—a coarse wool one, just like what he used to wear before his death. The rabbit *ushanka* is also from his final years.

He looks to be about thirty-five. It's hard to make out his exact age in the half-light of my dreams, but this postwar gauntness and general scruffiness, this casual carelessness or, as he'd put it, "nonchalantness," those glasses with round frames—the very glasses that were probably the first thing I saw on his curious face when I was brought back from the maternity ward and instantly loved forever—all this points to his being thirty-five. He's younger than my children.

Of course, they only remember him as an old man with chronic back pain, saggy skin on his face, and remnants of gray hair on his head—God, how he hated this about himself! He'd look in the mirror after shaving and straightening his hair with a wet comb, angrily waving himself away—"Ah! Can't stand to look at this!" And off he'd go, king of kings, tall and heavy, to have some coffee, followed, perhaps, by a trip outside to deliver a lecture at the university, or maybe simply for a walk in that awful rabbit *ushanka* of his, cane in tow.

They knew him as an old man. They thought: Grandpa. But I remember him as a young man, agile, loud; I remember him, a glass of red wine in hand, laughing at dinner parties at home with his jovial young friends. I remember how he would tuck me in and tell me all about the universe. About the orbits of electrons. About waves and particles. About the speed of light. About how, owing to the fact that all bodies have mass and that mass increases with acceleration ad infinitum, we can never travel at the speed of light. Bodies can't, but light may.

I was around ten years old when I asked him: But what is the world really made of? From what kind of stuff? As if one could truly answer that question. Father would tell me about gravity, about energy, about the theory of relativity, about the curvature of space-time, about forces and fields, but none of that would do it.

"*What* is the world made of, Daddy?"

He'd patiently sigh.

"Okay. What if I tell you that it's made out of copper—does that suit you? Or from cabbage juice? No? Look, there is something called the magnetic field. . . . You asleep already?"

I remember him happy, laughing, of course, but I also remember him angry, unjust, gloomy. He was afraid of death, and the thought of its inevitability would put him in a foul mood, as if it were an execution that had been scheduled for tomorrow, with no stays granted. I was an adult by then, I knew how to express myself, and I'd tell him that there is no death, there is only a curtain, and that behind that curtain is a different world, beautiful and complex, and then another, and another; there are roads and rivers there, wings, trees that rustle in the wind, spring with white flowers: I've been there, I know all about it, I promise. He argued, he refused to listen, he wouldn't believe me. He'd say: Unfortunately, I know how the universe works. There is no place in it for what you speak of. And I'd respond with what I had memorized in my childhood: Bodies can't, but light may.

A month before his death, he decided to believe me. Somewhat embarrassed—after all, it's all such nonsense—he told me that, since it appeared that he'd die before me, he would send me a sign from the other side. A particular kind of sign. A certain agreed-upon word. Telling me what it was like.

He never lied to me. Never. And he didn't lie to me this time.

In my dreams, he appears as a young man; he arrives wearing his wool coat and his rabbit *ushanka,* clothes from his future, yet-to-happen final years. Apparently, he doesn't much care. Under his coat—a red-checkered scarf, but maybe not. It could be that periwinkle shirt, my favorite. He has the gaunt, triangular face of a wartime goner, and round-framed glasses. The soles of his shoes don't touch the ground, as if he were levitating, undulating, although I can't be sure—it's dark and hard to see. His gaze is attentive and friendly. I know that look, I recognize it in the living and in those who appear in my dreams; I'll always respond to that look, get up and walk toward it.

He wants to say something, but he's not saying it; wants to explain something to me, but he's not explaining it. He appears amused. Perhaps it turned out that the universe really is made out of copper and cabbage juice, packed away in a suitcase with leather patches on the corners and interspersed with tiny little mothballs. And that this prevents nothing—not the unrelenting light of a billion diamantine stars, not the curvature of space-time, not the splashing of waves, not the stillness of time, nor the roads, nor the love.

The Invisible Maiden

We would arrive at the dacha in several shifts.

First—once the last of the black-crusted snow had melted, usually in April or early May—came Mother. Sometimes she'd take me along to help out, but I wasn't particularly helpful. I was fat, lazy, and prone to daydreaming; all of these attributes were poorly suited to working in the garden, much less lugging firewood from the shed, or water from the lake. Although Mother wasn't really counting on me for the latter. In fact, she wasn't counting on any of us; she simply did everything herself. Her silent hard work was to serve as a reproach, a lesson, and an example. But it didn't.

We would enter the damp rooms, thick with the wonderful scent of stale linen tablecloths; of blankets abandoned for the winter; of plywood from the walls and old glue that seeped from the furniture due to moisture; of ancient rubber boots that were exiled here, to the country, for hard labor. Mother always walked in first, pointing her flashlight, undoing the latches on the wooden shutters that covered the windows from the inside; we would take off these heavy plates together and the moldy rooms would get flooded with sunlight. We'd throw the windows open, the sharp outside air would whoosh in; we'd shiver, wanting to do nothing more than to drink hot coffee in the sunroom—hot coffee premixed with condensed milk, which we had brought with us from the city.

And so that's what we did. Mama would slice up some bread and cheese; we'd sit in the creaky wicker chairs, squinting at the garden through the clear glass panes and the ones of stained glass, of which there were two: a blood-red rhombus that made the entire world seem pale pink, like overcooked berries in compote, and a green rhombus, which in any season created the illusion of its being July.

Then Mother would get up to light the wood-burning stove, to boil water for cleaning, to lift and move heavy objects such as furniture, and I'd make pitiful contributions—open up drawers to smell the old paper lining, for instance. Or thumb through forgotten notebooks, looking among the mundane lists and business records (baking soda . . . sugar 5 kg . . . call A.F. . . . pulmonologist for Musya . . . K2-14-68 . . . brown ribbon), hoping against hope to find some mysterious name, a passionate exhale, an imprint of an unknown love.

I'd get stuck on each book on the shelf that I was attempting to sort through. And sorting after the winter was necessary, as there were rats living at the dacha, and they fed on the binders of *Novy Mir* back issues and the French novels written at the beginning of World War I. The rats feasted on the paste used in the old days to secure the spine; they bit through the canvas that held the binding and sucked on the light-blue ribbons that served as bookmarks. They shied away from synthetic adhesives but enjoyed starch tremendously. And so it was necessary to pick out that which had been gnawed at, to sweep away the rat droppings, to wipe down the shelves.

It was the time of the Khrushchev Thaw; *Novy Mir* was publishing daring and timely pieces, which, alas, did not hold my interest. But those French novels, which mysteriously found their way to our dacha shelves, spoke of eternal things: searing eroticism, nude women, deceit and betrayal perpetrated by men. When you're thirteen, that's all you want, really. And it encourages the study of French.

One of those novels was called *Une explosion d'obus*—A Shell Explodes. As I understand it now, it was a sort of metaphor: the pretty boy in white pants, his hair slicked back and his mustache twirled (illustration), has experienced an explosion of feeling for the graceful and shapely young lady in an enormous hat that covers her magnificent hair (illustration). Or maybe *she* experienced the explosion. Anyway, mutual passions came to a boiling point: lace, illicit embraces, two front teeth between parted lips . . . followed by the bitter realization, eyes cast to the ceiling—"*Mon dieu,* how could I have been so imprudent?"—hand-wringing and other thrilling French behavior. All this while you, in your rubber boots, are supposed to be lugging firewood.

I was particularly fond of one of the illustrations. The caption read "She boldly entered the sea, unashamed of her near-nakedness, as he greedily looked on." In fact, she was wearing a full-length gown with long sleeves and a high collar; upon getting into the water she had lifted the hem, which revealed striped pantaloons reaching just below the knee—perhaps that left her "near naked"; on her head was a bird's nest of ribbons and bows. In the background, the more timid and shy maidens were bashfully peeking out from the bathing machines, the pale lace of the waves lapping around the wheels. Publication year: 1914. The last peaceful summer before the war.

"Mom, what does *les cris de passion* mean?"

"The cries of passion," Mom would reply reticently. "Leave this rubbish and go pick up a rake."

But the picture that, according to the caption, depicted

these intriguing cries had been fiercely torn out, and all that was left of Claudine and her voluminous hair was a handful of lace on the floor and a carved leg of the bed where she'd been overcome by the invisible and mustachioed Albert. As always, the most precious, interesting—the most censurable—had been removed.

§

The second shift was Nanny's arrival with the children to a scrubbed and clean dacha. The house was already thoroughly heated, it smelled of fried potatoes and canned meat, of hot dried-fruit compote—it was homey, cozy, reliable: All shall be fed, all shall be warm. The wood-burning stove was on; the gas stove was used only intermittently, as gas cylinders were scarce; and the impossibly slow double hot plate, imprinted with a mantra of sorts—"Left only: low heat. Right only: medium heat. Both together: High heat"—was ever ready for action.

Nanny would tote the three-liter, cheesecloth-covered jar with the kombucha all the way from Leningrad and place it on the windowsill. From the day of my birth till the day of Nanny's death, I looked out our Leningrad kitchen window at the gray six-story building across from us, at the schoolyard with the volleyball net, at the endlessly distant matchstick-thin pipes of the Vyborgsky District peering through this symbiosis of bacteria and yeast, through this jar, through the little amber swamp atop which rested the puffy, pale, fat, layered pancake. It was alive. It needed to be watered with freshly brewed weak tea fortified with a spoonful of sugar. Three days later, this tea would turn into a stinging, tangy, yellowish drink that was allegedly very good for you. Where there is a kitchen, there is kombucha; where there is kombucha, there is caring, loving, nourishing, and anxiety. Kombucha needs to be watered! Did someone water him?

It was like another child in our family—seven of us, plus Kombucha. Us kids, who were blessed to be born with legs and arms, with eyes—and him, prematurely born, eyeless, unable to move, let alone crawl. Yet he was alive. And he was ours. Nanny's baby. (When Nanny died, there was no one to take care of him. One of the sisters took him in, but forgot to water him as needed; he started to wither, to get murky, and soon decomposed and died.)

Nanny used to place Kombucha on the dacha windowsill; his appointed neighbor was Onion, a mayonnaise-jar resident whose fibrous, whitish roots were dipped in water. The windowsill was where the empty glass jars from the green peas were drying, along with the jars from Nanny's favorite tomato sauce, which she insisted on calling "red stuff" and nothing else. Our kitchen was dark, sunless, and remote, because our dacha had been built by an imbecile.

All the sun, all the wind, all the flowers were over there, outside the window.

Over there, outside the window, was where the neighbor's property began; it had been like home to us, but it was no longer accessible. Over there, at the neighbor's house, we used to rent the entire first floor until Mom bought this dacha of ours, the one built by an imbecile. The neighbor's plot was enormous: there was a field with potatoes, another one with wild bluebells, and a "third field," where nothing in particular was growing, it was just there. There was also an apple orchard, a lilac garden, a zucchini patch, a thicket of yellow acacia, a grove of giant knotweed, an unusually large and thick birch tree, a spruce forest that rolled down the western hill, and a pine grove that rolled down the eastern hill. In the pine grove, under a thick carpet of red needles, you could make out the faint outlines of small graves, which resembled suitcases overgrown with moss: the original property owner used to bury his favorite dogs there when they died. All this, this entire world, used to be ours, but now it was cut off by a chain-link fence and we could no longer go there.

At the top of the hill stood the house itself—"the White House," as we used to call it. The apocryphal story goes like this: Many years ago, at the end of the nineteenth century, a certain Mister Dmitriev paid a visit to this narrow isthmus—a tongue of land between two lakes—on a hunting trip with his son. The younger Dmitriev so loved the pine grove and the sandy lakeshores and the thickets of willow herb and blueberry bushes that he said to his father: "When I grow up, I'll build myself a house here." Junior grew up, became an engineer, got rich and bought the isthmus; on one of the pine hills he built a hunting lodge (it was still there in my childhood but later burned down), and on the other—the White House. The hunting lodge was entered through a small porch, and there were deer antlers hanging over the front door. The White House had two entrances: the back one, through the porch, for routine comings and goings and deliveries, and the front one, through the portico with the white columns; the columns were of wood, covered with stucco. The second floor was a loft with slanted ceilings. They say that the façade was a replica of Tatyana Larina's house in the 1915 staging of *Eugene Onegin*.

If you're a young lady with a braid, of an age of yearning and expectation, and it's a white night June evening of unfading light, and no one is sleeping, and there is no death, and the sky seems full of music, it feels right to go stand on this portico, hugging a stucco-covered column, watching the sea of lilac bushes cascading down the steps, and breathing in the scent of its white misty foam, the scent of your own pure flesh, the scent of your hair. Life will deceive you later, but not just yet.

We used to live there on the first floor, and I remember the mysterious shadows of the common rooms, the Dutch stove with plain dark-green tiles, smooth and monochrome. Owing to someone's blunder, or whim, perhaps, two of the tiles were dark blue, and this imperfection evoked a certain pity—or, in other words, love. I remember the basin perched atop a wash-stand along with a timeworn pitcher, and the arched windows of the upstairs loft—those bedrooms weren't ours, they certainly didn't smell like us; when invited, we used to walk up the grayish-blue staircase to get to them. Up on the second floor, between the window frames, there were small shot glasses filled with dark-burgundy and dark-orange liquid; I used to know what they were for, but I've forgotten. They'd say it was some kind of poison—either to kill the flies, or to prevent the windows from freezing over in wintertime. When I was a kid, I feared the word "poison," and I don't like it now. I used to imagine poison to be the color of port wine, with the stifling, sugary smell of cough syrup.

They also had a trumeau mirror; I was dazzled by this nocturnal-sounding word—"trumeau." On a wall hook was Aunty Vera's robe of pale lilac, the color of sighs and murmurs, of white nights, whispers, and otherworldly emotions. Its scent was so enchanting that it nearly stopped your heart. It smelled of the White House, of 1914, of faraway, virginal, immaculate woods.

The hill upon which the White House stood poured down,

if you will, eastbound and westbound. At the east side, surrounded by pine trees, stirred a large blue lake with the Finnish name Hepojarvi, still unspoiled and unlittered: the worst
one could find at this wonderful lake were thickets of alder—
a nasty weed of a bush, the back of its leaves covered with red
dots, like warts.

To the west—down a steep path from the top of the hill—
was a quiet little black lake, or, more precisely, the bay or a
bend of the big lake, though we used to call it "the Little Lake,"
considering it the independent younger sibling of Hepojarvi.
Growing in it were yellow water lilies that smelled like mermaids. If you dangled your arm off the edge of a boat, submerging it deep enough, and then yanked at just the right
moment, you could pick a water lily by its two-meter-long
stem, and then, provided you tore the stem apart correctly, you
could—and absolutely should—make a cold, wet necklace out
of it. In the evenings, the black-mirrored surface of the Little
Lake reflected a long-blazing yellow Finnish sunset and fir trees
seemingly carved from black paper. A couple more toadstools
underfoot and you'd have an Ivan Bilibin illustration. In the
daytime the firs retreated, disappearing somewhere, and the
waterside was golden-green again, happy. There were leeches in
the lake; we used to catch but also fear them. There were water
striders that ran across the smooth plane of the water, dragon-
flies that hovered above it, and on the shore there was a bath-
house where Dmitriev Junior used to bathe—the nineteenth
century was slow to leave these shores; it hesitated, showing us
how it was before the First World War: the green, blue, sunny
world of the not-yet-killed.

Lucky for Junior, he wasn't killed in that war, or during
the purges that followed. They said that he was a VIP in the
world of energetics, that he participated in the GOELRO plan,

which sought to bring electricity to the entire country, and that this is what saved him. Russian Wikipedia says that in April of 1937 "the main engineer of GOELRO, G. A. Dmitriev, was arrested. Death by firing squad on September 14th." But this must have been some other Dmitriev, perhaps from Moscow. Neither the age nor the place of residence matches up with ours. If this had been Junior, then they would have come after his heirs, killing them or sending them to work in the uranium mines; the White House would have been turned into some kind of state-run tuberculosis clinic for the bigwigs of the trade unions, and they would have been hacking their *profsoyuz* snot all over the lilac garden.

Before the Revolution of 1917, Junior installed an electric generator on the shore of the Little Lake, and subsequently the White House had power. When I was a kid, you could still see the limestone slabs, a platform of approximately two square meters, upon which he placed the generator. The grass of oblivion—little three-leaf white clovers—was already forcing its way through the cracks between the slabs. It was sweet, we used to eat it.

Now I alone remember where the generator stood, where the nostrilled limestone slabs disappeared into the ground. The new folks don't need to know this. And I won't tell them.

The other thing that was left behind by Dmitriev Junior was a large, yellowing collage: photos of boring mustachioed faces in ovals—engineers, no doubt, who had graduated with distinction (or without) from some Polytechnic Institute and who were burning with desire to apply their knowledge for the glory and benefit of the Fatherland. A carved black frame, dead flies, glass. All those faces in ovals were most probably arrested and executed.

Junior's heirs held on to both houses for a long while, but

then the government started closing in—it was forbidden to have multiple properties—and so they sold the hunting lodge, and then one little piece of the land, and then another. Meanwhile the house grew too small for our clan—there were seven of us by then—and so mother bought the dacha next door. With a view of the White House. Few are so lucky.

§

A carpenter nicknamed "Curly"—the aforementioned imbecile—built our dacha. One of the kids gave him the moniker. "Mommy, Curly is here!" Finding it endearing, the carpenter started calling himself "Curly" after that. No one remembers his real name. He'd built the house right after the war, for the previous owner, a pharmacist named Yanson, who was planning to rent out the rooms. Curly's stupidity manifested itself variously; for example, all the rooms on the first and second floors, save for one, faced north, and not a single ray of sunshine ever found its way to them. And so the house grew moldy and rotten, all the quicker because Curly, unable to refrain from stealing building materials, constructed the dacha with no foundation. In the faraway corner of the garden he erected a roomy Finnish outhouse with two seats—a two-holer—but as he absconded with the partition wall, an interesting opportunity presented itself: you could now visit the shitter in pairs. Curiously, no one ever took advantage of this.

Curly was a jack-of-all-trades, gardener as well as carpenter, and he loved his work. Hammering, tearing things apart—he found it all equally interesting. After building our crooked house that listed to one side, he began to feel a sense of ownership: he'd come visit from the city uninvited; he'd enter without knocking, toolbox in tow, all his nails and pliers, and, with the mysterious air of an artisan, he would get to work on sense-lessly improving something. Sounds of hammering and the wheezing of a hacksaw filled the air, until he emerged from the basement or from the attic, or climbed out from the shed, squinting in the sunlight, and with a log or piece of plywood in his hands and that mysterious artisanal smile still plastered across his face, he'd take it all home. If you weren't on high alert you could end up losing a balcony: Curly was once caught removing the support beams that held ours up—the very same support beams he'd attached to the wall ten years earlier. We didn't notice, however, when he managed to disassemble the roof over the firewood shed.

Apparently he viewed any house he came across as a poten-tial source of building materials that might come in handy somewhere else: he did construction and repairs in other com-munities, and if he happened to arrive with some bricks or plywood, you could be sure that he'd hacked it off somebody else's house to attach it to yours. If after Curly's visit we dis-covered a shovel, it meant that in Vaskelovo, or in Gruzlno, or maybe even in Elisenvaara, a shovel was missing; if Curly, smil-ing assuredly, carried away a pane of glass, it was immediately clear that it would soon sparkle in somebody else's window. This man was carrying out a circular organ transplant, so to speak, attaching one person's ear to another's leg—I have no doubt he used our outhouse partition to fashion an inelegant garden table for the unsuspecting owners of a tiny plot of land in the unsavory village of Oselki.

So, as it was, the hallway leading to the bedrooms was on the sunny southern side of the house—one obviously couldn't live in it, as that would have been strange—while all the bed-rooms faced north and thus were always cold and dark. We did have woodstoves for heating, but they fell apart and stopped working back when I was a child, and no wonder: the dampers and some of the bricks had "disappeared." I'll let you guess where they went.

The upstairs hallway unexpectedly morphed into a sunroom midway through, mirroring the one below it in shape, and it, too, contained the magical rhomboidal panes of red and blue found in the downstairs verandah. I sometimes used to go there to look through the blue.

§

The third shift saw the grannies—Aunty Lola and Klavdia Alekseevna—come to the dacha. Aunty Lola was our deceased grandmother's friend. She also considered our dacha to be her home. She always sat in the same old chair, drank from her own special cup, and always slept in the same bedroom on the second floor—the dampest one—which she forbade anyone to use even in her absence, not that anyone wanted to. Anyone else would have simply succumbed to the dampness and died, but Aunty Lola was one of the "Alexander grannies"—born during the reign of Alexander III—and a very sturdy woman, who favored the cold-water cure followed by rubbing oneself with a waffle-weave towel, and so on. In Leningrad, Aunty Lola occupied a room of three square meters in a communal apartment—yes, three square meters exactly. It was originally the janitor's closet. Her previous home had been blasted to smithereens by the German air raids during the siege of Leningrad. *Une explosion d'obus.*

I've been to that tiny room; strictly speaking, it could fit only a bed. If one were to get up, another person couldn't even squeeze by. So Aunty Lola used to receive people on the bed: she and her guest would sit side by side, talking. Sometimes she'd go out into the hallway to put the teakettle on—in that case, her guest would lift their legs so Aunty Lola could get past. A minuscule table was wedged in by the head of the bed, because, after all, you need to put your tea down somewhere.

As a result, that damp bedroom in our dacha was like a palace to Aunty Lola. She'd stop by the neighbors who sold flowers and strawberries and buy herself a bunch of pink peonies; she'd spritz herself liberally with a Riga-made perfume called "Acorn," open the door to the balcony (the very one that Curly tried to dismantle), sit in her wicker chair, and, with her bad leg propped up, she would enjoy a novel in English. Or French. Or German. She was equally adept in all three.

Being a soldier at heart, Aunty Lola adhered to a strict schedule, even of enjoyment—as soon as her leisure time was up, she would limp down to the first floor (the creaking stairs announced her approach—run!) and grab one of us for Russian dictation, or to study English, French, or German grammar. An hour a day. That is, she'd teach one of us for an hour, and then another one of us, and then another. . . . (Of course, we all saw this as a chore and hated it, but only thanks to Aunty Lola was I accepted to university, and only thanks to her do I still have near-perfect spelling.)

Aunty Lola was obnoxiously honest, unbearably straightforward, suffocatingly slow. She spoke in an elevated literary language, as if she lived inside a Henry James novel, and punctuated what she said with her voice. She was a very good person. She never cheated anyone. Being teenagers, we ran from her for exactly that reason.

Due to Curly's architectural logic, all the bedrooms in the house were interconnected: if someone entered your room, you could quickly escape through a different door. But there were a lot of us, more than there were doors, so Aunty Lola was usually able to apprehend someone. Placing her cold hands on your waist, firmly holding on as your body tried to wriggle free, Aunty Lola would start up an empty, meaningless conversation: "When I was in the seventh grade at the lycée, we had a geography teacher who thought that the best way to learn the subject was to travel around the countries you meant to study. And I must say, I completely agree with him. Suppose you are learning about Germany or France—"

"Auntylola!" We'd laugh, yelling into her hearing aid, as she was practically deaf from that same *explosion d'obus*. "What year did he say that? Nineteen fifteen? What about Alsace-Lorraine? It's both Germany and France at the same time!"

"Well, of course not during the Great War," Aunty Lola would say, starting up a new thread. "One can only talk about such excursions in peaceful times—"

"Auntylola! Are these peaceful times? Just try getting a visa to stinking Bulgaria, Auntylola! The party won't allow it! *Lasciate ogni speranza, voi ch'entrate*, Auntylola!"

Directly underneath Aunty Lola's fortress chamber, on the first floor, there was what we called "the Green Room," its name taken from the green linoleum that Mother had installed there—installed with her two bare hands, of course: moved the furniture, unrolled the linoleum, and nailed it down as needed.

This room saw more foot traffic than any other room in the world. It had one window and three doors: one leading to the sunroom, one to the kitchen, and one to a bedroom shared by four people. It also had an armchair and a TV that was always on. Through this room we'd ferry pots of soup and pans of meat, salad bowls of greens and glass bowls of compote; we'd pass through to bring clean dishes and to carry back dirty ones. You couldn't possibly live in this room, and yet Klavdiya Alekseevna—Klavsevna—did. Somehow amid the constantly opening and closing doors, the chair and the TV stand, the bookcase and the window, a narrow, maiden's bed was wedged in. Klavsevna would sleep in it half sitting up, just as in medieval paintings.

A quick estimate: the house had fifteen people, half of whom were children, so that's more like twenty-five people—kids exist simultaneously in two places, the coordinates of which quantum mechanics does not allow us to identify precisely. Twenty-five people regularly taking their meals three times a day, and irregularly bursting into the sunroom for an apple or a cookie, so that's another two times—or five in total. Twenty-five times five—I get one hundred twenty-five, what about you?—so that's one hundred and twenty-five passes through the Green Room just for the food, not counting the TV watching, with shouting matches over what to switch on: cartoons or the evening news? And what if there's boxing on? Or a movie, especially a crime drama? And what about adults coming and going to sweep the floor, iron the laundry, or lug firewood, not to mention all the children running, screaming, playing tag or perhaps even something more dangerous? In the midst of this purgatory, the meek and docile Klavsevna was able to exist only on condition of her own invisibility—she had perfected the art of living unseen, almost to the point of disappearing completely.

It's impossible to imagine Aunty Lola invisible. Her special cup—better not touch it! Her special chair—better not move it! Loud and simpleminded stories of a partially deaf person— "And then the doctor says to me: 'Remember, you have a friend!' And I thought: He's talking about himself, and I was so very grateful to him. But he continues: 'Farmer cheese! Remember that farmer cheese is your friend!' " Aunty Lola would let her presence be known clearly and assertively. She made tracks in our lives; she was a force to be reckoned with.

Or take Nanny, a firm and stiff-necked person who loved us but disapproved of our lifestyle, and who was constantly nagging us—she, too, was a force to be reckoned with, and her presence hung in every room like a lingering scent. During the daytime we were "god-damned blockheads" or "rotten treasures," and come evening she'd sigh, "You are all so sweet when you're sleeping." When the older sisters began sneaking out on dates, she'd grumble, "You should get it all sewn up," and we younger siblings were dying to know: Get what sewn up, and where? But Nanny wouldn't elaborate.

Klavsevna, however, was invisible. There was an armchair in the sunroom that she really loved, but this chair was considered to be Father's, and when he arrived on the weekends she'd disappear into thin air as soon as he'd set foot in the house—only her shadow would flicker. I don't remember her in any of the rooms except for the green one; I don't believe she ever went up to the second floor; in the kitchen she'd blend in with the appliances, such as the hot plate with the "Left only: low heat" mantra; in the garden she'd blend in with the bushes. Sure, she was subdued and spoke infrequently, but that wasn't it—she didn't emit any interference, didn't send out any signals, didn't produce any energy waves.

Klavsevna had a distinctive appearance. She was close to seventy, but her face was lively and she must have been very pretty in her youth. A sleek turned-up nose, blue eyes that sparkled with laughter, peach fuzz on her otherwise bald head, impressive height—it was possible to picture, by straining your imagination, how svelte and comely she had once been. Klavsevna wasn't blessed with brains, however, and this was for the best:

thinking would have been a hindrance for her; she believed only Jesus and her doctor, who told her to put yellow drops in her eyes twice daily, to sleep propped up on a big pillow, and to avoid looking in the dark.

Avoid looking in the dark! Klavsevna took that literally, and it was impossible to dissuade her. She made her bed, which was situated at the intersection of all roads, in such a way that at the head was a fortress of pillows and props that precluded her lying down. She'd turn on the lamp and sit in her bed amid the horde, looking straight ahead with the tactful smile of one who doesn't want to disturb anyone else with her presence, until Morpheus finally would descend to dim her sight. This somewhat unnerved her, for when you close your eyes all goes dark, and the doctor had advised against that. When venturing out to the far corner of the garden to relieve herself into Curly's brainchild—the communal two-holer—Klavsevna was afraid to look into the darkness there as well, and so she'd use the pit of her choice with the door wide open. This allowed her to see from afar who was approaching with similar purpose via the walkway, and to immediately disappear before disturbing them.

Before her retirement, Klavsevna had been a typist at a company that sold loose face powder (White Nights, Carmen, Lily of the Valley), floral perfumes (Red Poppies, Chypre, Lilac), and other sweet-smelling womanly toiletries. Our neighbor from across the street, a sullen, greedy man by the name of Mikhail Bernig, used to work at the same company as a bookkeeper, and at some point, soon after the war—we were still living in the White House then—he told all his colleagues about the wonderful pine trees in our lake region, about the empty beaches of Hepojarvi, and suggested our slice of heaven as a place to take salubrious strolls with parasols. Klavsevna, then a not-so-young and lonely maiden, came to our community with some friends and, while walking, caught a glimpse of my sister Natasha, then four. Klavsevna's heart skipped a beat. Everyone's heart skipped a beat when they saw Natasha. All blond curls and gray eyes—she resembled a magical, sad doll, with a lost gaze, as if all her relatives are gone but she's not complaining, just quietly grieving. Even those with several children of their own wanted to scoop her up, cover her with kisses, and adopt her. Klavsevna was gone.

She started coming to Hepojarvi just to look at Natasha, who used to go for walks with Nanny. Klavsevna struck up a friendship with Nanny. Nanny was strict—she saw right through Klavsevna's foxlike cunning, keeping her at arm's length. But Klavsevna was quiet, harmless, meek, and enraptured; it was the right tactic—Nanny relented, deciding to let Klavsevna be.

A year passed, then two; it was time for Klavsevna to retire, which she did obediently. Her pension was thirty-two rubles for life. In the early 1950s that must not have been so bad, but every year prices went up and her pension remained the same. Being an experienced typist, she was able to find a bit of work at first; she'd take odd jobs home even though she was terrified of getting audited. But then her eyes began to give out, and her doctor prescribed the yellow drops and forbade her to look in the dark. And she couldn't really see that well in the daytime, either.

Another ten years passed, our younger brother and sister were born, and now *they* needed someone to take them for walks. Nanny was by then too old, and so she suggested to our mother her (by that time) dear old friend Klavsevna: she wouldn't be able to manage in wintertime, but in summertime—easy as pie. And so in exchange for room and board as well as a small stipend, Klavsevna began taking the little ones on their walks.

My sister Natasha was no longer that sad doll; she'd grown up, taken up sports, her favorite being the shot put. She was a girl of marriageable age, but Klavsevna still saw in her that erstwhile lost little girl, and when Natasha would come to the dacha, Klavsevna followed her like a shadow.

§

People in our family are divided into two camps: those who were stung by the White House and those who were not. I'm in the "stung" camp. Whether I'm walking down the street or lying in bed awake, whether my eyes are open or closed, at any moment can I walk up the wooden porch stairs into the back sunroom, open the door, pass through the narrow hallway with its random boxes, summer coats—called "dusters" back then, a forgotten term now—hanging from hooks, and breathe in that air: the infusion of flowers, children's tanned skin, household soap, and boiled milk; I can touch the railing of the staircase that leads up to the loft, feel its gray balusters, and then take a left into that room with the green-tiled Dutch stove, the one with the two errant blue tiles. It's July. I'm five years old. Nanny says our new little sister has just been born, her name is Olya, and we're going for a walk now to meet Mom and Dad, who are driving in with this new addition.

There is a long trek upward—it's a serious hill, a few years later a competition-sized ski ramp will be built up there. You can see forever from the top—even the faraway shore of the blue Lake Hepojarvi is visible, the far, empty shore. No one lives there and no one can, because of the shooting range where once a day thunder is heard—*l'explosion*. An invisible canon fires so loudly that the house shakes and the windows rattle, and afterwards we need to invite Curly to spackle. No one has been to the shooting range but everyone knows that it's there, beyond the hills and the valleys, beyond the marshes with the white mist, beyond the sea of fireweed, and the raspberry and blackberry bushes. We are standing at the top of the hill, looking ahead, blocking the sun with our hands: in the distance, in the outlying forest, is a remote meadow, and there, two trees side by side, like two siblings. That's where Eden is.

Nanny leads us past the teahouse with its inebriated men, past the kiosk where Mom buys the kerosene for the Primus stove—this is still the age of firewood and kerosene, they aren't selling gas stoves yet, and the silly mantra of "Right only: medium heat" hasn't been thought of. We walk into the pharmacy, and there—herbs, herbs, herbs—it smells of sage, chamomile, and dried linden flowers. This is where our Yanson used to work; we don't yet know that we will be buying his house, leaving the White House forever. Nanny picks out some kind of herb for herself, and we walk out onto the main dirt road. It's dusty.

Here they come, here is our Pobeda coming to a halt, and inside the car are Mom and Dad, and a satchel that is our new sister; Mom moves the lace away from her red little face. This is Olya. Thirty-six years is all she will get on this earth.

§

If you look through the blue glass long enough, someone will die. Not completely, not hopelessly—after all, death doesn't really exist—but they will no longer walk among us. You will no longer be able to touch them, kiss them, to inhale the scent of their hair and neck, to take them by the hand, to ask them a question, to look them in the eye—none of this will be possible any longer. They leave us for that gray, twilit land beyond the blue glass. By bringing my face close to it and looking long enough—through the rustling and the undulation of the garden, the swaying of the branches in the wind, through the melancholy bloom of gray jasmine and the sea of gray lilac—I seem to be able to make out their faces, their hands: they are looking at us and waving, they've noticed us. Perhaps there, on the other side, it's fun for them and bright; perhaps they are playing ball or simply sailing on airships above our gardens— submerging their arms deep into the warm air and yanking flowers by their long stems, and picking petals one by one to tell fortunes. Why wouldn't they try to tell fortunes? Perhaps from this side of the blue glass we appear to them gray and wistful, locked away and unattainable—I don't know. But the blue glass is the window of heartache, and one oughtn't look through it intently or for long.

§

A tragedy befell our friends, the upstairs neighbors at the White House, the ones living in the loft with the poison and the trumeau and the lilac robe: their housekeeper drowned. She went for a dip in Lake Hepojarvi, swam out into the open waters, and was sucked in by a maelstrom. I remember the frightful commotion that this news created, tearing through all the houses on our pine grove isthmus like a great gust of wind. Some of the grown-ups rushed to the lake; others, blocking the view, wouldn't let us look. I never saw the drowned woman. Of course, that was the right thing for the grown-ups to do—I wouldn't have let children of mine see the lifeless young maiden—but because I didn't get to see her then, now I see her always. I don't remember her face, I don't know her name—there were many of them back then, young ladies looking for jobs as house staff after the war to escape the villages they detested, where there were no young men; girls yearning for love, kisses, and freedom where only barnyard work was to be had. I remember these young girls only by the smell of their maiden skin, their sweat, the cheap pink loose powder they used. Men had a different scent, they smelled of motorcycles, you couldn't confuse the two. Young ladies would go on dates with soldiers from the nearby military base and then inexplicably dissolve into tears, quit their jobs, and disappear. There were Ninas and Valentinas; there was a Liuba, who liked to sew; a Klavdia; and a Zoya, who left behind a pink semicircular hair comb; and the beautiful Marusya, who stayed the longest—she had no suitors because of her withered leg, stricken with polio.

I don't remember which one of them drowned because the one that did—that invisible maiden, lying on the lake's shore, on the grass behind all the grown-ups fussing, leaning over her, and blocking the view with their legs—was all of them: Nina, Klavdia, the other Nina, and Zoya. She was all of them—lying on her back, on her side, and facedown; propped up against a tree, covered with a blanket, naked, wearing a blue wool swimsuit, or a cotton one with orange dots or tiny flowers; in her underwear—pink satin or white cotton—or, for some reason, with a long nightgown clinging to her pale young body. She was the sister Alenushka from the fairy tale, calling out from the water's depths: "My brother, Ivanushka! Heavy is the stone that pulls me down, silky is the seaweed that binds my feet, yellow is the sand that covers my heart!"

Afterwards, the grown-ups explained to us about the bottom of Hepojarvi: at first, everything is smooth and shallow, and then *boom!* A sharp drop-off, and not just a drop-off but a vortex, with a deep hole, a cave. If you swim above the drop-off, you can get sucked in under its smooth edge, as if under a roof or an awning.

§

Between the world of our parents—books, science, common sense, encyclopedic knowledge and education—and the world of the nannies—fairy tales, myths, fears, superstitions, things that go bump in the night—was the world of the children, who were trying to understand it all, and who didn't know how to talk about it.

Puzzling things, puzzling people. A soldier, for example. Say the kids overheard rumblings from the grown-ups' world about how one of the Ninas went out with a soldier late at night and how, uh-oh, nothing good can come of that. Nanny, in an effort to scare us, would say that a soldier was coming to carry us off in a sack if we didn't behave. This was alarming, and confusing, but alas, there was proof that this practice of carrying off children in sacks existed: illustrations from the folktale "Masha and the Bear," in which, as we all remembered, there was a bear walking upright and carrying a little girl through a dark forest in a woven basket full of savory pies.

What horror! The soldier, treading slowly, would enter from the back porch of the White House and gingerly take off his sturdy shoulder bag. Where would he take me? And why? What would happen afterwards? Would he throw me in the lake so that I'd get sucked into a maelstrom, my feet bound by silky seaweed? Would he start sharpening his knife? Or maybe, having mysteriously descended from the large, flyspecked photo collage graduates of the Polytechnic Institute, with their mustachioed faces framed in ovals, would cover me in stifling yellow paper so I would start to choke and kick and I'd wake up with my heart pounding, crying, "Nanny! Nanny!"

The room with the dark-green stove tiles and the two errant blue ones had no curtains. I remember that autumnal morning—gold and translucent—when I woke up from the light and, climbing up to kneel on the windowsill, looked out. The world outside was just as it must have been originally conceived: made of gold, quiet, and kindness. A leaf softly fell to the ground. I was around five years old. I had no thoughts. But I did have—from that morning when it appeared, and staying with me till this day—a sense of self, separate from the others.

And therefore what should have followed was an expulsion from paradise, and that's exactly what came to pass: we left the White House, and the gates that led inside it slammed shut, the way there blocked to us forever.

§

Of course, we all loved our crooked, damp, and absurd dacha. It belonged to us and we could do with it as we pleased. For example, Curly started building—though never quite finished—two more rooms in the attic. Each room did have a door and a window, and some sort of ceiling lining—we needn't dwell on the imperfections. I claimed one of these rooms and for some reason chose to paint the window frame bright red; the result was quite hideous, and I quickly repainted it white, but the red color still showed through, and so I kept covering it with more and more white paint until the window would no longer close.

I found that I enjoyed painting, and so, until I ran out of supplies, I painted everything I could: window frames, doors leading to the sunroom, thresholds. Even the black prerevolutionary cupboard—an heirloom from Yanson—was painted white, to my mother's dismay.

Every day we used to buy milk—a big, three-liter container—from one set of neighbors and strawberries from the other set. Initially Mother tried to plant some strawberries herself, but soon gave up on the idea. Yanson had left behind a great farm: it had everything from gooseberries to geese; it had chickens, a piglet, an apple orchard, cherry trees, and even a plum tree, which, for a long time, we considered to be some barren, useless alder tree until it went crazy, as trees are wont to do every few years, covering itself first in beautiful flowers, and then in fruit—inedible fruit, but fruit nonetheless.

He even used to have a cow—Yanson, that is—and so the house had a cowshed attached to it. But by the time the house was in our possession, the shed had long been turned into a large storage space with closets and shelves all along the walls, and there was no sign of it—the cow, that is—she had been forgotten and we don't even know what she looked like, what color she was, what her name was, if she had calves, and what happened to her: Did she end her days ground into meat patties or did she die of an illness or old age? Only on humid days before a storm, when scents begin to rise from the earth, could you smell the presence of an animal, as if blown in from pastures beyond Lethe, the river of oblivion. Through the small window a ray of light would shine, dust floating in it, neither taking off nor settling, but eternally there, eternally circling, as the cow's shadow would walk from one dim corner to the other, sighing and treading heavily.

There was a time when basically every house in the community had a cow—aside from the White House, which kept no livestock. But at some point the authorities once again imagined something or other, and directives were issued to chop down the apple trees and to surrender all the cows to the collective farm. The dutiful folk shed some tears, chopped up the trees and the cows—you wouldn't just hand them over to strangers, would you?—but some, deciding that the monarchy's rage would subside and that the dark skies would clear, kept their animals on the sly. One neighborhood woman, who truly loved her cow, ferried her by boat to an uninhabited island on Lake Hepojarvi—we used to call it "Lily of the Valley Isle"—and the cow would ramble there, chewing the flowers, confused, while the woman would go every day to milk her: in the morning fog over calm waters, and in the evenings, by turbulent waves out of Turner paintings, with a bucket and clean cans for this white, lily-of-the-valley-scented milk.

§

Yanson didn't have any children, just a wife—I remember a picture of her with a milkmaid's yoke, surrounded by chickens, a barn and a pig in the background—and so he was able to devote all his free time outside the pharmacy to the geese and the cherry trees. By contrast, our family had a small child army, and before the youngest had grown up the eldest already had kids of their own. Mother couldn't keep up with the gardening required, and so the pharmacist's farm slowly descended into disarray: the apple trees got to be as tall as the pines, the gooseberry bushes grew wild, the Persian lilacs refused to bloom and resembled a mop, the Turkish carnations crept away from their flower beds and we'd find them in the weeds by the fence sometimes.

None of us children liked working in the garden; we enjoyed sitting on the porch in the evenings, playing cards or charades, reading or making up nonsense rhymes, one person writing two lines and then passing the sheet of paper to the next. Sometimes Father would join in and the rhymes would acquire a certain compactness as well as a hint of political sedition.

Mama would walk past us with a pruner or a rake; she would work in the garden till dark, teaching us hard work by example—to no avail, as we never budged from our spots to help her unless she asked, and she rarely did. Occasionally a paroxysm of guilt would overtake one of us and we'd yell in her direction, "Mama, c'mon, I'll weed there tomorrow!" But she'd impartially answer, *"Morgen, morgen, nur nicht heute, sagen alle faulen Leute,"* which was German for "Morrow, morrow, not today, that's what lazy people say."

(Years later, when the Soviet regime fell apart and was succeeded by democratic times, when working for the common good was considered a laughable and contemptible anachronism, the courtyards of Saint Petersburg were choked with garbage, and no one came out to clean them. That is, no one except two people: the janitress and Mother. Mother was by then close to eighty. She'd put on canvas gloves, secure her hair with a headscarf, and set out to pick up the bottles peeking through the melting snow, to sweep up the frozen dog poop, to gather up paper, plastic bags, and discarded syringes. On TV, Sobchak was barking about democratic principles and we all watched in rapture; but Mother would walk past us, in silence. "Mama, c'mon, sit down, relax!" "Garbage doesn't pick itself up. We want to live with a clean courtyard, don't we?")

§

Besides that Lily of the Valley cow, there was the Eimans' cow, but we were too lazy for the long walk to their place—it was about a quarter of a mile up a road overgrown with thick grass.

The house belonged to a large extended family and one of the inhabitants was Vera Eiman, a mysterious woman, enveloped in sadness, who knew how to get rid of warts using a quarter of an apple: you secured one quarter to the wart and then buried the other three while saying these magic words: "You three, riding on a mare! Take this wart away from here!" A week later the wart would be gone without a trace—the three horsemen abided. At some point before 1914, this Vera was a personal dresser for the ballerina Anna Pavlova; she used to enrobe and disrobe this distinguished woman, clean her swan tutus reverently, travel the globe with her. She'd bring out autographed photo albums covered in velvet to show us: "For dearest Vera . . ." You're standing there, with a three-liter milk can tugging on your arm—"All right, can I please go now?"—but Vera is still flipping through the formerly cream-colored pages with trembling hands. "You see? And here again: 'To dearest Vera . . .'" Anna Pavlova decided to stay in England, and Vera came back to Russia to get married.

And get married she did, or rather, thought she did, but the consummation never occurred, *les cris de passion* never rang out in the dark vaults of Vera's bridal chamber: her husband would gently kiss her on the forehead and leave the room, closing the door behind him. Vera was an innocent maiden but nonetheless possessed some vague notions about the mechanics of matrimony; days followed days and nights followed nights.

Finally, tired of waiting for the caresses promised her at the altar, unable to understand what all this meant, and not knowing where to turn, she got up from her cold marriage bed and knocked on her mother-in-law's door for advice. Oh, the horror; oh, the depths of despair: the dim light of a kerosene lamp, shadows, lace, and scattered bedsheets. Yes, her husband was

86

indulging in passionate lovemaking with his own mother in the very same bed where she'd birthed him, and where, as it turned out, after making him her lover for thirty years she still wouldn't let go.

Vera hanged herself. But her husband rescued her from the noose, brought her back to life, and then promptly hanged himself. No one tried to resuscitate him, it should be noted.

She didn't remarry, and she grew barren among the velvet-covered albums full of someone else's exhilarating beauty. They say that after what had happened, men inspired only horror in her. I don't know—when handing us a full three-liter milk can, having carefully placed it inside a checkered bag, did she sometimes think about what could have been, that it was possible to forget, to overcome, to fall in love again, to have children, to nurse them with her own milk, her own body whose earthly time had been so uselessly spent on the side of life's road? Or did she completely dissolve into the swanlike whiteness of the past, into the dreamy sublime sadness, into those pointe shoes, ribbons, and flounces—the flounces and lace that she used to bleach with her very own hands, used to press with a sad iron?

Anna Pavlova's name has been immortalized by one KLM airplane, by an Australian dessert, and even, God help me, by some haptophyte algae; it still resounds, and all this is well and good; yet it might still please her—now on the other side of that blue glass—to know that even here, in the shade of the White House, amid the pines in the middle of nowhere, Vera, the eternal maiden, spent her long, sad life loving her, and that after each evening's milking she'd smooth out Anna's silky photographs the way she used to smooth out her tutus.

§

The house was overrun with children, and Klavsevna was hired to take the little ones—Olya and Ivan—for walks, so they wouldn't be in the way. You'd amble somewhere, not doing anything in particular, and here they are—situated by a pile of sand, next to a fallen pine tree, Klavsevna sitting down on the tree's roots, her red jacket visible from afar, while Olya and Ivan are making mud pies or playing with toy trucks: *beep beep*. I don't know exactly what she would talk to them about or how she entertained them, but at some point an imaginary character by the name of Fedor Kuzmitch entered the picture.

He, as I understand it, bore no relation to any historical figure. He just materialized out of nowhere and there he was. Fedor Kuzmitch was a role model: he always finished his supper, he never licked his plate even after raspberry jam, he never spat cherry pits out onto the table, but only onto his spoon, then carefully placing them on the edge of his plate.

Before entering the house, Fedor Kuzmitch always shook the sand off his sandals, as well as the pine needles from his clothes: he was considerate of Mother's having to sweep the floor. Fedor Kuzmitch didn't dangle his feet and kick under the table, didn't pick his nose, didn't draw on the tablecloth with colored pencils. And he never—NEVER!—brewed tea in the buckets of fresh water just brought back from the lake, as Olya used to do; never stomped his feet over the blueberry pies covered with tea towels on the table as, again, Olya did. And he never mixed salt and sugar—quickly and deftly—while looking with innocent and impudent eyes when caught in the act, Miss Olya! Sure, you're five years old, and yes, you're the most uncontrollable creature around for miles—button nose, corkscrew curls—but Fedor Kuzmitch, dignified and exemplary, does not approve of such shenanigans.

I'd overhear bits and pieces of this epos: Klavsevna gently rustling, the rug rats possibly absorbing some of the lessons.

§

Now that Olya is long gone, and we have lived out most of our lives and will ourselves soon be going beyond the blue glass, I called my brother Ivan to ask: What was all that about? And who was this Fedor Kuzmitch? Where did he come from and where did he go? But Ivan doesn't remember. Fedor Kuzmitch just was. So I guess, once again, I'm the sole witness of the existence of these titans and their dilapidated worlds.

Remember the palace of giants,
The silvery fish in the water,
The sycamore trees—goliaths,
The fortress of rock and mortar?

Remember the golden stallion,
Playfully rearing mid-canter,
His white shabraque and medallions
Adorned in an exquisite manner?

Remember, the heavens parted,
Together we found a ledge;
The stars, in the skies uncharted,
Like grapes dropping down unfetched.

I was twelve years old when I picked up a thin old book from the shelf and read these verses by Nikolai Gumilev. It seemed like they were speaking to me. When a line in a book says "Remember?" then it seems to me as if I do remember. Yes, I think I remember. Something rings a bell. I don't really know what a "shabraque" is and I'm still too lazy to look it up, that's more up your alley, Mister Gumilev, but "the skies uncharted"—let that be mine. I read this and dutifully remembered. Immediately the palace of giants appeared to me as the White House: the white columns, the dark-green tiles, the smooth blue-gray balusters disappearing high up the stairs, all seemed colossal in my childhood; and the loft window rested directly against the crown of the pine tree, the pine cones knocking against it in the storm—you could just reach up and touch the ledge where the heavens parted.

Fedor Kuzmitch must have come from a clan of Titans that populated the earth even before the appearance of man. He was a dazzling resident of the mythological Golden Age, close but not equal, of course, to Dmitriev Junior the Demiurge, who created our world according to his personal whim and who saw that it was good. Blind *aoidoi* in dusty and loud markets, in the shade of reed canopies, sang about the twelve labors of Fedor Kuzmitch; for a small price, cunning entrepreneurs showed the bluffs where Fedor Kuzmitch's cyclopean bed-sized feet stomped, and the vertical wall, overgrown with ivy, that Fedor Kuzmitch poked with his staff to create a spring of sweet water. Here Fedor Kuzmitch healed a quadriplegic, and over there is where he overcame the Minotaur. A rainbow in the sky, a thundering explosion on an invisible shooting range, twin trees on a faraway, unreachable shore—all these were the tracks of Fedor Kuzmitch that lingered long in this world, until the Golden Age ended. I blinked and missed how that happened and he was replaced with Krinda and Splat.

Ivan told me, in a sad telephone voice, that he remembers

clearly: after Fedor Kuzmitch were Krinda and Splat. Yes, he was five, and Olga was six.

Thus shrink generations, thus decline the tsars, thus great kingdoms meet their demise as the sands bury the Sphinx to her breast. Where temples once towered, all that remains are white column shafts, and they are beset with scarlet poppies come springtime.

§

Our sister Katerina had three children, and, being the eldest and by her own lights the most conscientious of us all, she decided to make things easier for Mom, and at the house in general, at least for a month. We were already sleeping there in layers and eating in shifts. She found a young nanny named Tosya, a sixteen-year-old girl with a tapirlike nose and the resulting nasal habits of speech. It was easy to see that she was an unreliable and dopey sort, but Katerina was fond of brave social experiments and firmly believed against all common sense—in the equality of all living beings. She bought train tickets to Feodosia: the end goal for all of us was always Koktebel, its essential value being not just the beach and the sea, but its sacredness. Our grandfather was friends with Maximilian Voloshin in the days of yore when this famous poet's house was still the only one on the deserted beach; the distant silhouette of the bluffs at the water's edge back then still resembled his profile perfectly. Father was friends with Voloshin's widow, and whenever he came to visit, she'd set up a bed for him and Mama in the studio. He later told me that this is where I was conceived, under the visage of the Egyptian princess Taïakh— her yellowish head blindly and mysteriously looking into the distance, her enigmatic features revealing nothing. It must have smelled of wormwood that day; all the grass had already dried out. Invisible cicadas clipped the hot air with tiny shears. August was under way; the waves beat ceaselessly against the empty beach.

Three generations had already visited this house, and Katerina was on her way with the fourth. Mother was a little worried; she was waiting for a telegram to find out how the journey went. On the third day after Katerina's departure, one of us went to the outhouse but found it occupied. It was still occupied ten minutes later, then twenty. We did a quick roll call—everyone was accounted for. After waiting a little while longer, we went out there to yank on the door, which was locked from the inside. Father pulled the handle strongly and broke into Curly's handiwork. Inside, white as a sheet from fear and desperation, was Tosya the nanny.

"What happened? Where is Katya?" exclaimed my parents.

Tosya was silent.

"Where is Katya? Where are the kids? What happened?!"

The nanny could only shake her head. She was pulled out and taken back to the house, given hot tea. Fearing the worst, we pressed her, demanding: What happened? What?

Finally she unclenched her jaw.

"Flw ld ff trn."

"What?!"

"Flw ld ff trn."

More tea, more alarmed exclamations, crazy thoughts, near-coronary panic. (Father: "Ooooh, I can't take this anymore, I demand to know what happened!" Mother, as always, cool as a cucumber.) Finally the vowels returned to the young lady, and, barely moving her tongue, she got the words out:

"Fellow lead off train."

Lead whom off? Lead where? At this very moment a telegram arrived. The post office lady was apprehensive about walking through the gate, since our dog Yassa was full of hatred toward all government employees: postmen, land inspectors, soldiers—basically anyone who came for official reasons and wearing boots; Father dragged the angry dog from the gate and frantically grabbed the telegram. Katerina wrote: "Nanny ran off with a Georgian comma everything OK comma fruit galore full stop."

Later, piecing together the mosaic of information, it came to light that shortly after Kaluga, but before the air turns sweet, southern, and languid; before the ladies selling baked potatoes and sour pickles become ladies offering sunflower seeds and hot corn on the cob through the open train windows, marriage grifters are already hard at work. The gorgeous Georgian "fellow," twisting his sable brows above his intensely piercing eyes, performed a well-rehearsed routine of sudden passion, allegedly inflamed by the short-legged and long-nosed Tosya, promising her love till death did them part and giving her a pair of lacquered heels as proof. "Come with me, and even death won't separate us." Tosya ran to Katerina: in a rickety old train car, between the boiler with metallic-tasting hot water and the WC with rattling hinges, gear-locking mechanism number 3, and such, a Love was born. That's exactly how love comes. "Please let me go!" Katerina tried to stop her: "Do not fall for men's cunning tricks!" But the young lady was head over heels in love, and in tears, a state that did wonders for her looks; so Katerina, who gave her blessing to all emotions, let her go.

After that, everything happened fast, too fast, and according to the script: the Georgian sat Tosya down in the Bryansk train station waiting room, taking all her money and the lacquered heels as well; he needed to buy tickets to his native Sukhumi.

"Wait here." She waited until nightfall before accepting that this was it. The end. It's unclear why she came back to our dacha, how she made it there with no money, and why she locked herself, cowering in fear, in our outhouse.

We talked about her for a long time after that: How would she live in this world, being so naive. How do such people survive?

How does anyone survive?

§

It's easy to enter the past: just keep looking straight ahead and walking. There will be no fences, no locks, the doors will open by themselves to let you in. Flowers won't wilt, berries will know no season, apples won't fall from tall-as-pines apple trees but will reach the ledge where the heavens part and turn into stars and grapes. Here is old man Dobroklonsky, an art historian, taking his four dachshunds out for a walk. He also lives in the White House—he must have moved in after us, because I can see him only from our side of the fence; we can no longer go for walks and play ball on the enormous field with its bald spot in the middle, but he can; he's bending over, unclasping the leashes so his frail, bowlegged dachshunds can run every which way in the grass. One of them, with cloudy cataracts in her bluish old eyes, hobbles my way to yap from across the wire fence. Yassa, locked inside the house, is worn out from indignation, she bangs her paws on the window, her bark hoarse: How dare they??? How dare they???

Mother walks to the lake with water buckets; Dobroklonsky greets her by lifting his black academic's skullcap. Mother says: He was friends with Benua and Yaremich, he used to be the director of the Hermitage. Father says: He lost both his sons in the war.

Dobroklonsky crosses the meadow that no longer belongs to us, he disappears behind the lilac bushes that are also no longer ours; I won't see him again. You don't know, do you, the names of his dachshunds. But I do! Another fifty years from now—even a hundred, or two hundred—and I'll still be able to hear his noble clarion voice:

"Myshka, Manishka, Murashka, Manzhet!"

Those were their names, and always in that order.

§

First Nanny passed and it was unclear how to go on. Nanny had lived in our family since my mother's birth in 1915, that faraway and already not-so-peaceful year when the first hammers started clanging at the future site of the White House. She'd leave, come back, suffer from asthma; she'd light a red lantern by an icon at night. She darned cotton stockings on a wooden mushroom; she kept a tin filled with various buttons, bits of lace, and flat elastic bands for rethreading into warm flannel pants. She let me sort the buckwheat: I'd scatter it on the oilcloth, and make a circle with my fingertip around the foreign elements: black thingies, oat-seed thingies, and tiny barrel-shaped thingies—all that weird stuff that you inexplicably find in buckwheat. Nanny smelled of clean, warm groats heated up in a pan. The lines on her face were checkered and soft.

"How you used to cry 'Nanny, don't leave! Nanny, dearest, don't leave!'—but it was time for my vacation, I had to go back to my village, to see my brother Petrusha, he was waiting and waiting for me, my little brother Petrusha . . ." " 'Nanny, don't leave!' " she'd repeat dreamily to me, or oftentimes to herself: she'd stand by the window, looking out somewhere in the distance and repeating my impassioned pleas to herself. Yes, I did cry—we were still living in Eden then, and I still believed that you could make someone stay with tears and love.

Then Aunty Lola passed, we no longer heard the *tap tap tap* of her cane on the staircase; it was now possible to sit and relax in the sunroom without the fear of being caught and taken upstairs for French lessons. Her personal cup—the one she drank her tea from and forbade us to touch—now idled in the sideboard; now you could just take it, but no one wanted to anymore; it seemed to be a peculiar porcelain gravestone, white with orange maple leaves and worn-away gilding. The smell of pink peonies and Acorn perfume lingered for years in Aunty Lola's bedroom, or perhaps it just seemed that way, was just our wishful thinking.

Once, long ago, Aunty Lola's nephew came to visit her at the dacha. He was an art student, and he spent the day at the lake drawing a study of sky and clouds. Nothing else. The grownups had little to say after looking at his creation. But I liked the clouds, they were of the cumulus variety, my favorite, eternal wanderers, clean celestial mountains. They'd hung above Lake Hepojarvi for a while that day, and then left. The cardboard painting was placed on top of the sideboard; it soon fell into the crack between the sideboard and the wall.

But then—a few years later—I found it; bending some wire into a poker, I pulled it out, along with a thick layer of dust, dead flies of years past, and a green leg from a plastic toy hippo. I took the cardboard picture and thus appropriated a singular day of eternity. In it is summer, and midday, and immortality. Certainly immortality.

Then others passed away—first this one, then that one. Each one had their own important life theme, their own love—real or imagined, happy or unrequited. Each one had a person, or a dream, or an idea, or a garden, or a house around which their life orbited, as if around the sun. They passed on, their personal suns went out, and there was no one left to speak of them, to think of them and to tell stories, to laugh and shake one's head while remembering.

Even Curly, whose life's purpose seemed to be to continually prove the law of conservation of mass—whatever is removed in one place is invariably added back in another—even he was, as we found out accidentally, an ardent supporter of Nikolaev, the one who killed the prominent Bolshevik leader Kirov (or was appointed in name as his killer; it's all terribly dark, unclear, and complicated). I was already an adult, Curly was old and frail, and Mother sent me to bring him some medicine. I found his apartment on the Petrogradsky side, hidden in one of the gloomy courtyards: a narrow room with windows that didn't open, dust, summer, and stale air. Tables, stools, shelves fashioned out of planks, all do-it-yourself, all from stolen boards and appropriated plywood; every surface covered with ancient magazines, stuffed and overflowing envelopes, documents that had descended from the sofa to the floor like glaciers.

"I keep writing!" Curly complained woefully. "I keep sending letters to historical magazines! To professors in Moscow, to party bigwigs, trying to explain that it wasn't him, it wasn't him! I knew him! Nikolaev just couldn't have done it, he was slandered! And they keep sending rejection letters: 'Thank you for your interest. . . .' They don't want to get to the bottom of this."

He wanted to talk, to explain to me his theory about what actually happened; the people around him must have grown tired of his truth by now: "What's it to you, it's over." I was a fresh—albeit unexpected—visitor. But I, too, couldn't be bothered to listen, and all the while, even as I walked down the dilapidated, treacherous staircase, Curly kept talking from the dimly lit landing; he kept talking and talking, his gray, but still curly, simpleton's head hanging low.

And then he passed away, too.

§

Natasha usually brought Klavsevna a kilo of sausages; Natasha was forever Klavsevna's lost little girl. This time she couldn't make it: students, kids, heavy bags, the need to transfer from one trolleybus to another. So she asked me to go instead. It was the first time she had, strangely enough. It took me awhile to find the entrance. It was an old building on the Griboyedov Canal, on the seventh floor of a walk-up, and as I was climbing up this unpleasant stairway off the back entrance, out of breath, I kept thinking: How does she manage? She must be eighty-six by now.

This was one of the cleanest and most spacious communal apartments that I ever did see, and in Klavsevna's room, where she lived and lived, time magically stood still; it was the emptiest of rooms and it got the most light, and I didn't immediately realize why. A narrow bed with two stiff pillows and a thin blanket was nestled by the wall. In the space between the two windows, a table made of yellow plywood and a mirror in a plain frame, and, fastened with a thumbtack, a fan of post-cards: the operetta star Georg Ots in a carnival mask for the role of Mister X, the Blessed Virgin Mary, and a portrait of someone unidentifiable. No drapes on the windows—the doctors advised against "looking in the dark"—so the white night evening was equally bright outside, on the empty street, and inside, in the empty room. In the window, faraway rusty roofs, chimneys, a tree growing through someone's balcony.

She was still pretty, Klavsevna, nimble and snub-nosed, and even leggy. We had nothing to talk about, but convention seemed to dictate that we talk, and so she unexpectedly told me her life's story—out of the blue, seated on her maiden bed, the sausages in her lap.

In 1914, Klavsevna had a fiancé—he was handsome, he was in love with her. They were walking hand in hand along Nevsky Prospect, not far from where we were sitting, by the way. On the bridge across the Griboyedov Canal they came upon some Gypsies. They laughed, decided to get their fortune told. The Gypsy told Klavsevna that anyone who married her would die. They laughed some more. Then the war started. Klavsevna's fiancé was killed.

And in the 1920s, after she'd had time to mourn and to move on, a wonderful young man, an engineer, asked for her hand. She was planning to marry him, but he died. She remembered the Gypsy woman and became alarmed. And in the 1930s, while traveling somewhere by train, in the compartment she met a lovely older gentleman, a professor. He kept looking at her, and then followed her into the rattling train corridor to say: "You're so beautiful! Would you be my wife? I am a widower, my kids are grown, I have money, I'll turn your life into a fairy tale."

She asked for three days to think it over. After the three days were up, she declined the professor's offer: he was so lovely and she didn't wish to be the cause of his demise.

And that was that. No more suitors, no more love, and no children—nothing but vitamin drops in her eyes and big stiff pillows in her bed.

"Would you . . . would you buy a postcard from me? And a plate? I need three rubles," said Klavsevna.

I gave her three rubles for the postcard and the plate.

On the plate, the edges of which were wrapped in kitschy gilded lace, trembled a poorly painted skylark; a reproach was written in Slavic script: "Still asleep, little man? Spring has sprung, get to work." The postcard was of a soldier with a harmonica, with an inscription that read: "Farewell to my family, farewell to my friends, farewell to my lady, all's come to an end."

What was written on the other side, with a piece of paper glued over it, we are not meant to know.

"How is little Olya doing?" asked Klavsevna.

"Wonderful," I lied.

"What a chiseled figure she has," sighed Klavsevna.

"Yes."

I wanted to remind her that it's best to keep the sausages in the fridge, but she, most likely, didn't have one.

She didn't have anything.

That's why her room was so spacious and full of light.

"Something to remember me by." Klavsevna motioned with her eyes toward my pitiful acquisitions. "Maybe you'll think about me sometimes."

Once at the threshold, I turned back to look, but she had already dissolved into the air and blended in with the white evening light.

The Square

In 1913, or 1914, or maybe 1915—the exact date is unknown—
Kazimir Malevich, a Russian painter of Polish descent, took
a medium-sized canvas (79.5 cm. x 79.5 cm.), painted it
white around the edges, and daubed the middle with thick
black paint. Any child could have performed this simple task,
although perhaps children lack the patience to fill such a large
section with the same color. This kind of work could have been
performed by any draftsman—and Malevich had worked as
one in his youth—but most draftsmen are not interested in
such simple forms. A painting like this could have been drawn
by a mentally disturbed person, but it wasn't, and had it been
it's doubtful that it would have had the chance to be exhibited
at the right place and at the right time.

After completing this simple task, Malevich became the
author of the most famous, most enigmatic, and most frightening painting known to man: *The Black Square*. With an easy
flick of the wrist, he once and for all drew an untraversable line
between old art and new art, between a man and his shadow,
between a rose and a casket, between life and death, between
God and the Devil. In his own words, he had reduced everything to "the zero of form." Zero, for some reason, turned out
to be a square, and this simple discovery is one of the most
frightening events in all of art's history.

Malevich knew what he had done. A year or so before this significant event, he, along with some friends and like-minded peers, participated in the first All-Russian Congress of Futurists. It was held at a dacha, in a bucolic, wooded area north of Saint Petersburg. Deciding to write an opera called *Victory over the Sun,* right there, at the dacha, they immediately got to work carrying out their plan. Malevich was in charge of scenic design. One of the set pieces was black-and-white, and it somehow resembled the future, still-unborn Square; it was used as a backdrop for one of the scenes. What would later spill out from his wrist, impulsively and with inspiration, in his Saint Petersburg studio would be recognized as a fundamental achievement of theory, an apex of accomplishment—a discovery of that critical, mysterious, coveted point after which, because of which, and beyond which nothing exists and nothing can exist.

Groping about in the dark with the brilliant intuition of an artist and the prophetic insight of a Creator, he found the forbidden figure of a forbidden color—so simple that thousands had walked past it, stepping over it, ignoring it, not noticing it. . . . To be fair, not many before him had dared to plan a *Victory over the Sun;* not many had dared to challenge the Prince of Darkness. Malevich did—and, just as is supposed to happen in tales of yearning Fausts bargaining with the Devil—the Master gladly, and without delay, whispered in the artist's ear the simple formula of nothingness.

By the end of 1915—the First World War was already in full swing—the sinister canvas was displayed alongside others at a Futurist exhibition. All his other works Malevich displayed on the walls in the traditional manner, but *The Black Square* was afforded a special place. As can be seen in one of the surviving photographs, the painting is displayed in the corner, under the ceiling—right where it is customary to hang Russian Orthodox icons. It's doubtful it eluded Malevich—a man well versed in color—that this paramount, sacral spot is called "the red corner," the word "red" here, in the original Russian, having the additional meaning of "beautiful." Malevich quite purposefully displayed a black hole in a sacred spot, calling this work of his "an icon of our times." Instead of red, black (zero color); instead of a face, a hollow chasm (zero lines); instead of an icon—that is, instead of a window into the heavens, into the light, into eternal life—gloom, a cellar, a trapdoor to the underworld, eternal darkness.

Alexandre Benois, a contemporary of Malevich and an excellent artist in his own right, as well as an art critic, wrote this about the painting: "This black square in a white frame—this is not a simple joke, not a simple dare, not a simple little episode which happened at the house at the Field of Mars. Rather, it's an act of self-assertion of that entity called 'the abomination of desolation,' which boasts that through pride, through arrogance, through trampling of all that is loving and gentle it will lead all beings to death."

Many years before that, in September of 1869, Leo Tolstoy had a strange experience that would have a powerful effect on the rest of his life, one that would be, it appears, a turning point in his entire outlook. He left his house in high spirits to make an important and profitable purchase: a new estate. He and his servant were riding in a horse-drawn carriage, happily chatting. Night fell. "I dozed off but then suddenly awoke: for some reason I felt afraid. . . . I suddenly felt that I don't need any of this, that there is no need to ride this far, that I'll die right here, away from home. And I felt frightened." They decided to spend the night in a little town called Arzamas:

> We finally approached some lodge with a hitching post. The house was white, but it seemed horribly sad to me. And so I felt a great sense of dread. . . . There was a hallway; a sleepy man with a spot on his check—that spot seemed awful to me—showed me to my room. Gloomy was that room. I entered it and felt even more dread. . . .
>
> A whitewashed square room. As I remember, it was particularly painful to me that this room was square. There was one window with a red curtain. . . . I grabbed a pillow and lay down on the sofa. When I came to, the room was empty and it was dark. . . . I could feel that falling asleep again would be impossible. Why had I decided to stop here? Where am I taking myself? From what and where to am I running? I'm running from something frightful that I can't escape. . . . I stepped out into the hallway, hoping to leave behind that which was tormenting me. But it came out after me and marred everything. I was just as scared, more scared even.
>
> —What nonsense, I said to myself. Why do I feel anguish, what am I scared of?
>
> —Of me, came the soundless voice of death. I am here. . . .
>
> I tried to lie down but as soon as I did, I jumped up in horror. The anguish, the anguish—the same dread as comes before nausea, but only spiritual. Frightening, terrifying. Seemingly it's fear of death, but if you recollect, think about life, then it's actually a fear of a life dying. Life and death were merging into one. Something was trying to tear my soul to pieces but was unable to do it.

I went to look once again at those who were sleeping; I tried to fall asleep, too; same kind of dread—red, white, square. Something being torn apart but not tearing. Painful, painfully dry and malicious; not a drop of kindness could I sense within myself. Only an even, calm anger with myself and with that which had made me.

This famous and mysterious event in Tolstoy's life—which was not simply a sudden, major depressive episode but an unforeseen kind of meeting with death, with evil —was named "the Arzamas horror." Red, white, square. Sounds like a description of one of Malevich's paintings.

Leo Tolstoy, who personally experienced the red-white Square, couldn't foresee, or control, what happened. It appeared before him and it attacked him, and under its influence— not right away, but steadily—he renounced the life that he'd led before; he renounced his family, love, the understanding of those close to him, the foundations of life around him; he renounced art. This "truth" that was revealed to him led him into nothingness, into the zero of form, into self-destruction. On a "spiritual quest," toward the end of his life, he found only a handful of banalities—a version of early Christianity, nothing more. His followers, too, walked away from civilization, and likewise didn't arrive anywhere. Drinking tea instead of vodka, abstaining from meat, rejecting family ties, making one's own boots—poorly, crookedly—that, essentially, is the result of this personal spiritual quest that passed through the Square. "I'm here" came the soundless voice of death, and life went downhill from there. The struggle went on; Anna Karenina (mercilessly killed off by the author, punished for her desire to live) was still ahead of him. Still before him were several literary masterpieces, but the Square had won.

Tolstoy banished from within himself the life-giving power of art, moving on to primitive parables and cheap moralizing. He let his light go out of him before his physical death, in the end astonishing the world not with the artistry of his later works but with the magnitude of his genuine anguish, his individual protest and public self-flagellation on a hitherto unprecedented scale.

Malevich also wasn't expecting the Square, although he was searching for it. In the period before the invention of Suprematism (Malevich's term), he preached "alogism," an attempt to escape the boundaries of common sense; preached "the struggle against logism, naturalness, philistine sensibilities, and prejudices." His call to action was heard, and the Square appeared before him, absorbing him within it. Malevich had every right to be proud of the celebrity afforded him by his deal with the Devil. And proud he was. I don't know if he noticed the paradox of this celebrity status. "The painter's most famous work" meant that his other works were less famous, less important, less enigmatic; in other words, they were less worthy. And it's true—alongside *The Black Square,* all his other works lose luster. He has a series of canvases of geometric, brightly colored peasants with empty ovals for faces that look like transparent, unfertilized eggs. They are colorful, decorative paintings, but they come across as a tiny and insignificant stew of rainbow colors, finally swirling into a colorful funnel before they disappear into the bottomless pit that is *The Black Square.* He has landscapes—pinkish, impressionistic, very run-of-the-mill— the kind painted by many, and often better. Toward the end of his life, he tried to return to figurative art, and those attempts look predictably bad: these aren't people but, rather, embalmed corpses and wax dolls, tensely peering out from the frames of their clothing, as if they've been cut out of colorful bits of fabric, scraps and leftovers from the "peasants" series. Of course, when one reaches the top, the only way is down. The terrible truth was that, at the top, there was nothingness.

Art critics write lovingly about Malevich: "*The Black Square* absorbed all painting styles that had existed before it; it blocks the way for naturalistic imitation, it exists as absolute form, and it heralds art in which free forms—those that are interconnected and those that are not—make up the meaning of the painting."

It's true that the Square "blocks the way," including the way for the artist. "It exists as absolute form"—that's true as well, but it also means that all other forms are unnecessary by comparison, since they are, by definition, not absolute. "It heralds art"—this bit turned out to be false. It heralds the end of art, its impossibility, its lack of necessity; it represents the furnace in which art burns, the pit into which art falls, because the Square (to quote Benois again) is "an act of self-assertion of that entity called 'the abomination of desolation,' which boasts that through pride, through arrogance, through trampling of all that is loving and gentle, it will lead all beings to death."

A "pre-Square" artist studies his craft his entire life, struggling with dead, inert, chaotic matter, trying to breathe life into it; as if fanning a fire, as if praying, he tries to ignite a light within a stone; he stands on his tippy toes, craning his neck in an attempt to peek where the human eye cannot see. Sometimes his efforts and prayers, his caresses, are rewarded: for a brief moment, or maybe for a long while, "it" happens, "it" "appears." God (an angel, a ghost, a muse, or sometimes a demon) steps back and acquiesces, letting go from his hands those very things, those volatile feelings, those wisps of celestial fire—what should we call them?—that they have reserved for themselves, for their wondrous abode that is hidden from us. Having solicited this divine gift, the artist experiences a moment of acute gratitude, unhumiliating humility, unshameful pride, a moment of distinct, pure, and purifying tears—both seen and unseen—a moment of catharsis. But "it" surges, and "it" retreats, like a wave. The artist becomes superstitious. He wants to repeat this moment, he knows that, next time, he may not be granted a divine audience, and so his spiritual eyesight opens up, he can sense with deep inner foreknowledge what exactly—avarice, selfishness, arrogance, conceit—may close the pearly gates in front of him. He tries to wield his inner foreknowledge in such a way as not to sin before his angelic guides; he fully understands that he's a co-author at best, or an apprentice—but a crowned co-author, a beloved apprentice. The artist knows that the Spirit blows wherever it pleases. He knows that he, the artist, has done nothing in his earthly life to deserve being singled out by the Spirit, and so if that should happen he ought to joyfully give thanks for this wonder.

A "post-Square" artist, an artist who has prayed to the Square, who has peeked inside the black hole without recoiling in horror, doesn't trust muses and angels; he has his own black angels, with short metallic wings—pragmatic and smug beings who know the value of earthly glory and know how to bite off its most satisfying and multilayered chunks. Craft is unnecessary, what you need is a brain; inspiration is unnecessary, what's needed is calculation. People love innovation, you need to come up with something new; people love to fume, you need to give them something to fume about; people are indifferent, you need to shock them: shove something smelly in their face, something offensive, something repugnant. If you strike a person's back with a stick, they'll turn around; that's when you spit in their face and then, obviously, charge them for it—otherwise, it's not art. If this person starts yelling indignantly, you must call them an idiot and explain that art now consists solely of the message that art is dead—repeat after me: dead, dead, dead. God is dead, God was never born, God needs to be trod upon, God hates you, God is a blind idiot, God is a wheeler-dealer, God is the Devil. Art is dead and so are you, ha-ha, now pay up! Here is a piece of excrement for it; it's real, it's dark, it's dense, it's locally sourced, so hold it tight and don't let it go. There is nothing "loving and gentle" out there and there never was, no light, no flight, no sunbeam through a cloud, no glimmer in the dark, no dreams, and no promises. Life is death; death is here; death is immediate.

"Somehow life and death have merged into one," Leo Tolstoy wrote in horror, and from this moment on, and till the end, he fought back as best he could—it was a colossal battle of biblical proportions. "And Jacob was left alone; and there wrestled a man with him until the breaking of the day." It's terrifying to witness the battle of a genius with the Devil: first one seems to overcome, then the other.

The Death of Ivan Ilyich is such a battlefield, and it's difficult to say who won. In this novella, Tolstoy says—tells us, repeats it, assures us, hammers it into our brains—that life is death. But, in the end, his dying hero is born into death as if into a new life; he's freed, turned around. Enlightened, he leaves us for a place where, seemingly, he'll be given consolation. "New art" derides the very idea of consolation, of enlightenment, of rising above—it derides it while taking pride in that derision, as it dances and celebrates.

Conversations about God are so endlessly complicated that it's scary even to engage in them, or, on the contrary, very simple: if you want God to exist, He does; if you don't, He doesn't. If He is everybody, ourselves included, then for us He is, first and foremost, ourselves. God does not impose himself on us.

Rather, it's His distorted, falsified image that's imposed upon us by other people, while God simply and quietly exists within us, like still water in a well. While searching for Him, we search for ourselves; while refuting Him, we refute ourselves; while mocking Him, we mock ourselves—the choice is ours. Dehumanization and "desacralization" are one and the same.

"Desacralization" was the slogan of the twentieth century; it's the slogan of ignoramuses, of mediocrity and incompetence. It's a free pass doled out by one dimwit to another bonehead while trying to convince the third nincompoop that everything should be meaningless and base (allegedly democratic, allegedly accessible), and that everyone has the right to judge everyone else; or no one does—that authority can't exist in principle, that a hierarchy of values is obscene (since everyone's equal), and that art's worth is determined solely by cost and demand. Novelties and fashionable scandals are surprisingly not that novel and not that scandalous: fans of the Square keep presenting various bodily fluids and objects created from them as evidence of art's accomplishments. It's as if Adam and Eve—one suffering from amnesia, the other from Alzheimer's—were attempting to convince each other and their children that they are clay, only clay, and nothing but clay.

I'm considered an "expert" in contemporary art by an arts fund in Russia that's subsidized by foreign money. Artists come to us with projects and we decide if they should get funding or not. There are actual experts working alongside me on this panel, true connoisseurs—old art, "pre-Square." We all can't stand *The Black Square* and the "self-assertion of that entity called 'the abomination of desolation.'" Yet they keep submitting projects that consist of "the abomination of desolation," solely of the abomination, and nothing else. We are obligated to spend the money allocated to the fund or else it will be closed. We try our best to fund those who come up with the least pointless and annoying ideas. One year, we funded an artist who placed empty picture frames along a riverbank, and another who wrote "ME" in big letters that cast a beautiful shadow, as well as a group of creators who organized a campaign to clean up dog feces in Saint Petersburg's parks. Another year, it was a woman who affixed stamps to rocks and mailed them to various cities in Russia, as well as a group that made a pool of blood in a submarine—visitors had to step over the blood while listening to the letters of Abelard and Heloise via headphones. After our meetings, we members of the panel step out for a silent smoke, trying to avoid eye contact with one another. We then silently shake hands and hurriedly walk home.

Judith with the Sword

Toward the end of the 1980s—when everything seemed possible, in bloom, and promising—I was interviewed by some newspaper. They asked about literature and history, and I said that, if I could, I'd publish a book portraying twentieth-century Russia in letters, with each missive corresponding to a single year.

This would have been nearly impossible because there were whole decades when letters lied; you couldn't write down anything truthful. People even lied in their personal diaries, fearing searches and arrests, and so, of course, lying in one's letters was natural. But perhaps with a massive effort it would still be possible to put together such a book, said I. There are literary archives and attics with trunks, aren't there? And how simultaneously wonderful and disquieting it is to read other people's letters. It's like peering into a stranger's window: you feel awkward, you feel curious, it's better than the movies. Inside there is somebody else's singular, sui generis life.

Shortly after this interview, a man (I still don't know who he was) found me and presented me with a thick stack of letters: Please read. "Perhaps you'll find them useful," he said. I read them and returned them: alas, useful they were not. All of them were written by the same woman—I don't remember her name, so let's call her Maria Vasilievna—who lived in the

ancient provincial Russian town of Ryazan. I couldn't quite figure her out, nor did I catch to whom she was writing, and the
mysterious messenger didn't care to elaborate. Maria V. worked
as a trolley car driver, but her life was full of spiritual and cultural inquiries. Grammatical errors abounded in her writing,
but her interests were all-encompassing: from simple rhymes
she read in the local newspaper, to reminiscences of the famous
Russian philosopher A. Losev's funeral, which she considered
an important cultural milestone, and for which she had traveled to Moscow to stand, full of reverence, in the crowd.

One of her letters I did ask to keep. The story that it told
somehow pierced my heart. Twenty-five years have passed, but
I'll tell it now.

Retell it.

In her town of Ryazan, in one of the dilapidated houses
across from the bus depot, there lived an artist with his wife
and kids. He spent years salting away money for a bedroom
furniture set. His wife dreamt of having it all—a night table
on either side of a double bed, a wardrobe with a full-length
mirror inside, intricate carvings—and for all of it to look ever
so expensive, ever so artistic. Finally he'd saved up enough to
go to Moscow to explore the antique shops.

Back in those days, all of the Frunze Embankment was basically one big antique market. All kinds of lovely junk was being
sold there for a pretty penny: flame mahogany, black stuff with
gold, white stuff with gold, stuff on crooked claw-feet, and stuff
with the wings of a griffin. They had beds, chests of drawers,
armchairs, oval and octagonal tables, centipede tables, kidney-
shaped tables, consoles, vases, chandeliers, leaf-shaped crystal
garlands, statuettes, paintings, and clocks, and everything was
just so, so lovely.

As he walked amid all this splendor—a thick stack of bills

tucked into the inside pocket of his jacket, fastened with a safety pin so it wouldn't get stolen in the metro—he was using his keen artist's eye to pick out the best. Meanwhile, back home in Ryazan, his wife, as you can imagine, was anxious about that stack of bills, which had taken years to accumulate—anxious but at the same time daydreaming, imagining how magically their marriage bed would be transformed, how mysteriously the lacquer on the nightstand would shine in the moonlight, how their love would be renewed, how her girlfriends would die of envy.

In one of the shops, by the back wall, he saw a sculpture. White, marble, the height of a woman. *Judith with the Sword.*

And he was gone.

Undoubtedly he had heard of Pygmalion, who carved Galatea and fell in love with her; they used to teach it in school back then. A standard sampling of romantic myths was offered—harmless and thus available to the Soviet citizen: Orpheus and Eurydice for the young; the faithful Penelope awaiting her husband's return for women of Balzac age; and Pygmalion: *My Fair Lady*—who doesn't know that one?

But it is one thing to know, and quite another to fall in love with a marble statue till death do you part. And when I say till death, I truly mean it.

The artist asked: How much? "This much." He haggled, but it was still too expensive—he didn't have enough; he dispatched a telegram to his wife: Send more. In a tizzy, she ran around borrowing from friends and neighbors: must be mahogany, must have curlicues and bronze inlay!

He bought his beloved, paying for her an outrageous sum; he barely had enough for the movers and his ticket back home. Judith was wrapped up in rags, but the movers were Soviet, drunk, unqualified; while they were dragging her along the train platform and shoving her into the train car, the tip of her sword broke off.

He dragged her home by himself, to the second floor, I believe.

Imagine, you're the wife, you're expecting your husband with a magnificent master bedroom set, including the nightstands—sacral objects, as it were. Mentally you are already luxuriating, stretching out on the bed, young and libidinous once again. And then he tumbles in through the door—with another woman. So what if she's made of marble? That's even worse.

The wife—writes Maria V., if you still remember her—ran out on him in a hurry, with kids in tow. They haven't seen her in Ryazan since. And we—continues Maria—finally managed to get an invitation to come visit him. Brought a cake, the kind with green cream roses. Surprisingly tasty! He put the kettle on. He's a lovely man, very polite. He has interesting paintings. Lives alone. And *her*—writes Maria V. in holy awe—we saw her, too. *She* stands by the wall—white, her gaze averted, hair parted neatly and pulled back into a bun. The tip of her sword is missing. The apartment is nice and clean—goes on Maria V.—but under the wardrobe I saw a strange gray rug, which I bent down to examine closer: it was dust. He must have not dusted under there for eight years! Otherwise he's perfectly normal.

So that was the letter. And all of it has been left behind the barrier of time, all of it must be gone by now: Maria Vasilievna, the artist, that world.

There is only love, unexpected and inexplicable, and it's always the same story: embarrassing, pointless, down to the last penny. And silent.

Stay silent, but stay.

Aetherial Worlds

"You do understand, don't you, that from this moment on, all the rights as well as all responsibilities and liabilities associated with this property will become yours," the lawyer patiently repeated. "This will no longer be David and Barbara's responsibility, it will be yours."

David and Barbara were watching me sullenly, without blinking. In my hand was a pen with black ink, and all I had to do was imprint the purchase agreement with one last signature. David and Barbara were getting a divorce and selling their Princeton, New Jersey, home. I was the buyer. And we were all sitting in a lawyer's office. A heavy American downpour raged outside, the weather bearing similarity to that of the flood of Saint Petersburg in 1824; it was coming down with a particular kind of vengeance, you couldn't see more than thirty feet ahead of you—there was just a wall of rain—and what you could see inspired consternation: the furious waters had already climbed halfway up the tires of the cars parked outside and were rising as fast as a second hand sweeps the face of a clock.

"Yeah, we may see some flooding," the lawyer said indifferently, following my gaze. "In New Jersey, thousands of cars wind up at used car lots after a downpour like this. But I wouldn't recommend buying one. They're all lemons. However, that's entirely up to you."

"What about the house?" I asked. "Might the house get flooded?"

"The house sits on a hill," David interjected, fidgeting. "The neighbors do get flooded, but not us, so far—"

"Mister P., please!" came a strict reminder from counsel.

This lawyer forbade David from speaking to me and me to him. Perhaps he feared that David would let something slip, possibly exposing the hidden flaws of the house, whereupon I'd gasp, and the sale price would immediately plummet. David would suffer a loss. Or—just as now—he would ply me with false promises, like the one about the hill allegedly ensuring the safety of the property, and I'd believe him, only later to walk into the house and find water undulating in the basement. This would mean that David had lied to me in the presence of two attorneys and so I would file a lawsuit, there would be litigation with no end in sight. No, according to the playbook, David was supposed to be cold, reserved, and neutral. Courteous but distant.

But this David? This David could scarcely hide how tickled he was that somebody wanted to buy his pitiful—at least by American standards—dwelling: a long gray unfinished barn with a leaky roof, tucked away in the back of an overgrown plot in an unprestigious rural corner. The address may have said Princeton, but really it was Bumblefuck, New Jersey—dense forest, a rutted road leading toward neglected, dilapidated structures. At the end of the road was a shack I would come to call "the End of All Paths": boarded up, broken windows, decayed to the color of ash, it would have collapsed long ago if not for two dozen thin but sturdy young trees that pierced it like spears and improbably, impossibly, un-fucking-believably held it upright.

David was simple and honest, so very simple and honest

that his eyes would bulge from the fear that he might cheat me or hoodwink me, even by accident. He showed me where the floor was rotted in the kitchen: the linoleum was so worn it had holes in it, having gone unchanged for thirty years. But the wood underneath was still holding up. He proposed that we both get on all fours to look under some cabinet, where a big chunk of the floor was missing. He'd yank at the window frames by the latches now formless from all the coats of paint—"Look, these are no good! They'll need to be changed!" He thoroughly described where the roof leaked, where I'd be obliged to put buckets when it poured. He told me about the patio fiasco. That is, David didn't have a patio—it existed only in his dreams. "Go see for yourself." After banging his hip against it several times, he was able to open the swollen, warped plywood door that lurked in the back of this squalid abode—and there . . . a most magical room!

You take but a step and escape the semi-dark, narrow, low-ceilinged pencil box of a house for this airy sunroom, suspended just a bit aboveground. On both the left side and the right were floor-to-ceiling windows overlooking lush gardens where little red birds fluttered, and something in bloom entwined in the trees swayed in the wind.

"You see, I had the door and window frames made by a great craftsman—he has a two-year waiting list," said David apologetically. "I ended up spending a lot of money. Maybe two grand. Or two and a half. Didn't have anything left for the patio."

He pulled at the sliding glass door—transparent and patterned, like the wing of a dragonfly—and the whole thing moved to the side. Beyond the threshold there was a green abyss, and a little beyond that, a lone pine tree. Beneath that tree, a latticework of sun rays on a carpet of last year's needles, through which had sprouted lilies of the valley, their gaze shy and averted. My heart skipped a beat.

"No patio," repeated David ruefully. "Right here is where it should have been built."

Like a true fucking lunatic, David had begun building his Garden of Eden before making a budget. And so this absurd, wonderful addition, this airy, translucent box promising entry into an aetherial world, was stuck in our terrestrial one, weighty and stifling.

"But it can still be built!" he said. "All you need to do is to apply for a permit at our local municipal building; they'll grant it."

"And why are you selling, if I may ask?" I asked.

"I want to buy a ranch and ride horses," said David, lowering his gaze. Behind us Barbara began to weep quietly, stifling her sobs, and by the time we reentered the dimly lit house, she had already pulled herself together.

"I'll take it," I said. "It suits me fine."

And now, once I imprint this American document with my illegible scribble, an entire acre of the U.S. of A. will become my personal property.

It was 1992 and time was flowing by—just whirling, raging past—as I had recently moved here from Russia, where everything had fallen apart, where the rug had been pulled out from under us, where it was impossible to tell what belonged to whom, and where nothing belonged to me. But here, in the New World, I could buy a green rectangle of dependable land and own it in a way that I'd never owned anything before. And if somebody dared to break in, I'd have the right to shoot them. Although I should probably look up the Constitutional rights of thieves and robbers first.

So David and I came to an agreement that I would defi-

nitely be buying his house. We even sat down to have a cel-
ebratory drink, trying not to pay any mind to Barbara weeping
alternately in the bedroom and in the backyard. David told
me that the house's original owners were a childless African-
American couple, and that all the flowers—he encircled the
fading, autumnal yard with his hand—all these flowers had
been planted by the wife; what the husband did, no one knew.
"She had a real green thumb, as you'll see later, when spring
comes—you will see it all."

The sale dragged on through the entire summer: first the
college had to confirm my future employment, then the bank
had to approve my future salary and calculate what mortgage
terms I qualified for, then the lawyers had to figure out David
and Barbara's divorce and the distribution of proceeds from
the sale of the house—there were a lot of bureaucratic steps, by
which time the summer had passed, the foliage had wilted, the
house was left sitting dark and cheerless.

We figured out all the terms ourselves and even became
friendly—Barbara no longer bothered keeping up appearances;
she'd walk around the house hunched over, eyes red and face
puffy, her arms dangling limply, resigned to her fate and awaiting the inevitable. David had already showed me all his manly
treasures, which he kept in the garage: jack planes, chisels,
screwdrivers, and drills. Men like to show these instruments to
women, and women like to pretend that these instruments
are absolutely fascinating. He even took down his grandfather's sled from the wall. His grandpa had used it back in
the 1920s, as a rosy-cheeked, chubby five year old; when he
started school—a mile and a half on foot in the freezing snow—
his mother would get up before dawn to bake him two potatoes, one for each pocket, to warm his hands during his long,
unaccompanied journey. David gave me the sled as a gift and I

didn't know what to do with it. He also gave me his proposed alteration plans, which he no longer had any use for—a whole binder of them on tracing paper, one more fantastical than the other: here is the house, all in ruin, and here it is growing wings on either side; here is a loft with an oval window taking flight above it; here are terraces encircling it like ruffles. In short, David poisoned me, lured me, entrapped me; he sold me his dreams, his fantasies, his ship in the sky with no passengers and an invisible captain.

Meanwhile, I was renting an expensive and no-longer-necessary apartment, where I kept all my belongings, accumulated during my three years here. Our stuff wasn't anything special, but a family of four does acquire quite a few earthly possessions: earthly suitcases, earthly dishes, and earthly clothes, not to mention our earthly table and our four chairs, which were the earthliest of all. I asked David if I could keep all this crap in the house—David's house, but mine, too, in a way—perhaps shoving it all in the basement. David didn't mind. But, just in case, he consulted his attorney, who immediately reacted, restricted, and rejected the idea: the storing of my things in this yet-to-be-purchased house would create, under the laws of New Jersey, some sort of tricky loophole, the victim of which would be David, since I would thereby have the right to simply take his house without paying, or otherwise rob, bind, and deprive him, the owner.

No, we couldn't do that, and so I watched in dismay as the last of my savings were depleted—I guess I won't be fixing the roof this year, or putting in a new bathtub to replace David's old trough. Wouldn't have enough for a lawn mower, either, which I knew was a must here, but at least the linoleum—that I could afford, as I'd be installing it myself, and not buying it as a single piece but in those dirt-cheap squares instead. The black-and-white ones, just as in the painting of Nikolai Ge's, wherein Tsar Peter interrogates the Tsarevich Alexei.

Looking out the window once again, I saw that the waters had already roiled up to my car doors, and that if I didn't sign right now I wouldn't have anything to drive away in. And so I bit the bullet. The house became mine, and I—its.

All the participants, who either received or parted with their money, experienced their complicated and contradictory emotions and went their separate ways: David disappeared into the wall of rain, conveyed by his pickup truck; Barbara glided off into the waterfall of her unhidden tears, and my family, we made our way toward our new home, unsure whether it was still standing.

It was completely empty, naked, and old. The floors were drab and worn, the windows swathed from the outside in dark spruce branches. I don't like pine trees—to me they feel like the trees of the dead. Blue pine trees are the worst; they are the color of a Soviet general's uniform, and so they plant them where those high-status corpses lie. Our neighbor had one such pine. And so I was forced to look at it, see.

Brown spiderwebs were already dangling under the ceiling, in the corners. The agile American spider produces a high-quality web overnight, and since Barbara had long stopped taking care of the house, the accumulated layers of web could easily support the weight of small household items, if somebody decided to place them there for some reason, as if in a hammock. My boys gloomily inspected their dimly lit cubbyholes, unpacked their computers, and proceeded to stare at their screens.

The magical room was also sad and cold. And its glass doors opened onto nothingness.

I alone loved this house.

§

Spring in the states, on the East Coast, is basically crazy. Overnight, everything that just yesterday stuck out its dead branches is resurrected. Cherry blossoms adorn the green lawns like pink fountains, forsythia bushes are sprinkled with yellow flowers without a single green leaf—the leaves come later. And the pear trees—my God, I can't take such beauty! By the time the magnolias begin to bloom it's already too much—a simple heart does not require such splendor. Flowers should be crumpled, torn, and ragged, like peonies, for instance.

The original owner—the African-American lady about whom I know nothing—had, as promised, truly planted the entire property with flowers. Along the walkway from the street to the front door was a long row of irises. Under the tree they call "catalpa" she had a small rose garden: it had grown wild, and when I ripped out the gigantic American weeds and cut down the monstrous American thorny bushes—spirals with spikes that could easily have served to secure the perimeter of a gated property—I discovered lovely white roses, surprisingly fragrant considering that in America flowers usually have no scent, vegetables no taste, and that, generally, smells of any kind are culturally unacceptable.

In the middle of the front lawn she had planted a Japanese maple, the kind with little red, filigreed leaves. That was a great thing she had done! I often thought about her, imagining her for some reason in a sky-blue dress: here she is, walking out of our little house, squinting at the sun, walking over to the white roses, to the purple irises wildly gynecological in their construction; touching red leaves with her dark-skinned hand and looking around to see that, behold, it was all very good. I also found out that she had planted daffodils, but over the years they had migrated south, and I would find them on the border of my neighbor's property, in thickets and vines, in places where my legs couldn't go but my hands could still reach. Of course, I dug them out and moved them back to the house—that was where she'd wanted them from the very beginning. And I had an intimation of her walking by, casting a glance.

I could see traces of her presence everywhere on the property—and the property was huge. I soon found out what she had planted on the south side and what on the east, what she'd hidden under the pine tree—such as those lilies of the valley—and what she'd wanted to make visible from the front stoop, our flimsy little three-step porch. When lush American summer came, I finally saw her vision in its totality: an immense wall of bushes rose up at the edge of the property and completely shielded us—from the street, from the cars, from the fumes, sounds, and prying eyes. We couldn't see anyone and no one could see us. If you didn't know that our house was just there, behind that green wall, you'd have never guessed it. After sunset it disappeared in the crepuscular light, so that I myself could easily miss it from the street.

In the hallway, from the ceiling, there hung a rope. I tugged at it, and a squeaky folding staircase came down. It led to the attic, of course. There, boxes filled with junk from the 1960s were drying out and falling apart—blouses and aprons, the kind one wouldn't have wanted to wear even then but couldn't bring oneself to throw out. Nothing interesting. A whole mess of postcards—Christmas, Easter—also boring and unremarkable: "Merry Christmas, dear Bill and Nora." So her name was Nora. Funny, I had imagined her as a Sally.

Once again she walked by, undetected, running her hand over the droopy branches of the Liquidambar—a beautiful evening-hued tree, full of sweet sap. But Bill didn't walk by— he never walked in the garden. He stood, camouflaged by the wall, semi-transparent, eyes glistening in the dark.

According to custom, our neighbors came bearing pie. We already knew that this is what happens when you first move in but weren't sure if we were supposed to reciprocate. These neighbors had a farm.

"Do you eat meat?" they asked.

"Yes, of course," we answered naively.

"Then come by and pick out a baby lamb. We will slaughter it for you and you'll save some money."

We were city folk, and this offer somewhat paralyzed us. Not that we were considering becoming vegetarians, but the idea of coming to a farm, pointing to that one—sweet, curly, innocent—and . . . what? "Kill it, I want it"?

I reckon they ascribed our sudden stupor to that general idiocy of foreigners.

"Then come by for blueberries, you can pick all you want. We have so many this year, don't know what to do with them."

Blueberries I could agree to. I grabbed a basket and off I went, taking the long way through the fields. The distance between our houses was no more than five hundred feet, but those feet were densely forested. The thicket between my neighbors and me was absolutely impassable. Little Red Riding Hood and the Wolf, entering from opposite sides, would never have found each other.

I looked around for the blueberries, but couldn't see any. The missus walked me over to some sort of aviary—in the Moscow zoo, such cages are used to house sullen feathered creatures with complex Latin names.

"We have to keep the berries under a mesh or the birds will eat them," she complained.

I walked into the aviary. High above my head, on the upper branches of the bushes, there were, indeed, berries, but not the cute little blueberries we Russians crouch and kneel to pick. These were industrial-sized, overgrown, American monster-berries. And to pick them, one had to get on tippy toes and reach high overhead. The sun was blinding. The birds desperately stalked the mesh roof but couldn't reach anything. I didn't last long. After picking a small boxful, I stopped and decided to head home. Watching me go, the neighbor's wife concluded that I was a moron, but politely concealed it with a fake smile. Thank you, Lord. I am free! Under a canopy there was a little black boy with a frightened and unhappy face. The husband was busy instructing the child.

"We adopted him." The neighbor's wife pointed her finger in the direction of the little one. "Say hi!"

The little boy hurriedly got up and gave a nod.

"He had a bad life before, but he's happy here," said the husband, and then turned back to finish his lecture: "First you work, then you eat."

I took the long way home, through the fields. You could say that nothing bad had transpired, but as often happens with introverts, I felt as if my soul had been trampled on. Was it the birds . . . ? The path veered off into the forest, where houses stand empty, propped up by trees that pierce them like spears.

"Nora," I said to an empty house in the empty forest. "Nora, he had a bad life before them, but he's happy here."

But she was looking far into the distance, and was almost no longer here.

§

I was working at a small college way up north. Two days a week—Mondays and Wednesdays—I was to teach creative writing. We'd tell the students right away that it can't be taught, but they'd only smirk, thinking that the grown-ups were lying: "Somebody must have taught *them!*"

Few of them truly applied themselves, but that wasn't what irritated me. Much worse was that they didn't really know how to read and couldn't be bothered to learn. Didn't care about what was actually written down on the page.

I'd assign them a five-page story to read. Hemingway. Or maybe Salinger. "So, Steven, can you tell me what this story is about?"

"I dunno. I didn't like it."

"Thank you for sharing—your opinion is very valuable to us. Can you tell us specifically what you didn't like?"

"I didn't like that the guy was cheating on his wife. That's just wrong. I don't like to read about such things."

"Tell me, Steven, do people sometimes cheat on each other?"

"Yes."

"So why not write a story about that?"

"Cheating is wrong and it doesn't teach us anything."

"So you're saying that literature must teach us? An interesting and debatable point of view. Can you please elaborate?"

I didn't give two shits about what Steven would say. What I gave a shit about was not letting this smart-ass little punk—who'd spent the entire night before smoking weed (and still reeked of it) and who'd just cut me off in his Porsche to take

127

my parking spot—think he'd hoodwinked me about even having read the story. Must have just asked his girlfriend outside:
What's this story about? And she said: Some dude steps out on
his girl. Now here he is, answers at the ready. Don't piss on my
leg and tell me it's raining, I'll corner you and eat your brains
for breakfast.

But here is the conundrum: if you simply and guilelessly
expose a student as a liar and fail him for being unprepared,
he'll avenge himself at the end of the semester. Every single one
of them gets a teacher evaluation form from the dean's office
twice a year. They sit down and, diligently bending their wrists
unaccustomed to writing, fill out said forms with block letters
and slanderous accusations. "Professor didn't hold my interest."
"Didn't create an entertaining atmosphere for me." "What's
with those crazy ties?" "Gave me Cs and Ds but didn't explain
why. Overall, I was disappointed."

And so the instructor must find more nurturing and beguil-
ing ways to make the student realize he is a lazy ignoramus (if
that is, indeed, what she wants him to realize), so that very
student will be forced to admit it to himself and his friends will
be able to corroborate it. Any earnest appeal to principles, to
conscience, to exemplars worth aspiring to, or other such high-
falutin crap that's so popular in my homeland, doesn't work
here at all. Here one must provide nonstop entertainment for
the group while simultaneously making each and every student feel they are number one, the subject of boundless and
incessant care. All this without familiarity. And without ful-
some praise. If a professor attempts to weasel their way into a
student's favor with too much fawning or too high a grade in
the hopes of receiving a good evaluation, the student will only
come to despise them and, upon getting the last word, shit all
over them.

It's also advisable to put aside one's intellect: intelligence is annoying. Employ a simpler vocabulary—the students already complained I was using too many words they didn't know. Try being Puss in Boots infused with the Stanislavski method.

An experienced educator knows: there's no point in teaching the students. What you need to do is make them feel taught by term's end.

I turned out to be a poor instructor, but at this psychological trickery and buffoonery calibrated for local conditions, I excelled, though not immediately. At the end of the first year, the students, to whom I'd stupidly and earnestly given my all, gave me poor marks and wrote negative evaluations. The other professors, my friends who cared about me, were devastated.

"You're a foreigner, Tatyana, you don't get how it works here. Let us help you, train you, try to fix this."

"It's okay. I can manage."

"But if you get poor evaluations next year, they'll fire you! And we don't want to lose you!"

And I don't want to lose my house, I said to myself. I need this job, and I will keep it. If I need to get on all fours and bark, I'll get on all fours and bark. Because I love my house, and it loves me.

The following semester I received top marks from all my students. My friends marveled as if I were Uri Geller and had just made a stopped watch tick.

"How did you manage that?! In a single semester? That's never happened in the entire history of the college! What did you do?"

"I dunno," I lied, impudently looking them straight in their earnest eyes of liberal intellectuals. I mean, I couldn't very well admit to them that I had indeed got on all fours and barked for love.

§

Door to door, it's two hundred twenty miles from my house to the college—four hours of driving. It's winter.

On Monday, may it be damned, the alarm goes off at 5:00 a.m. I jump up like a soldier; half an hour to shower and brew five cups of strong Turkish coffee: one for now, four for the thermos. Sandwiches are prepared the night before; a pack of Benson & Hedges menthols is always in the car. Apples are quartered and thrown into a Ziploc bag. Cassettes of Russian rockers Grebenshchikov and Khvostenko, angels of the divinely absurd. Also recorded lectures about something obscure and complicated, so my brain is forced to work and not sleep: Chinese philosophy, the history of opera, quantum mechanics. Also audiobooks of British detective novels (can't do classic literature, too soporific; to avoid conking out during the drive one needs simple impatient curiosity: who dunnit?). If you assume that five hours of sleep is enough, you are assuming incorrectly.

So as not to wake up my family, I sleep in the magical room. It has a door that opens straight into the garage. A cold draft whooshes in under the door, making the room feel uninviting during winter nights, but only for those who don't know and can't see: there is entry here into aetherial worlds. The house is surrounded by snow, piled high; when the sun comes up, it illuminates the room from one side to the other, from the pink southern snowbanks to the pale blue northern ones, and the room will be like a ship, swaying in the air. We don't know where happiness comes from, but places do exist where it's sprinkled into heaps. Each time I take off, I leave happiness behind.

I walk out into the garage, get in the car, slam the door, turn on the headlights: the shelves with old crap from David and Nora, the cans with dried-up paint, Grandpa's sled, curled-up green water hoses, rusted rakes—all is illuminated. I'm an automaton, all my moves repetitive, economical, and calculated.

Opening the garage door with the remote, backing out, closing the door with the remote. Peeling out into the street, making a U-turn, and going north —by feel, slicing through the inky darkness, diving down hills into valleys, on empty narrow roads, past sleeping villages and lonely farms demarcated by tiny beads of light.

This pitch-black hour is the most horrible in my life; it repeats week after week, year after year. I am half reclined in a sarcophagus scattered with litter, as if a long-forgotten, distant relative of some pharaoh, surrounded by her ushabti and her vessels for drinking and eating, which are supposed to last until the Day of Judgment, when one is called and asked: Didst thou steal? Didst thou take from a widow? Didst thou add to the weight of the balance and didst thou falsify the plummet of the scale? There is no greater loneliness, no sharper coldness, no deeper despair. No one is thinking of me in this emptiness—my father is dead, and the rest are sleeping. I have no friend, and no place to find one.

But this death alights upon me for only an hour, and then it's annulled, as all death is annulled, its sting removed, as we've been promised. I know what intersection I am about to cross and under which trees I'll be stopped at a red light when the heavy, heatless crimson sun appears over the horizon. I know which road I'll be turning onto as it rises up in the sky in all its morning glory—raging and white, as in those ferocious Turner paintings—blinding all who are speeding northeast behind me.

Lower the visor, put on the sunglasses: an entire army of drivers gears itself simultaneously; we are all automatons, all gnawing our way through this difficult world with our crumbling teeth.

No, five hours is not enough sleep, and so the entire journey is devoted to keeping myself from nodding off and hitting the divider; from flipping over, crashing into an oncoming car. Methodology is as follows: continuous coffee-drinking and smoking, cracking the window to let in the frigid air, munching on something and listening to Grebenshshikov at full blast, or, better yet, singing at the top of my lungs and drowning out my idols. This car full of crazy is speeding down American roads, flying onto the four-lane highway, and I can see that I'm not the only one: there is smoking and singing in other cars, too, while the most passionate are dancing at the wheel, drumming away with one hand or both. Finally the highway goes its own way, whistling and rattling, as I veer north; the sun is already high up in the sky, back to its normal size, nothing special.

The air outside is razorlike, the landscape now of cliffs, pines, and new types of birds—perhaps eagles, even. From the mountaintops one can see spectacular valleys, rivers snaking through them, and new skies opening up; everything is different, and beyond the blue mountains—Canada.

§

By November's end my students completely stop applying themselves. The other professors tell me:

"What do you expect, they had an entire week off, they spent it skiing in the Adirondacks—you must know how hard it is to get back into it after vacation! If you want learning, writing, thinking out of them, you've got to get it before Thanksgiving. Because now, the plague is coming."

"What do you mean, 'the plague'?"

"You'll see, their aunties will start dying off; grief will prevent them from coming to class and taking tests."

And what do you know, two groups of students suffered the loss of three aunties, a few uncles were writhing in agony, and the fiancée of one of the most arrogant pretty boys was rotting alive.

"Rotting alive?" I asked again, fascinated.

"Yep!" he confirmed shamelessly. "At first it was just, like, her legs to the knees, then it kinda, like, spread further up, and now she's literally in her last hours. One more week, I think, is all I need. Such a tragedy, you know?"

I took pity and gave him a passing grade for such beautiful fiction. Yes, I have added to the weight of the balance. Yes, I have falsified the plummet of the scales.

§

During my years there I did have some talented students, if unexceptionally so, a few of those even planning to make a career out of writing, stocking store shelves with their uninteresting, timid stories tinged with soft-core porn. Most often, they'd pick my brain about getting published in *The New Yorker*—what and how did one need to write to make that happen? I'd tell them that I didn't know, that getting published is a different skill altogether. But they wouldn't believe me. One young lady grumbled: "Fine, I get that you need to sleep with the editor. But what else?"

Every student was supposed to write three stories per semester. And to rewrite, for improvement, each story at least once. This means that during my time teaching there, I read five hundred and forty short stories. And reread them. By the end of my sentence, all the delicate passageways by which I found access to aetherial worlds had thus become clogged with nonbiodegradable plastic waste. Full of ennui, I'd pick up the next one: "Susan felt a strong connection with George. They preferred the same brand of toothpaste, they both enjoyed listening to the Smashing Pumpkins. . . ."

During this entire time, I had only two encounters out of the ordinary. There was one girl completely free of any storytelling constraints and conventions—the others all eyed her with fear. She wrote a story about how much she liked shoplifting: both to ease things when cash was low and for the intrinsic joy of it; how, when planning to shoplift cheese, she'd put on a thick sweater with wide sleeves and traipse through the store with the most carefree expression, bending casually over the cases with prepackaged triangles of *formaggio* as if searching for something, but then, surreptitiously, with her sleeve held taut, she'd scoop up a package of Roquefort, or something just as expensive, never actually touching it, and holding something else in her other hand as a decoy. If someone bothered to look, they wouldn't even notice. Once the cheese slid down to the elbow, she had only to lift up her arms, as if to fix her hair, which had deliberately been left disheveled. At this stage the cheese would pass through the armhole and into her baggy sweater, securely cinched at the waist.

This wasn't even so much a short story as it was an étude, a study, yet it was more than any of the others—the lazy and the diligent alike—were capable of. They couldn't feel what the trick was, and I didn't know how to explain it: a culture that makes blanket pronouncements such as "Yes means yes and no means no" and orients itself squarely toward a puritanical ethic fails at parsing metaphors and acknowledging paradoxes; it fears play and runs from even fictive sins. I grew attached to this girl, who though from a wealthy family enjoyed shoplifting and lying precisely because, with nothing denied her, she was bored. She'd look into thin air and see visions. She yearned for different worlds and, by her own admission, had a way to reach them. She had a mild form of epilepsy, and every once in awhile she'd have a seizure, petit mal—almost unnoticeable by others. And as we know—from Dostoyevsky, for example—other worlds opens up right before an epileptic seizure. Everything around you begins to make sense: the workings of the universe, all causes, all meanings, everything. But then a dark veil descends and you thrash about in convulsions, and when you come back you don't remember anything. She told me that as a little girl, whenever they gave her anticonvulsives, she'd purposefully not take them, so as to be "elucidated," "to keep things interesting." Oh, how I envied her! Sure, I was also able to go there, but not deep inside and not without effort; there was no elucidation or convulsions, the key to the entry gates being tears. Or, occasionally, love.

The second exception was a lad who, in his standard academic classes—and this was an academic institution after all, albeit one of liberal arts—was widely considered an idiot. His looks didn't help—the physique of a potato sack, a backwards baseball cap, a rumpled white sweatshirt, coarse features and heavy tread. His parents, farmers, apparently belonged to some reclusive religious sect. It seemed that prior to college, the most sentient being he had come across was a cow. I suspected he was autistic.

When I saw his writing, I couldn't believe my luck. I can't reproduce it now and the manuscript has been lost—those New Jersey floods finally did reach my basement, annihilating my entire archive—and to be honest, I don't even remember what the story was about. But there was something wondrous in its brute savagery. A brother and sister. She's sitting at a wooden table, eating pea soup. He throws an ax at her. He misses. I don't remember why. The atmosphere is downright Bruegelesque. It wasn't so much the plot—but the smell of stables, peas, and smoke veritably emanated from the pages and I could just see those people, slow-moving and oafish. This bumpkin was possessed of an inexplicable ability to glide effortlessly through walls of words to those subterranean fields where intentions are sown, where the winds of meaning blow, and where motives rustle. But his story didn't end. It simply stopped.

"Yeah," he said. "I don't know yet what comes next."

We were sitting in an empty auditorium; no one was disturbing us.

"What if you lift it here and pull this way?" I asked carefully, and pointed with my finger. He looked.

"That could work," he said after some thought, "but won't it sag there?" He also indicated.

"Yes . . . but if you pad right here, la la la, maybe four lines or so, no more, and then trim the beginning?" I couldn't, I simply couldn't believe that this was happening.

"Yeah, I see it! And then thread it through like this." He chuckled with delight. "I got it, I got it! That works! And then I'll add some heft right about here."

He pressed his finger into the paper, as if adding weight.

"I'd get rid of this phrase . . . or maybe move it. Seems too pink, and right here, it's too smoky."

"No, I need that. I'll move it into the shadows. And, and . . . and I'll add a *J,* it's nice and graphite."

I was completely besotted. An astral twin had been sent to me in the form of a potato sack. I could have spent hours next to him, although not eye-to-eye—there wasn't much to look at—but voice to voice, so that we, like Dante's Paolo and Francesca, could read any book, sifting it with four hands as if it were sand from the ocean, laughing with the joy of little kids who, when the grown-ups weren't looking, had snuck in through an unlocked door that leads to Eternity.

"What are your plans after college?" I asked him.

"I want to apply to the Iowa Writers' Workshop."

"I'll write you a recommendation letter."

"But I haven't even finished my story yet."

"But you know that you will, because the story is already there, it just isn't visible yet."

The potato sack brightened and nodded his head. We were speaking the same language. Then he gathered his pages and walked out, treading heavily, blending in with the wall.

I don't even remember his name. It was a square one. Maybe Carter? Let's call him Carter.

Every Wednesday I drove back home from the college. It was the same commute as on Monday, but in reverse. The sun took a long time to set, the sky grew darker, early twilight washing out the surroundings before darkness fell; the main thing was not to crash my car and flip over—Sing, Boris, sing, help me out. A long road through the cliffs, then the wide highway, then a country road, and then the final stretch, almost by feel—from unseen hills into unseen valleys, then hills once again, past sleepy villages and lonely, dimly flickering farms. And I was daydreaming about how, who knows, perhaps inside one of those gloomy houses—maybe that one, or possibly this one—another Carter was sitting, his heavy hands resting on the wooden table, the clock ticking as he lowered his heavy ear to the ground, listening to the pea pods sleeping under the snow, and thinking of how a cow is staring at the wall, about how the wax cloth smells, about how the night flows.

And he won't say anything to anyone, because no one will ask him.

§

Meanwhile, my family quietly fell apart—dried out with time, everyone going their separate way. My kids had families of their own. And nobody needed my house anymore—not the green door with the round brass handle, not the off-white walls, which I painted with my own hands, nor the birch parquet, which began to shine like old gold after I, on all fours, scrubbed it clean of all kinds of crap with a special American oil formulated for scrubbing the parquet clean of all kinds of crap. I also had a glass table, which allowed one to examine one's knees, an interesting endeavor. And I had purchased an old china cabinet at a flea market; it was the color of dark cherry, with curlicues on top. One of its drawers contained an unexpected bonus: a green-felt-lined case containing two protractors. The unknown, long-gone owner had possibly drafted something—perhaps he'd sketched a patio for his house. And so I decided I too would add a patio to the house, just as David intended.

I went down to the municipal building expecting long lines, misery, inexplicable restrictions, and insurmountable obstacles, but there was nothing of the sort. I paid all the necessary fees, the inspector came and, measuring my house, he gave the patio his approval. He also gave me a list of licensed carpenters, pointing out which ones charged more and which ones less, and advising me against hiring someone just off the street. That was because a licensed carpenter knows that the most important thing about patios is the distance between the balusters. It can't be less than a certain number of inches, or some kid is bound to get their head stuck in there. The year before, the inspector told me, they'd made the standards stricter, reducing the distance further. Apparently the average American head had grown smaller. And all the licensed carpenters have been notified about this. When the patio is finished, the inspector will come and survey the job.

That's how simple and boring this process turned out to be. Where were the bribes—the sliding envelope, the lowered gaze, the anxiety that it won't be accepted or that he'll take a look and deem it too little? Where were the nervous jitters about removing stolen goods from a warehouse, as I had done in Moscow? I remember how, early one July morning, the construction workers I'd hired took me to a yard near Myasnitskaya Street, to a door, and behind that door were rolls and boxes of supplies; the workers gesturing to it all: Choose whatever you want.

"What is this?" I asked

"A warehouse. Go ahead."

"Whose warehouse?"

"The military prosecutor's office. It's Sunday, so go ahead! But quietly . . ."

We loaded up on tiles and parquet flooring as well as rolls of mesh, its purpose unknown: I asked, but the workers had no idea, they simply took some because it was there. They found some sort of yellow, bubbled glass and offered some to me as well; the temptation was great, but my renovations did not call for bubbles, so it stayed behind, about which I still feel pangs of regret, and God, what year was it?—1987? Yes, I think so. The early-morning pedestrians were scurrying down streets made wet by watering trucks, July was waking, fresh and luxuriant, life was in full bloom. We stole quite a bit that day, cleared out the prosecutor's office quite nicely; I still feel the thrill and gratitude.

My Moscow construction guys were certain that I was an actress; all protestations to the contrary were dismissed— they knew better. Hair to the waist, red lipstick, unstructured behavior—must be an actress! In the end, I suppose it didn't matter, but the problem was that having fallen into a kind of proletarian cultural paradigm I was expected to act the part, though of course I couldn't possibly live up to standards I wasn't familiar with. I could see that this offended my workers; everything I did defied their expectations. What, oh what, did they want from me?

Another heroine from their proletarian folklore was the General's Wife, a character that existed primarily in the fantasies of such men. The myth of the General's Wife was basically that she—of Yugoslavian negligees and German bubble baths, surrounded by rugs and lacquered dressers, and bursting with passion—is waiting for him, a simple worker, a plumber. She would leap into his arms, perfumed and ready: Take me! I'm yours!

The General is obviously "in the field," so to speak.

Women, too, were conduits for this lore. Take Galina, who, by the way, hung my wallpaper upside down. She surmised that her crew's last job had been for a General's Wife. There was air freshener in the loo—it had to have been a general's shitter.

"Just imagine: plop—whoosh—orange blossoms."

Unfortunately, I was already familiar with all the details of Galina's personal life, her complicated relationship with her lover and his mistresses, none of whom, of course, could hold a candle to her.

"I told him—you listening? I told him: 'Fine, I'm a slut, I'm a whore, I suck cock, but I am still a WOMAN.' Was I right or was I right?"

As an actress I was expected to have an artistic opinion: about a woman's dignity, about the craftiness of men, about fashion.

"Ain't too bad, right? Sewed it out of two shawls." Galina

was examining her skirt, but, secretly, of course, she was admiring her wizened fifty-something legs. The skirt wasn't half bad. Galina and her team weren't even planning on working: they positioned some wooden scaffolds around the room, climbed on top of them, and were playing cards while incessantly and virtuosically cursing. They'd send the elderly Kostya to go get booze, and I should note that Kostya, as a parquet artisan of the highest caliber, consumed only cognac.

"When will you be able to finish hanging the wallpaper?" I'd bleat.

"Can't do it now! The spackling hasn't dried! Notice how damp your apartment is? Takes time to dry. And by the way, actress! You owe us two hundred rubles."

"Two hundred? For what?!"

"Prepayment!"

Around the twelfth century BC, Mycenaean civilization was obliterated by flooding and fires. The fire baked some of the clay tablets that contained accounting notes, thus preserving them. When in the twentieth century AD these tablets were excavated and painstakingly decoded, what wisdom of the ages had scholars discovered? "Carpenter Tirieus didn't come to work today," and such like.

Exactly! The eternally flaky carpenter is fickle and unpredictable. A Russian carpenter (or plumber, tile layer, spackler) stretches out his arm to his Mycenaean brethren across millennia: Workers of the world unite, if not in space then in time. Anyone who decides to build or rebuild their home knows that they are entering into a different world, one full of instability and surprise, and that there can be no knowing that the work paid for will be finished, or indeed even started. Just as with Schrödinger's cat, there is only the probability of this event happening. And in my case, I didn't even have that.

The spackling paste had been drying for the second month when I concluded that my workers had no intention of getting on with it. They considered my apartment, which had suddenly fallen into their lap, to be their private den of debauchery, and here they would drink themselves silly in three shifts; at some point a harmonica even entered the picture. Of course, I tried to get them to leave by appealing to their conscience, even bringing in my husband and father-in-law as reinforcement— but all was futile in the face of this construction gang. Whenever other people came to the apartment, the proletariat would do an energetic impression of activity: they'd furiously run the paint rollers up and down the walls, move boxes of parquet from corner to corner, struggle hauling buckets of cement, bang the ceiling with sticks, as if to loosen the old plaster. But as soon as my visitors had gone, the fuckers would jump back on the scaffolds, where a feast was already set: canned sprats, salami, beer, vodka—food for every taste—and the crème de la crème of parquet layers would be off and running to buy the most expensive of cognacs.

"It's still drying! It's all part of the process. No way can it be rushed. We even turned on the space heaters."

I had stopped paying them long ago, but therein lay the rub: "If you don't pay us, we won't leave." Basically, this has been the modus operandi of our entire country for the past six hundred years.

Finally I gave up and asked my older sister, Katerina, for help. She was a formidable woman. Formidable! I explained: This and that, they think I'm an actress, a subhuman, they're not working, they are bleeding me dry. Anything you can do?

"Who's in charge there?" asked Katerina after giving it some thought.

"Galina."

I brought Katerina to my apartment. She threw the door open and walked up to the scaffolds with a deliberate, slow, and heavy step, her feet firmly and widely planted, as if wearing a pair of shiny general's boots. With the low rumbling voice of a herald, Katerina bellowed:

"Galina! I vanquish thee and cast thee the fuck out of here!"

Galina grew apoplectic on the wooden platform.

"What the hell? Who are you?"

"I'm the Devil."

There was a silence in response, and, for a second, the platform gang froze. Katerina darted into the corner, lifting her hands up, each forming a set of horns. She declared:

"I call upon the forces of darkness to unleash the evil eye!!! Everybody—out! One . . . two . . ."

Sure enough, they jumped off in unison and made a run for it, shoving one another and cursing under their breath as they bounded over the creaking floorboards; Galina's wizened legs carried her the fastest, as she hollered shrilly: "The Devil, the damned Devil!" as if she'd met Him before and knew that she'd run up a tab with Him. I never saw any one of them again.

"What did you do?" I asked. "How?"

"It's the proletariat. You can't talk to them in any other way," shrugged Katerina.

But the American carpenter was not "the proletariat"; he didn't nap in his parka with his mouth open, did not indulge in riotous fun at the job site, attempted no entry into aetherial worlds with the aid of moonshine and a processed cheese product; a hot and bothered Venus disguised as the General's Wife did not haunt his dreams—mythopoeic power bubbled up inside him not at all. And so he approached building the patio drily and diligently. He didn't try to pad the bill, instead charging me the agreed-upon amount; he didn't belatedly discover that the terrain was somehow unruly, or that the logs were unusually difficult to work with and so it was only fair to add a little sumpin' sumpin'. For that matter, when the time came, the municipal inspector didn't cast an eye on the ceiling and indicate with a polite cough that it wouldn't hurt to have a drink, nor did he suggest that I invite a priest and a cat—the priest to christen the new space, the cat to absorb the negative energy. No, he simply patted the beams with his hands, measured the distance between the balusters to ensure that some average American kid's head didn't get stuck there, and that I, as owner, wouldn't get sued for triple the value of the house on account of someone else's microcephaly.

§

My patio—the deck of a ship that's stuck on earth—was finished. What next?

I spent summer evenings there, reading and smoking, as the sun set, and as the filigreed lilac leaves of the Liquidambar blended with the twilight, and as a deer roamed the woods, or maybe it was a unicorn—who's to say?

Can't make out the words on the page anymore.

Every person has their own angel, for protection and compassion. The angel comes in different sizes, depending on the circumstances. Sometimes he's the size of a dachshund—if you're visiting a friend or if you're in a crowd; sometimes he's the size of a person—sitting in the passenger seat of a car, if you're hurtling down the highway, shouting and singing; sometime he comes in his full size, approximately as tall as one telephone pole atop another, and hangs quietly in the air, the stuffy and empty evening air of a pointless July in a year unknown. In a certain light, with your peripheral vision, you can glimpse the micaceous glint of his wing.

You can talk to your angel. He'll sympathize. He'll understand. He'll agree. That's his way of loving you.

What next? you ask him. What comes next? *Exactly,* he'll agree, *what next?* You love and love someone and then you look up and the love is gone, and if you feel sorry it's not for him but for your feelings—you let them out for a walk and they come crawling back to you, all bruises and missing teeth. *Yes, yes,* he'll agree, *that's how it is.* And also people die, but that's just nonsense, isn't it? They can't just disappear, can they, they still exist, you just can't see them, right? They must be up there, with you? *Yes, yes, they're here, all here, no one's disappeared, no one's been lost, everyone is well.*

A transparent sort, hard to make out, like a jellyfish in water, he hangs in the air and undulates as fireflies pass right through him; and if starlight is refracted when piercing his aetherial body, it is refracted just a little.

§

Almost all the money that I was earning at the college was going toward the upkeep of the house. And working at the college was killing me. Only a few years before, I had the ability to see through things, but now a mental glaucoma descended upon me, dark water, as they say, and I needed to put an end to it and to go home—to my old apartment, to Moscow, for instance. Or to Saint Petersburg. Okay. Once my contract ends, I'll leave.

I allowed tenants to move in. I rented out everything but the magical room to an elderly Russian couple. They were kindred spirits—he was a theoretical physicist, she was a journalist—such kindred spirits, in fact, that I felt uncomfortable taking their money. Every Wednesday evening, when I returned from the gulag up north, I'd climb out of the car, my legs weak, and see them already waiting for me, table set with a bottle of wine; they were happy to see me, and I them, and we'd sit around discussing everything we knew, even my knowledge of quantum mechanics, pumped into my brain via books on tape during long and grueling journeys north.

He'd come to our United States of America for medical care, but the doctors couldn't save him. And the house stood empty again.

That's when I decided to rent it out entirely and to find a cheap apartment for myself near work. Turns out, it's not so simple to rent out a house in America. That's not because there are no takers, but because all of those people are your potential enemies.

The law comes down squarely on the side of the renters. For instance: I, as the owner, must abide by a certain sense of *égalité,* may it rot, and consider everyone to be equal. A nice intellectual couple, let's say two Princeton professors, shouldn't in my eyes be more desirable than a family of strung-out junkies, or a gang of Gypsies with shifty eyes, or a foreign couple who don't speak any English. If I express too distinctly my displeasure at the possibility of their inhabiting my house, in theory, they can sue me. So one's forced to express regret: Oh, so sorry and what a shame, but the space has just been rented.

There is a danger of renting to people too poor to afford it. If these people have nowhere to go (and can't pay you), they have the right to just stay in the house until their situation improves, and of course it never will. Meaning that I can't just kick them out. That I myself may have nowhere to live; the law doesn't give two shits about.

There is also a danger of renting to a handicapped person, or to a family with small children, who'll stick their head through the balusters, those rascals, or slip and fall, breaking their leg, and it'll be my fault for not making sure the place was childproof.

So I kept my eyes open. First to arrive were a couple, both Indian programmers. Exactly what I wanted: a young married couple, with beautiful British English, clean-cut and very sweet. But they were looking for something else. They wanted carved door frames and marble everywhere. My barn was too simple for their tastes.

Then an elderly black couple, both around sixty, came by. He walked through the door with no problem, but she took one step and got stuck in the door frame, couldn't move. He, apparently used to this, grabbed her by the hand and pulled her in—about 650 pounds in all, I'd guess. We exchanged smiles and on they went to inspect the rooms. I didn't follow them—I was afraid that my house would tilt. The wife tried the bathroom but couldn't fit through the door. Trying again, sideways this time, she fit, although a quarter of her remained in the hallway. A muffled consultation between them could be heard. They continued on their tour and I sat there, full of trepidation that she would decide to check out the basement. She decided to check out the basement.

I sneaked in from the other side so I could eavesdrop and not miss the impending disaster.

"This won't work. Let's go," said the husband.

"No, I want to look downstairs."

"This house is clearly not an option for us."

"So what, I still want to look."

"I'm telling you, it's best we go."

She began squeezing herself through the narrow basement door, and . . .

"Benjamin!"

"I told you."

"Okay, sir, less talk, more action!"

He leaned against her and with both hands forced her through the door. The stairs were next. She took one heavy step and I heard the wood cracking.

"Vanessa, damn it!"

"Language!"

She was clearly the queen of the household, and he was just a footman. A few more ominous tremors from below. Then silence. I tiptoed back to my den and pretended to be working on the computer. Benjamin peeked in and asked nonchalantly:

"Um. Is there another way out from the basement? Or just the one?"

"Just the one."

"Oh, okay, just wondering."

He disappeared again, and I turned on SimCity; I loved laying underground water pipes there and watching them come to life, elbow after elbow, blue musical water streaming down them at last. Besides, I had some cheat codes for the game and I didn't need to be stingy with my virtual money when irrigating my virtual cities. And those two will probably be down there for a while anyway. Benjamin popped in once again:

"Do you happen to have a screwdriver?"

"Maybe in the garage? It's through this door. I also have ropes there and other things."

"Got it. What about a hammer?"

"Also there."

About half an hour later—I was already running electricity to the prison, university, and hospital—they reappeared together. I had my best poker face on, and so did Benjamin. Vanessa looked a bit disheveled.

"The house is lovely, simply lovely. But we're going to think about it. What a wonderful, wonderful garden!"

"Thank you! Yeah, let me know."

"So lovely meeting you!"

"Same here!"

He pushed her through the green front door to the street, and through the window I could see them walking down the brick path: she, marching regally, and he, scurrying behind, weaving around her from side to side. They still had loading into the car ahead of them.

And then Nielsen came. He was twenty-two. Shrimpy, pasty white, with bleach-blond hair and the hands of a prepubescent boy, an expression of mild disgust on the flat face of a mealworm.

"It's dusty in here," whined Nielsen.

"Dusty?" I responded, surprised. The house was spick-and-span—scrubbed with renters in mind.

"I need the house to be sterile," grumbled Nielsen. "I am allergic to even the slightest bit of dust. Once the entire house is sterile, I'll take it. And I need this fireplace to be completely clean, like new."

Oh, curses! The fireplace? More expenses! By definition, a working fireplace cannot be "sterile." Thirty years of soot on its stone walls, traces of ash—and anyway, it's not like you'll be performing open-heart surgery in there! And what could be cleaner than fire, Nielsen?

In New Jersey, sterility was provided solely by two Belarusians. They were here illegally and so they took on any hard labor that the local Russian-Americans would hire them for: from housecleaning to roof repair. They overcharged woefully, but at least no job was too dirty for them. These two terminators were also married to each other, and it should be noted that against any expectation the wife's last name was Kock and the husband's Chik. This, seemingly, was not their only perversity. Keenly aware of their irreplaceability, cruel and adept in their united front, they always performed the same routine: give an approximate, acceptable estimate, but warn that there might be unforeseen adjustments, and shortly before finishing the work, just when everything is torn apart and upside down, jack up the price to a horrific sum. Chik looked to be the brutal sort. Kock had an elfin face, and her case history included work in a bar: perhaps this was why, when it came to arranging glassware, for instance, she would line the glasses up not randomly but strictly by type, one behind the other and deep into the cupboard, away from the owner's eyes.

Kock and Chik finished their work—polished all surfaces, horizontal and vertical, with their potent acids and ammonia, destroying all that lived, sterilizing the fireplace—and Nielsen, after playing hard-to-get, at last rented my house for a year and gave me a security deposit of fifteen hundred dollars. Legally, I was supposed to keep this money in an escrow account, and not to touch it until the end of the lease. But I had no money at all to my name. And I needed to rent something for myself, and even a dog kennel required a security deposit. So I borrowed his money unbeknownst to him. What difference would it make? I'd return it at the end of the year anyway.

Yes, yes, I've falsified the plummet of the scales, played foul with bank accounts and cheat codes; I've exceeded the speed limit at times, driven under the influence, and stolen from the military prosecutor's office; I've given false testimony in court; and I've committed adultery in my heart, numerously. What's more, I intend to keep on doing so in the future. Dear Lord, what obnoxious messengers You send to remind us of our sins, and of our promises made to You and then forgotten. Even so, not according to my will, but Yours. You truly do work in mysterious ways! Please forgive and forget.

Something was wrong with Nielsen. I must have made a mistake.

This was my house, after all, a living thing that I loved, and that had put its trust in me; where the sun danced on the golden floor; where the invisible glass table, the one I loved to sit at, existed: when I was away, the shadows of the dead and departed would take my place at it, no longer alive but still refracting the light that went through them, like prisms—where else could they gather to converse and drink wine? And now Nielsen was walking through this house touching everything with his sterile, prepubescent hands.

Perhaps it was Nielsen permeating my nightmares. He appeared as worminess, as decay, as rot, white fungus, pustules, lichen. A meaningless path that veered left onto a dimly lit road, or a treacherous scree—that was him. Houses with open doors, strange faces in the twilight, wet shoes—that was him. Ominous beaches, lost keys, leftovers, missed trains, a threat from above—that was him, all him. This house was my earthly pod, one of my shells. He infiltrated it, making his way under the skin. And he called upon the forces of darkness to unleash the evil eye.

I'd betrayed my treasure and I alone was to blame.

§

It was a bad year. I lived near the college that was sucking my soul dry, bleeding me of all that was alive inside me. There was extraordinary beauty everywhere: tall spruces, white snow; Beauteous Death. I was already in the habit of waking up at five in the morning, but there was nowhere to go at that hour, and nothing to see other than my ceiling. Hang in there, I'd tell myself, the year will go by quickly. Nielsen will leave, then I'll sell the house and go home. This isn't the right place for me. Once again it's not right. I should know by now that the right place is inaccessible; maybe it exists in the past, over the green hills, or maybe it's drowned, or, perhaps, it hasn't materialized yet.

What if the Lord wants us to know that we can't get anywhere on this earth, can't own anything, can't hold on to anyone. Perhaps only at five in the morning, though not every day, is the truth revealed to us: everything, everything that we've ever desired is simply a mirage, or a mock-up. Maybe . . . But then the night begins to vanish, the outlines of rented furniture come into view, and it's time to get up and make coffee, strong, the way they brew it in the East, not this muddy American dishwater, and then set off for the college to give out unearned grades: I'm leaving soon anyway. I have already decided.

I gave an A to a Haitian girl for a short story that wasn't worth a C. She knew this and freaked out when she saw the A, expecting there to be a catch. There was no catch. It was just the story of her escape in a boat, illicit, with bribes, from her island to the United States. The crew—their guides—collected payment in the form of dollars and sex: they raped all the women and girls on board. They gave no water—that was also paid for with sex. A baby died and was thrown overboard. All these details seemed matter-of-fact to her: "Does it happen any other way?" She made the journey with her mother, grandmother, and boyfriend; everyone suffered the same fate, but all were happy: they'd made it from a grave world into an aetherial one. Not everyone gets to finish that journey.

The story was simplistic, poorly put together; showing no imagination, she told everything exactly as it had, alas, happened. I sat with her for an hour after class, asking questions. Her family members were well settled here: the grandmother back to practicing voodoo, the mother taking in laundry. The boyfriend had already bought a Mercedes, and we don't want to dwell on how he managed, but we have an inkling. As for the girl herself, thanks to a government program, she was taking a creative writing class to rack up credits toward a degree.

She was gathering her papers into a pile with trembling hands; I was collecting mine and also trembling. She couldn't understand why she got an A and so she had come to find out; my job was to hide the reason—My goodness, I'm a dishonest Russian person, I'll throw ten As your way: go ahead and rack up the necessary credits, you sunny, pure being who holds no grudge against her tormentors!

Oh, these scales of mine. What weights and plummets!

My lying was inspired—yes, I'm good at that!—and she bought it, trusting me that there was value in her composition, that the details had been ably chosen, that the beginning was great and the ending even better—Of course, you can improve slightly here and rewrite a bit there, but you do understand, don't you, nothing's ever perfect, and some writers rewrite their novels six times, if you can believe it!

I acquired a taste for this sort of thing and broke bad. I walked around with a horn of plenty, pouring out splendid grades, generously bestowing them upon anyone whom I perceived to have even the tiniest of dreams, the slightest timidity before the darkness of being—howdy, folks!—the smallest desire to get on their tiptoes and peer over the fence. Mean idiots got Ds from me, kind idiots got Bs. I forgave some slackers and not others, according to whim. When, at the end of the semester, my teacher evaluations came from the dean's office, I tossed the entire package without even taking a look. I was done!

Goodbye to the North, to the snow and the cliffs, to the fairy-tale wooden cabins, to the faraway blue mountains, beyond which Canada lies, and to you, my friends—ours were real friendships, and I did love you, but now it's your turn to become translucent jellyfish, now fireflies will pass right through you, as starlight is refracted just a little.

I came back to this Princeton of mine, which wasn't really Princeton. Nielsen had already left. I walked into my house and began to inspect the rooms. I was gripped by terror and dread.

Everything that could have been broken was broken, everything that could have been damaged was damaged. This was no accidental destruction, not the result of boisterous horseplay, which could be expected from a young man—no: this was premeditated, demented, and bizarre. It was as if a worm, or a large arthropod, or a mollusk, had inhabited my house, and in some obscure stages of its life cycle hurled heaps of roe, sprayed the walls from its ink sac, laid eggs high up under the ceiling, stopping, perhaps, for a week or so in its pupa stage, and then, cracking its chitinous cocoon, emerged in new form and with a fresh need to crawl through things.

He carved holes the size of dessert plates in the walls, holes big enough for an adult's head, let alone a child's, to fit through; every wall had a hole at eye level. Wooden window frames, David's pride and joy, were defaced with deep grooves, as if Nielsen had suddenly sprouted a polydactyl paw with bone claws and a desperate need to scratch against something. Upon finding a screen door, Nielsen apparently enjoyed shredding that, too, until it dangled like a ripped spiderweb. Perhaps he slept in it, or maybe hung in it upside down.

He liked to chip away at the bathtub with a hammer and chisel, but only in the near left corner. The bathtub was cast iron, and he must have been trying to get to the metal through the enamel. Apparently he didn't find the other corners palatable.

The basement had housed some air ducts below the ceiling; they carried warm air to heat the house. Now the basement no longer housed them: Nielsen had cut them out. He ripped out sections, three yards in all, according to a plan he alone understood, a plan that no human brain could comprehend. Thinking that my eyes deceived me, I dragged a certified American contractor in to inspect the damage: What is this? Can you, please, explain?

"Holy shit," whispered the certified American contractor, backing away in fear. In American B movies, that's the facial expression that earthlings have as they stand there looking and not knowing what to do next when suddenly—*thump!*—something covered in spiderwebs and goo jumps into the frame and carries off in its jaws a young actress of average looks, the one that you always knew was going to get quartered and eaten after getting entangled in something sticky.

Sure, the house was also dirty, but what difference did that make? It was finally clear why he required sterility specifically, and not mere cleanliness: if you're a messenger from hell and you're building a pentacle, you need to purify the space of all specters, of all the lares and penates, both the household and the basement variety. That's when you need demons-for-hire to arrive with their fumigators—Kock and Chik, transvestites joined in matrimony, if not in surname; I should have figured this out earlier, when I saw Kock arranging glassware contrary to all human convention.

Bushes were pulled out by the roots in the garden, roses were cut down to resemble ski poles, and at the border with my neighbors there were signs in the soil of indiscriminate digging. The mailbox contained two letters. One a month old, in which Nielsen gives notice that he has vacated the premises and demands the return of his security deposit of fifteen hundred dollars. And the other letter, informing me that, because of my failure to return his security deposit, he is suing me. *He is suing* me.

§

So there you have it, girlie, that's the finale: you find yourself alone in the middle of the great American continent, not a penny in your pocket, and a crazed arthropod bent on suing you. Have you ever tried to wrap your mind around the behavior of, say, cephalopods? Consider, for example: "The fourth left arm in the males is distinctive in its formation and is used for fertilization purposes." Clearer now? The above is a scientific fact, by the way.

I found the address of a Princeton law firm in the Yellow Pages. Drove to their office. I picked the lawyer whose last name to me hinted at a knack for cunning pettifoggery. Described my situation.

"And why didn't you keep the monies in an escrow account, as the law prescribes?" inquired the lawyer.

"I just borrowed it, no big whoop."

"I see. Well, now he has the right to demand from you not just the security deposit, but also a penalty—I would guess around three thousand dollars. My fee, by the way, is two hundred dollars per hour."

"Shit. Um. Okay. So what's the plan?"

"I would be delighted to handle this case." The shyster's eyes lit up. "I think we can expect a very interesting fight in court."

American courts are not as they appear on TV—things proceed a little differently. In my nonprofessional opinion, everything could have been handled in just an hour. But at two hundred dollars for my lawyer and probably the same for Nielsen's, it would hardly be worth showing up for. So both shysters delight in playing for time. After a few hours, it's our turn to question Nielsen. Here is my lawyer, leisurely getting up from his seat, strolling ever so casually, as if contemplating something, then sloooowly spinning on his heel, slooowly asking:

"Your full name?"

There followed ten minutes of irrelevant questioning, then Nielsen's lawyer doing the same—and how polite, how respectful toward each other these shysters are. You don't need to be a detective to know that they take turns driving their bimmers to each other's house to sip whiskey on the rocks after work. Weekends are for barbecuing by the pool.

"Do you recognize the damage, as shown on these photographs, as the damage you caused to the walls?" slooowly asks my guy.

Nielsen is silent.

"Were you the one who damaged these walls?"

"I don't know."

"Did you cut an opening in this wall?"

"I did."

"And did you cut an opening in this wall as well?"

"Yes."

"For what purpose did you cut these openings, as shown in exhibit A and exhibit B?"

Nielsen is quiet, as the meters continue running. We are playing double or nothing: If I win, Nielsen will have to cover all my fees, including those for my attorney, in addition to the repairs. If he wins, I'll have to return his security deposit, pay a penalty, and cover his attorney's fees, and my house, desecrated by this beast for his séances of evolutionary regression, will hang around my neck like a millstone. What to do?

They stall and stall and then break for lunch. Another hour, another two hundred dollars. After lunch I ask my guy: So? How is it looking? He goes to confer with Nielsen's shyster. Through closed doors I can hear them laughing, obviously discussing other things and not just my case. This is how it's looking: Nielsen was unable to answer any of the questions clearly—his lawyer is furious. Furious! It's a special kind of lawyerly fury, because it doesn't cost him anything. But this doesn't mean that I am sure to win this case! It remains a fact that in failing to deposit his check into an escrow account I did violate state law. My chances are fifty-fifty. But we can end all this right here.

"He is willing to withdraw his claim," says my guy. "In exchange, he wants you to withdraw yours. That's the cautious way out. But I would be delighted to fight this!"

Of course you would! But I can't risk it. To hell with him. Let's end it right here. To leave and to not look back. After all—"forgive us our debts as we forgive our debtors."

"What a shame, what a shame!" calls my guy after me. "It was just getting interesting. I was looking forward to a good fight!"

§

After somehow repairing and cleaning up the house, I was able
to sell it to a Latino couple. They weren't particularly friendly,
never smiled, not even out of politeness. So I didn't tell them
about the leaks in the basement. They never asked and I never
said, just as my realtor had taught me. "I don't want to know! I
don't want to know!" he'd exclaim, putting up his hands.

I sold all my belongings at a yard sale. Dragged some tables
outside, set out my forks and corks, curtains and schmertains
and other crap—just like the stuff they sell in the subways in
Moscow. I put my furniture up for sale, too: a sizable crowd
came to check it out; hard to keep an eye on everyone, so
many things were stolen, including the draughtsman's kit, but
it wasn't mine anyway. I was pleasantly surprised to see that
Americans also pinch stuff, not just us Russians. The patio had
lost some of its color over the years, the wood turning silvery,
and it was almost time, according to the licensed carpenter's
schedule, to treat and stain it. Won't be me—I'll leave it to the
buyers! Their kids, by the way, had enormous heads.

I sold my car to a neighbor down the street—he had a grimy
little shop in his backyard: taking apart junk for spare parts,
tuning up engines, and selling it all to auto supply shops. I
asked for five hundred dollars but he turned me down. In the
end he paid me one buck, and this was fair: the bottom had
rusted out so much that, between the pedals, you could sometimes spot the remnants of skunks who hadn't quite made it.
He actually did me a favor: you can't simply abandon an old car
here—they'll fine you. Unless maybe if you take it deep into
the woods, to a forgotten plot of land, to a shack called "the
End of All Paths," and leave it there until the cows come home,

until the fat lady sings, until Columbus's second coming, until the day when they come for us all.

Thou comest naked into this world, and naked thou shalt leave.

I stood at the fork in the road, looking.

Yanked out the needle from my heart and walked away.

Doors and Demons

Throughout my life, Paris has been marked on my road map in a distinctive red color: maybe it's karma, or misaligned feng shui, maybe the Catholics jinxed me or someone shot me the evil eye or put a spell on me, but in Paris specifically, unseen dark forces lunge viciously at me, wreaking havoc in an unusual, sophisticated manner.

To wit: I arrive. It's April. I'm on my way to buy some fancy tea for which I acquired a taste after giving up cigarettes. As Polina Suslova—Dostoyevsky's muse—said, "Tea is my every-thing—my lover, my friend, my raison d'être." There is some-thing to that.

Being a Taurus—as everyone knows, Tauruses like buying in bulk—I purchase enough tea to last me several years: four kilos, to be exact. To drink myself, to give away, to have some nicely wrapped New Year's gifts handy. So I'm ready to head back, dragging my bale of dried *Camellia sinensis* leaves, when by the tea shop I spot a nice little boutique amiably located next door. Everything there is silk, just my size, and on sale. And if things are affordably priced, well of course you end up buying a ton: mountains of necessary things and oceans of unnecessary ones, for, as everyone also knows, sale prices intensify greed.

So here I am, buying a blouse the color of the Virgin Mary's mantle. And a mint one, even though I already have a dress that same exact color—but how can one resist the color mint? And a third blouse that reminds me of eggplant at night. I'm also purchasing a thoroughly unnecessary jacket simply because it's not just any shade of white, but . . . how should I describe it? It's as if someone had eaten a boatload of steamed salmon and then gingerly breathed on the crème fraîche. That color.

I don't have enough cash on me, it's back at the hotel. All I had planned on buying was tea.

The boutique proprietor is very stylish and handsome; he is around eighty but still sprightly, silver haired, with a scarf around his neck. If there is a wind, or when autumn comes, the Frenchman is never at a loss, the Frenchman has a scarf. Things, of course, get a bit more complicated in winter—he has to raise his collar.

I say to the owner: *Wait for me, I'll go get cash.* He's all: *Pas de problème, d'accord.* I go with my eyes: *I'll be back, trust.* He goes with his eyebrows: *But of course.*

I walk out with my head turned back 180 degrees: oh, the heaps of beautiful things that I'm leaving behind, unpurchased. That splatter-of-white-on-black dress, for instance.

I come back to the hotel, unload the tea, and go back out with a fist full of cash and a head full of dreams. I'm walking, dancing along the way, feeling all the feels: Paris! Paris! Boulevard Saint-Germain! The sun is shining wonderfully, as it often does in April. Look! There is a monsieur standing in the middle of the street, having a conversation with some other gentlemen. He's holding a lovely long stick, which he keeps swinging around: waving it, drawing it up like a fishing pole, slashing left and right. . . . How strange, I say to myself, as I pass a few feet away from him, giving him a sunny April-in-Paris smile. How str—but I do not have a chance to finish my thought: with a swing of his stick, the monsieur knocks me down, and I fall slam-bang on the pavement of Boulevard Saint-Germain. My favorite street in Paris, by the way. But perhaps that's irrelevant.

First I fall to my knees, skinning them against the pavement, and then I sprawl out, purse to the side, euros fanned out, iPad sliding out of my bag like a bar of chocolate. Parisians do not react.

In the early-morning fog,
Fuckers whack me with a log;
As I slump and curse my luck
No one seems to give a fuck.

At this point, of course, I start laughing hysterically: I'm spread-eagled, dying of laughter, when it finally dawns on me: the monsieur's stick is white—he's blind and so are his companions; they, too, I realize, are holding long white sticks in their hands. And through my laughter I can make out their conversation: "I think I knocked someone down," the monsieur says, sounding pleased. And his friends, likewise tickled: "Oh!" As if to say, "Oh great, the morning is off to a good start. Perhaps the rest of the day will be good, too."

I reassemble myself, dusting off and inspecting the damage, and limp to the nearest pharmacy, where they clean my wounds and stanch the blood. I look myself over in the mirror: my tattered tights are a good match with my dirty coat and its half-torn sleeve. The boutique proprietor does his best to suppress bewilderment when, with my blackened, bloodied hands, I hand over a pile of stained euros: *She strolled out a lady and crawled back a tramp. . . . Well, times are tough.*

One could say that this entire incident was pure chance. I, however, am inclined to see signs and symbols everywhere. Perhaps the universe was trying to tell me: "Watch where you're going" or "You've fallen victim to blind passion." Or something simpler: "Why on earth do you need all those blouses, especially when the blue one doesn't even fit?" But nothing remotely similar ever happens to me in other cities, does it? This is Paris, a particular kind of place.

And then again, just a few days ago, I stopped over in Paris on my way elsewhere. Only a few hours: an overnight layover and then back on the road. Time was tight, so the demons swarmed around me without delay. I arrived late at night. Gracefully flitted into the Métro with my twenty-kilo suitcase. (Go ahead and ask me why I need so much stuff to visit a quiet resort!) *Flitted* in, I say, exhaled, and all seemed well. Riding along. The train well lit, lots of people around me.

Then suddenly I get a text message: "Boris, door is locked, bell isn't working, call my cell. Asya."

I don't have friends named Boris, and Asyas have thus far stayed out of my life. Who are these people? Or maybe they're not people? Perhaps the demons are communicating? Sending each other coded messages? Door, you say. Something wrong with the doors. I cheerfully text back: "Asya, you have the wrong number!" but no one responds. The demons are silent. *When your demon is in charge, do not try to think consciously. Drift, wait, and obey.*

My train was to arrive exactly by my hotel, with no transfers. I planned it that way to avoid any late-night vicissitudes.

So I'm sitting on the train, when suddenly, behind my back, from the space between the train cars, I hear a series of thunderclaps. They sound like small explosions. The train comes to a halt. Starts and stops. Slowly begins to move again. Then stops in a tunnel. Then moves again. The claps become louder and more frequent. People crouch and look at the dark windows with apprehension. On the panel over my head, emergency lights are illuminated. The conductor grumbles something indistinct over the PA system; the tourists start to get nervous: "What did he say?" "What did he say?" Then, finally, a horrendously loud rumble, the lights go out, the train slowly crawls to some platform, and the gentlepeople hastily exit. I run out with my twenty kilos. Where are we? I ask. I hear back from the platform: "Gare du Nord."

Okay, Gare du Nord, no big deal—I can get a cab. I follow the arrows toward the exit. The crowds have mysteriously dissipated; I am alone in the half-dark train station. There are levels and escalators and more levels and more escalators and the signage is worse than what we have in Moscow, I shit you not. Arrows leading to dead ends, into blank walls, toward stairs without escalators. Finally I make my way to the top level: the arrows have lured me with promises of Parisian lights, of cozy taxis and friendly people.

Now, to exit the Métro, you need to use your ticket again, just as when you entered—you insert it into the gate for the doors to open to let you out. Tall plastic transparent doors. So I insert my ticket and I'm exiting with my suitcase dragging behind me when suddenly the doors slam shut. The photo sensor counted my suitcase as a second, unticketed passenger. The doors didn't sever my arms—we live in humane times, after all, not everyone gets the guillotine. I'm holding on to my suitcase through the slit between the doors, and I can see it, but my access to it has been lost.

And there, behind the doors, in my suitcase are my laptop, my iPad, my passport, all my cash and my credit cards, my phone, and basically everything I have of value. I had put it all in there back at Charles de Gaulle, you know, out of fear of those famous Parisian pickpockets.

So here I am, alone at night, in some deserted and dimly lit back corner of the Métro, separated from my belongings by an impenetrable, albeit transparent, wall. I'd suspect that similar emotions are felt by very wealthy people right after their death: just moments earlier you had everything and then— *bang!*—here you are, dead as a doornail, all incorporeal with rays shooting through you, and your bank accounts and real estate now belong to someone else, bwah-ha-ha.

Must be what Boris and Asya were quietly discussing.

Then a large man descends from the semidarkness. He grabs my suitcase, lifts it up with one hand high over the doors, and lowers it down beside me. I, of course, am very thankful— *grand merci, merci beaucoup*—but the man follows the suitcase over the doors; I don't even understand how he manages it, and I don't like that one bit.

He says: You're not in a hurry, are you? Let's get acquainted, get to know each other, be friends. I'm in a frightful hurry, I say, where is the nearest taxi stand? It's past midnight, everything around us is locked up and parked, surrounded by dreary railroad fumes, and farther out, where I can see people's faces, it's also not so lovely: "Gorilla calls and parrot screams," as the jingle of my student days goes. Those congregating outside are a liberal's wet dream: transvestites, prostitutes, fresh arrivals, and the disadvantaged with difficult childhoods and even more difficult prospects for old age.

I run toward my saviors, the hookers and the trannies; the man runs after me, continuing our conversation:

"My name is Joaquinto. Are you a miss or a missus? I propose we immediately get to know each other, talk and spend some time together. You're not in a hurry, are you? Wait, here is my phone number. Take it, please. Why don't you want my phone number? Why don't you want to get to know me? What are your reasons?"

It's hard to explain right off the bat what my reasons are. Sometimes it's hard to find the right words, Joaquinto.

Finally I manage to break free. I see the taxi line! At the head of it is a hunchback of slight stature, quizzically raising his finger at everyone in line: One? Two passengers? In New York airports there is always a dispatcher like this, shoving a slip of paper in your hand, guiding you to the right taxi, keeping the peace in the queue. Who knows—maybe it's the same here?

It's my turn; the hunchback raises one finger and immediately begins to wrestle my suitcase and purse from me. A slight altercation—I manage to hang on to my purse while he tightly grabs hold of my suitcase and drags it the five feet to the car. His hand shifts shape from a raised finger to a cupped palm: Pay up, lady. Me: Oh no you don't, you little crook. You don't get shit. I don't pay for service that was imposed on me. Besides, I only have large bills.

An ugly scene follows: the hunchback, screaming and spitting, lunges after me into the car, I push him away with my foot, he pulls at the car door, I wrestle it free and slam it shut; shrieking and cursing accompanies the car as it finally pulls away. On my grave I'd like the following inscription, please:

She also wrestled with Quasimodo in Paris
at midnight
and won.

Okay, we're on our way.

"How do you want me to go?" asks the driver, a product of the collapse of colonialism.

"Pardon . . . ? Just—get me there, please. Whichever way. To my hotel."

"No, but how would you like to go? Fast? Or . . . ?"

Things just aren't getting any better. I don't even want to know what options are available to me here. A lady gets into a taxi, gives the driver an address. What questions could there be? What else can one expect from a lady at a train station?

We arrive. The driver looks at the euro notes I hand him, sulks.

"I don't have any change," he says.

That won't work, Buster. I've taken taxis from the airport in Jerusalem, and even from Sheremetyevo in Moscow, God help me. I get it. No change? I can wait until it appears. I turn on my inner Buddhist.

We sit.

We wait.

Three minutes later he miraculously finds a five-euro note in his back pocket. I guess change really does come from within.

Hurray! I'm almost there. A lovely concierge at the hotel— a gorgeous man from Morocco who looks to be a student at the Sorbonne. He doesn't need my passport, or my credit card, or my reservation number: it's all good. Here is your key, here is your elevator, sweet dreams!

I insert the key card into the lock with the blissful feeling of having finally arrived safely, against the odds, of finally stepping off the ship onto terra firma, where Boris and Asya are no longer a threat. I press the door handle down and step into the room. A soul-piercing scream. It's occupied! For a second my eyes are exposed to an unexpected performance: a huge black man is pounding some lady. Or a mademoiselle. Or God knows what.

Finally, having obtained a new set of keys from the concierge, I find myself in the privacy of my hotel room; I lock the doors, kick off my heels, power up my laptop, and open a bottle of wine. My hands shaking, I pour Bordeaux generously into the soft plastic cup provided by the hotel. In a split second the cup tips over, the entire contents splashing onto my laptop keyboard. The laptop survives for three minutes and, just before dying, tries desperately to tell me something. It first changes languages, however this results not in letters, but in mysterious symbols I didn't know existed. I keep desperately trying to press the buttons as Russian letters turn uncontrollably into zodiac signs, waves, stars, ships, and crescent moons. And then the window with the text curls up as if into a tube and slides away.

Drift, wait, and obey.

Without

What if there were no Italy? What if it simply never existed—no such geological configuration in the shape of a boot? Perhaps it was flooded in Noah's days. Or perhaps it collapsed as a single block, with its Alps and Apennines, with its rosebushes and lemon trees, and—why not—along with Sicily and Sardinia, into blue waters during an earthquake, the sea formless and empty, only the Holy Spirit hovering above the salty abyss. Where would the Albanians, who steal laundry from clotheslines, steer their rubber boats? Let's pull out a map and duly look: the closest laundry is hanging in Corsica—too far to swim, and the locals might respond with a knuckle sandwich, although there wouldn't be any locals, would there, and no Frenchmen, either, only Gauls, unconquered and thus never having been ennobled by the Romans. Ipso facto, farther west there would be no Spaniards and no Portuguese, only wild Iberians, most likely under the reign of the Moors. Obviously there wouldn't be any Romanians or Moldovans, and Chişinău would be inhabited by an altogether different tribe, perhaps one unable even to mix lime paint in a bucket or to replace a windowpane. The English language as we know it—that is, with its almost sixty percent of words derived from Latin—simply wouldn't exist. And there wouldn't be any Latin letters, either; we'd write everything with Greek ones, although I'll grant that, practically speaking, the difference is small.

Greeks would be everywhere, there having been no Romans to conquer them—though that would, most likely, have been done, with great satisfaction, by the Persians once Alexander the Great died. Persians are pretty clever engineers; they are wonderful at building bridges and know how to irrigate, so no need to worry about pavements and water supply. The post office would also run smoothly, especially when serving the royal family. But when it comes to marble statues, mosaics, encaustic painting, and small bronze statuettes, things don't look so good. No doubt the Greeks can invent anything, make anything, build, write, and paint anything, but what about the small matter of taste? Persian style can be somewhat heavy-handed. Lapis lazuli. The battle of a king with a lion. Golden floor-length robes and hats piled high reflecting the ethos of Ivan the Terrible's court. Same goes for social mores. Abuse and tyranny, dark anger bubbling underneath: "Everyone! On your knees, bow with your forehead to the floor!" Keep all the women under lock and key and no funny business; drill a hole in the prisoner's shoulder blades and thread a rope through it. And where is political thought? Consuls, proconsuls, the senate, political parties, the patricians, the plebeians, and, last but not least, the Republic? Where is Roman Law? Helloooo? Where are orators? The historians? The theaters? Would the Persians really give a crap about the accrescent hum of an assembling crowd, the crepuscular sky above the amphitheater, the sweet scent of the oleander, the last bit of light from Venus, the evening star that's not really a star at all? About historical scrolls, the adversarial legal system? Would they be captivated by Ciceros, or, given the absence of such, by Demostheneses;

would they come to respect them and create public forums where any deadbeat can let his big mouth run? Impale, impale on a stake, clean the forums with quicklime, and farewell, civil rights leaders and advocates. Where are the baths, the flowing summer robes, the shaved chins, the terraced villas? Where are respected women, worthy mothers of worthy citizens? What about honoring agreements? Projects for the common good? Poetry, where is the poetry? Satire!!! Would a Persian tolerate satire? Or privacy of correspondence? Or doing sports in the buff? Or a relaxed attitude toward the gods?

Subtract from our culture the Roman and Gothic styles; subtract arches, vaulted structures, keystones; take away city planning, gardens, fountains, all European cities, castles, fortresses, spires, humpback bridges, colonnades and atriums; erase Saint Petersburg from the picture and shake its ashes from your hands as if it never existed. Send it all to hell in a handbasket. Off with the Renaissance. Giotto, Michelangelo, Rafael—shoo shoo shoo. Forget about pictorial art—it was but a dream. Down with opera, singing in general, just puncture your eardrums. Pour away the wine, you'll be drinking barley hooch from now on.

Tear up Dante, erase the *Mona Lisa,* raze the Vatican to the ground. There are no Catholics, no popes, no antipopes, no cardinals, no religious hypocrites, no Galileo or Giordano Bruno and none of their tormentors, no Guelphs and Ghibellines; there's no Western Roman Empire, and then no Eastern one, either, for there is no West. Absolutely no West at all. There are no brutal gladiators and no poisoning seductresses. There are no Seven Hills of Rome; the stripy Siena Cathedral does not exist; the blue expanse of Tuscany can't be seen from any window. It's not crimson bellicose Mars, not diamantine Venus up there in the sky.

Nothing, nothing exists—there is no pasta, no Fellini, no pizza, no bel canto, no Pinocchio, no Sophia Loren, no teary-eyed Maksim Gorky in Capri, no Cipollino the Onion Boy, no Neapolitan mastiffs, no Carrara marble, no carnivals, no pesto sauce, no Romeo and Juliet, no mozzarella, no cappuccino, no eruption of Mount Vesuvius, no perdition of Pompeii, no Italian mafia, no Italian fashion, no Mussolini, no Armani, no Pontius Pilate, no *Benedicta tu in mulieribus, et benedictus fructus ventris tui, Jesus.* The leaning tower of Pisa isn't leaning; the sinking town of Venice isn't sinking. There is no Catullus's sparrow. There is no one to discover America. No one to build Moscow's Kremlin.

Gogol has nowhere to run from the encroachment of Mirgorod, no sunny haven where he can lie supine, arms stretched out, gazing for hours into the blueness of the sky, purifying his dark, northern, frosty soul from the debris and detritus of his pale, sluggish, fat-assed homeland. "It's mine! No one can take it away from me! I was born here. Russia, Saint Petersburg, the snow, the scoundrels, the office, the university, the theater—it was all but a dream! He who has been to Italy will say farewell to other lands. He who has been to heaven will not want to come down to earth. . . . Oh, Italy! Whose hand will pluck me from here? Oh, the sky! Oh, the days! It's not quite summer and not quite spring, but better than any springs or summers that exist in other corners of the world. Oh, the air! I can't stop drinking it in. There are skies and paradise in my soul."

Without Italy, there *are* disputes in matters of taste. Money *does* stink. You *can* speak ill of the dead.

And all roads lead to nothing.

Faraway Lands

A letter from Crete to a friend in Moscow

Green clouds, the foul air of the fatherland, and especially its heart—Moscow—are behind us, and so here we are, giddy with joy and from lack of sleep, drinking ice-cold white wine and looking out at the sparkling desert of the sea, not caring to know anyone below Odysseus. And here is one, bringing us fried fish and tzatziki, as well as some horta (boiled bitter greens, in case someone forgot what horta are), and the pearly gates are once again open to us for two weeks. Perhaps we didn't sin all that much in the previous year.

The role of gatekeeper this time was played by Aegean Airlines, which sold us tickets for a laughably small sum but omitted a caveat, and of course there was one. The night before our departure we got an email: Your flight is not tomorrow afternoon as you had hoped, dear passenger, but at six in the morning. And you'll have a twelve-hour layover in Athens, with nowhere to lay your sleep-deprived head. Nothing to be done but sorrowfully sprinkle that head with ashes, throw some stuff into our suitcase, and race to the airport at three in the morning.

But somewhere along the way the Creator had mercy on us, and in Athens we were able to rebook our tickets for an earlier flight to Heraklion; not only did our luggage arrive safely, but we even got the rental car we'd reserved, although, as we arrived earlier than expected, the car wasn't ready and there were still spiderwebs on the back seat, a visual manifestation of the ongoing European economic crisis.

The crisis was also evident at familiar places and store counters. The paucity of choices at the supermarket, the joy of the greengrocer on seeing us—he almost kissed me, touched by my repeat custom, and I left his shop weighed down by bags full of vegetables and oranges for only three and a half euros in total.

Our hotel was half empty: a handful of mothers with children under ten. Maybe the season hadn't really started yet, but in years prior it was difficult to find a table with the view of wisteria. (Or was it jasmine? Palm trees? Rhododendron? Our friend Pasha would be appalled at my ignorance if he ever sobered up.) But now you can sit and peck at your paltry complimentary breakfast wherever you want: for instance, they rationed only one thinly sliced cucumber per meal. That is, one cucumber for all the hotel's guests. Cross my heart. Fortunately, I had brought my own for dieting purposes, at a cost of seven or eight euro cents; and besides, I didn't want to pilfer the provisions of the owners—stingy Stavros and his German wife. They also didn't set out any boiled eggs—what if no one ate them?—but if you asked, they obliged. I got a whole egg, and had I asked for two, I would have gotten two: Come quick, dear friend, this is a land of plenty. "Live your myth in Greece."

I'm sticking to my self-imposed Ramadan by eating canned turkey at night; I loathe it, and this particular brand has an unnatural look to it: petal-like pieces in some sort of preservative brine. But at least it's not pork or garlicky salami, which we used to gorge on in our more zaftig days. There aren't any Greek strawberries in the markets, they must all have gone to the markets of Moscow. Would a Frenchman eat truffles in lean times? No, he would sell them to a rich oil sheik instead.

Yesterday we went to a seafood place and ordered a whole platter of various fried fish. Twenty-nine euros for two, everything fresh out of the wine-dark sea. There were two sea breams, mother and daughter; a piece of swordfish; some sardines, which by default smelled of their wood-smoked fate; two unidentified fish; and a few giant prawns. All this was drizzled with lemon and delicious homemade olive oil—so long, diet—and garnished with green salad leaves. Turns out greens are yummy if they are fresh picked and not as they're served in the Fatherland. They're meant to be crunchy and not to sluggishly wrap around your teeth. Oh, there was also a side dish, but we, as you'll understand, had to abstain. The side dish was rice.

Yesterday's dinner meditations compared the behavior and motivations of a Russian to those of a European. Here is a classic theme: the drinking man. European literature, cinema, and anecdotal observations all paint the same picture: a lonely middle-aged soul in a bar, drinking alone but with dignity (which sometimes excuses his bluish nose, blotchy cheeks, trembling hands, and ancient scarf) at a table or at the counter, solitarily looking into his glass; if he does raise his eyes, perhaps only looking wistfully and forlornly like Pierrot, he doesn't stare, doesn't catcall, doesn't grab anyone's ass. He drinks slowly, staying past last call. He is contemplating his loneliness, we surmise, the meaninglessness of existence, the impossibility of emotional attachment, and the passing of the more-or-less good ol' days. My poor old mother, *ma pauvre vielle mère,* as well as the long-gone young lady in white bloom. If he has a dog, it's also as old as the sea, and he's sure to bring it, as the dog is always allowed. Imagine! A dog allowed in a bar! Because European canines don't jump up on people, tearing their pants and humping their leg—no, they lie under the table with toothless dignity and sightless wisdom, mirroring their owner's quiet heartache. One of the best stories about this is Hemingway's "A Clean Well-Lighted Place"—although there is no dog, the solitude is total and complete.

My sister was right in observing that the female hypostasis of the lonely European is a lady over forty, often bitter, having coffee and a dessert alone in a pastry shop at lunchtime. Inescapable sadness in her eyes: her feminine charms are no longer in demand, there has been no happiness, or perhaps, having deceived, it drained away like water through a sieve, and there lies ahead an endless desert, where even an encounter with a camel's prickly thorn is not guaranteed. We saw one woman just like this in Baden-Baden, in a pastry shop where we stopped for apple pie (with the shyness and audacity of a horny teenager at a brothel). She was sitting by the window— a plate with the ruins of a mille-feuille beside her—looking out into nothingness with such intensity that she was burning through all the oxygen in her line of sight. We saw another one like that in Florence—she was drinking espresso at a table outside in the square, that is, smack in the middle of the biggest crowds, the maze of flower beds, under the shining sun, in the midst of the vortex.

The Baden-Baden lady was hopelessly unattractive, and her heart couldn't soar over this wall of unsightliness, barrenness, and social leprosy. And as it couldn't soar above it, neither could anyone make their way through it, even if they tried. The Florence lady was not young—over sixty, but still capable of traveling solo. Varicose veins hadn't yet carved up her legs, her nose hadn't yet turned into a strawberry from a daily drinking habit; still, she was separated from this sunny world by her age, which she visibly hated and cursed, and in hating her age, she raged against the sunny world around her.

Sure, we might observe and ponder why a lonely woman is more likely bitter while a lonely man is more likely sad, although it's pretty simple, really: an unwanted man is a buyer with no money, and an unwanted woman is a seller with empty shelves. That's how, seemingly, the theme of the European financial crisis comes full circle.

Although we shouldn't jump to any conclusions.

Meanwhile—as you rightly know—a Russian man who is lonely and sad in a bar is unimaginable. Upon entering any establishment for the purpose of drinking, he immediately seeks out company, instantly infiltrates it, and, without delay, forges a quick, if shaky and dangerous, friendship while stepping on everyone's toes and violating personal boundaries that his drinking buddies didn't even suspect existed.

If a group of men are drinking, he'll plop down next to them, uninvited, instantly "logging in," so to speak, with widely accepted passwords: "This is some game, huh?" or "Those Sauerkrauts don't know shit from clay." And *bam*, he's already found like-minded countrymen; *bam*, he's entered a vague financial relationship fraught with catastrophe, such as "This round's on me!" thus uncovering a snaky path to a snafu to be followed by fisticuffs. If there are ladies drinking, he'll rush to them—the outcomes are obvious if diverse. Police reports usually detail only the fallout, the crowning glories of these encounters: perpetrator was drinking, got acquainted, continued party at new acquaintance's apartment (or park, or basement), started an argument, assaulted victim (new friend / lady friend) with a wooden stool (or kitchen knife, ax, etc.). But the intentions, the intentions were perfectly openhearted and pure.

You can't escape a lonely Russian on a beach: he doesn't hide behind a distant boulder, as a European would, but instead unrolls his beach towel overlapping yours, and upon hearing Russian spoken proceeds with a tactless line of questioning. Thank God for iPods: these days everyone is wearing headphones, but just think, a mere ten years ago they used to bring boom boxes to the beach, NSYNCing for all to hear.

Russian women, as you and I have often discussed, love to flock together. The stereotypical picture of old ladies congregating on a bench by their building's entrance is improbable in Europe—I mean real Europe, Western Europe. Not sure about Eastern Europe, but didn't see it there, either. In Greek villages, however, you have solitary old ladies in black sitting solemnly and wordlessly on folding chairs by their open front doors, red chintz curtains drawn. Only once, in the magical village of Margarites, did I see a group of such ladies in black quietly talking, and they, upon seeing me, a stranger, fell silent. Greek men, by contrast, are forever and routinely congregating; they drink coffee outdoors, fingering their worry beads and talking about women, football, high prices, and politics. More precisely, they begin with politics, and only then move on to the rest. They people watch with lively interest, and so outdoor cafés by bus stops are especially popular: folks get on the bus and they get off the bus; this provides endless entertainment.

Today there was a German family at dinner: mother and father and two boys aged around eight and ten. All four of them ate and drank in complete silence—it made me want to reach out and turn up the volume. On their faces—I looked at them closely—was good-natured indifference, and in twenty minutes of chewing nothing transpired: no remarks, no smiles, no jokes. At some point one of the boys reached over and seemingly pinched the other, but I rejoiced for naught: there was no reaction. And soon, silently and synchronously, they got up and left.

I couldn't help thinking: Fifty years from now, when their parents are gone and those boys are old themselves, everything good already behind them, they will go to sit alone at separate bars, somber drink in hand, among other dignified, lonely old gents, each of them honoring the great European tradition of respect for other people's privacy, staying mute till his very last breath.

Oh, the life they could have had—fighting with their neighbors, banging on the radiator with a stick, writing querulous petitions to the courts, spoiling the fun of youngsters, imposing themselves on others with recollections of battles in Königsberg, and enjoying other debauched behavior.

No, if for some reason I were forced to choose—"Are you with us or with them?"—I would, after protesting, resisting, and throwing a tantrum, still choose our boorish yet warm, loquacious, and insufferable way of going through life, if only to avoid the polite, dreadful, and deafening silence.

§

Bought a local Russian-language newspaper. From the classifieds:

JOBS
—Night shift at funeral home.

GIVING AWAY
—Will give away iguana with aquarium and heat lamp.
—Will share my kombucha.

LOOKING TO SELL
—Wedding dress, sequined. Comes with veil, gloves, and tiara.
—Two-bedroom apartment in Athens, Kallithéa, 2 balconies, 75 square meters, €75,000.
—Apartment in Ukraine, Village of Nikolaevka, €60,000.

LOOKING TO BUY
— Roly-poly Russian tumbler toy.
—Arctic fox or badger grease.

PERSONALS
—Carefree gal, full of laughs, seeks a fiancé, plump, tall, under 75.
—I'm a doctor, 41 years old, attractive, slender, married. Looking to meet a beautiful young woman, not predisposed to weight gain, without insecurities or reproaches, for pleasant encounters 2–4 times per month. Will cover rent. Please call only on Monday and Friday mornings, or Tuesday and Thursday evenings. Can't wait!

JOBS
—Russian-speaking family looking for a housekeeper under 40, hardworking, with a clean heart.

MISCELLANEOUS
—Have you consulted a weight-loss service only to be swindled out of your money? Please give me a call to discuss.
—At a remote and faraway monastery on Mount of Temptation (Israel) there lives a solitary monk. In

serving our Lord, in seclusion from other humans does he spend his days. He has virtually no means. By his spiritual endeavor he atones for all our sins. If you're inclined to help, please do so generously. Father Gerasimos Vourazanidis will mention you and your loved ones in his prayers. Phone # ****, Fax # ****, Ethniki Trapeza bank acct # ****, PO box ***, Jerusalem, Israel. Archim. Gerasimos Vourazanidis.

§

Many, many moons ago—twenty-five, to be precise—I first came to Crete and lived on the outskirts of the town of Rethymno. Back then, Rethymno was small, its border right by the old university. Past there were ditches and gullies, the rattling of a backhoe digging the foundations of future buildings, which now stretch out for fifteen kilometers from that very spot.

Basically, everything was still fresh, young, and untouched. The roads on Crete were impassable; some were simply dirt roads, and I enjoyed taking off my sandals and walking on the cooling evening dust that felt like flour. Nowadays, asphalt is everywhere and it's easy to drive places, but not just for me—and that's the problem. These disgustingly convenient highways were built straight through magnificent and mysterious mountains full of birds and trees; there are no more trees and no more birds there, only heaps of red stone in the whistling wind.

So there I was, on the Island of Crete for the first time, sitting at a restaurant in the harbor, right on the water, people watching. The restaurants there were crap—tourist traps with frozen fish and jacked-up prices—but there was one authentic spot, low-key and right under your nose. Everything was homemade and done right, the giveaway being that Greeks ate there. The tablecloths were blue gingham, and you could crumble bread straight into the sea to feed the fish without leaving your table as the sun shone down.

About ten feet away from me, in one of the tourist traps, there was a Swedish woman—around thirty-five, orange hair brushed straight up, T-shirt with no bra the way they like it in Scandinavia—surrounded by three Vikings of enviable height and heroic good looks: rosy cheeks, golden locks, and piercing blue eyes. All four of them were three sheets to the wind, very jolly, most noticeably the woman, who was laughing loudly with her mouth open wide. You couldn't miss her.

A quarter century passed and the Crete of yesterday, so inviting in its pristine remoteness, bucolic and patriarchal, had faded and surrendered to cement hotels and boardinghouses. Its distant outskirts, where summits once afforded mind-blowing vistas of sparkling seas and uninhabited shores, were now dotted with greenhouses and covered in abominable white film, all to grow tomatoes, say, for the visitors of those cheerfully painted cement hotels and boardinghouses.

And no longer did you feel like getting behind the wheel and driving farther, farther, farther, because in the distance, there, too, were asphalt and white film and convenience. The joy of these wild expanses that I got to experience was gone forever.

And so, twenty-five years on, I am once again sitting at a homey restaurant in the small harbor of Rethymno, my elbows resting on that blue-checkered tablecloth. Maria, the proprietress—now long in the tooth—is making her way toward me with my meal while I, as usual, deliberate the relative merits of driving drunk. But how can one not drink with dinner? And then from the table next to me comes this loud, drunken, mouth-wide-open laugh. I turn around—my God!

Thinning orange hair brushed straight up, peeling skin, T-shirt worn over a bra-less wrinkly body, leg in a cast sticking out like a bazooka, arm wrapped in some bandages—it's that very same Swedish woman, now in a wheelchair! Surrounded by the very same three Vikings, now slouchy and ruddy-faced, the remnants of golden locks blowing in the wind, eyes faded almost to white.

All of them shit-faced, all of them laughing hysterically; one is plagued by a smoker's cough, he's waving his arm— "Enough!"—which only makes the rest howl louder with jolly boozy laughter, and she, that faded carrot-haired beauty, the loudest and jolliest of them all.

And the sight of these invincible people filled my heart with awe and my eyes with tears.

§

The blood feuds here are like those of Sardinia. You visit some tiny mountain village in the year 2000 and then, ten years later, you read in the latest travel guide: they all perished, killed in a standoff. Toward the end of that standoff, the police came, surrounded the house where the shooter was hiding. They yelled into a megaphone: *That's it, Cousin Manolis, surrender!* And he yelled back: *This is none of your business, let me just shoot the last one and I'll come out myself.* How do you not respect that? They are all related down here.

We know one such family. About fifteen years ago we used to frequent a taverna run by Yorgos, a young man of uncommon good looks. If you've ever seen those preclassical kouros sculptures—that's Yorgos: tall, heavy hipped, with an inscrutable Mona Lisa smile that isn't really a smile but a natural crease of the mouth, for Yorgos was never amused. His eyes were also preclassical, Mycenaean, wrapping around his face like a pair of sunglasses and aiming somewhere behind his ears; their color was pale grape, perfect for staring blankly into the distance.

He was the son of the proprietor of the taverna, as I say, and as it was customary here, the entire family—all ten—toiled away during the high season from dusk till midnight: they bought, they brought, they peeled, they chopped, they served, they cleared. And everything was cooked by one immortal granny; well, there were two dark-haired short ladies helping in the 100+ degree kitchen, but the chef was Granny, all in black and shaped like a question mark. She's still toiling away there, fifteen years later.

So here is Yorgos, balancing on one tanned arm six oval plates of seafood and potatoes, the wine and six glasses held in his other tanned arm—the sun is setting, everything is bathed in golden light. The Germans already had ordered their *Schweinekotelett* and Mythos beer. Paradise. With his pale eyes, Yorgos is looking out over the German heads and ours—always above the tourists' heads—his eyes glancing over the mountains, the rooftops, the balconies and treetops.

"Sit with us, Yorgos, have a drink!" we say; we have known him for a long time. Or we think we know him.

Yorgos sits.

"The world is full of evil," says he.

"Sure, that's true," we respond lightheartedly. "But the weather is delightful."

And then it all comes pouring out. Yorgos is first in line; someday a bullet will come for him. Or not. It might be a knife. They are from a mountain village about twenty miles from here up a small green road. (We've driven past it, by the way, there was nothing sinister. A mini-mart, ice cream kiosks, gas station.) But in the nineteenth century, somebody stole somebody's sheep. The victim's honor was insulted: A sheep? Rustled from me? And so he stole two back. The initial offender was outraged in turn. Soon somebody's second cousin once removed was, well, removed. So it was necessary to retaliate by killing that clan's next in line, a daydreaming sixteen-year-old boy: you snooze, you lose. And so it went. Yorgos's family ran away from the village to the shore, a little safer there, no one is going to just start shooting in a crowd full of tourists, that's not manly, completely out of the question, the most important thing here is honor! But when the crowds have dissipated, then maybe.

Yorgos wanted to major in architecture and got into some European university. But his father yanked him away from his studies come peak season: You need to work, there are hordes of tourists coming. You can go back in the fall. Father spoke, son obeyed: from April till the end of October, Yorgos carried, stacked on his beautiful tanned arms, platters of tourist feed. "My heart's in the Highlands, wherever I go." They have a good restaurant. It was the best in the area. Year after year, the money flowed.

By November, visions of architecture fade: you close your eyes and *Schweinekotelett* is all you see. No impetus even to try. So he makes his way to Switzerland, to Germany where he spends lavishly, skis, frequents casinos. They could kill him there, too, of course, and there is no knowing who the killer might be.

His brother is also a target. His sister is married and living in a neighboring village; they wouldn't kill her, that's bad form. By killing a woman, you lower yourself, losing your place at the top of the social hierarchy. Same for old people. The best is to kill a killer, but, failing that, killing a young man before he's had a chance to father any future avengers.

And so Yorgos and his brother look out into the distance, scanning the mountaintops with their pale Mycenaean eyes.

"We never tell the truth about where we're going and when. If we need to leave at noon on Monday, we always say that we're leaving at two p.m. on Wednesday. We never know who's listening. Never know who might come. Never know how long we'll live. The world is full of evil."

All Cretans are liars, it's said. Maybe that's why? He got up and left: too much work to do. Can't leave him a tip; he's the owner, not simply a waiter. The Germans don't know, they tip. But are Sauerkrauts people?

Blood feuds are studied from every angle as a particular type of ancient institution that supports the clan structure of society and as a post-traumatic reaction—this leaves a wide berth for all things Freudian. There is something called "afterwardsness"; those who are interested can delve further. Wherever the concept of honor exists, so does the concept of insult. Where there is insult, there is revenge, spilled blood and the avenging of said honor. It's not only sheep that can trigger a conflict—it could be a woman, or disrespectful speech, or a disrespectful glance, even. "Sing, Goddess, sing of the rage of Achilles, son of Peleus." Rage—θυμός—is a typically Greek quality. It's as if it is stored somewhere deep inside, kept fresh forever.

An example: A man gets killed and is survived by his wife and baby. The wife hides his bloodied clothes in a dower chest; throughout his childhood the boy keeps asking: Where is my father? "You'll know when you grow up." When he finally does, his mother hands him clothes caked with blood. He puts them on and goes out looking for vengeance.

Or another: In 1987, a shepherd killed a hospital orderly he encountered at random. They were chatting, and the orderly, for some reason, shared that a long time ago, his distant relative killed a man with this or that last name. The shepherd realized that the victim in question was his uncle. The orderly's last name was the same as that of his uncle's killer. That meant they were related, and that meant the blood feud applied. "Suddenly, blood rushed to my head, my brain was cloudy, I just knew I had to kill him." Astonishingly, this shepherd was born twenty-two years after his uncle was murdered.

I went to see Yorgos this week, too. He's still alive. His face puffy, his eyes paler than ever, habitually scanning the balconies and rooftops. He looked at me with indifference.

"Yorgos," I said. "You don't recognize me?"

"I do."

He set my food in front of me and walked away. Not being dangerous, I was of no interest to him whatsoever.

§

In Greek villages you always find: white walls, blue doors, and a grim-faced old lady sitting on a rickety stool, looking out, possibly at you or possibly into the obscure depths of a life lived. She'll be wearing a black dress, or a black top and skirt—hard to tell; her head will be covered in a black scarf, her wizened black-stockinged legs set wide apart for stability. She will also be leaning on something: a walking stick or a shepherd's staff.

That must be the tradition. How many centuries have they been sitting like that? And at what age are they expected to exchange their colorful clothes for full-body black, forever abandoning femininity and full living?

At first I thought that this was prolonged widowhood, transformed into death during life. But no, these grannies often coexist with layabout husbands who never sit by the door but spend their days hanging out at the café in the town square with other slacker grandpas. Pale azure short-sleeved shirts, beige trousers (washed and ironed by the grannies in black), thick heads of hair—old Greeks rarely go bald. Some even proudly sport fancy mustaches. Worry beads—hands need to keep busy somehow. Cigarettes and tiny cups of very sweet coffee are de rigueur.

The grandpas in beige congregate at café tables in the shade of a tree—there is always a tree in a town square—where they discuss local, as well as world, politics. With lively curiosity they observe people getting off buses—at every village a bus stops twice a day, dropping off new, interesting, bewildered foreigners and their women. A few of the foreigners ask for directions, and the grandpas oblige with dignity, slowly gesturing with their hand: Go this way, then that way, and then turn there. They follow the clueless tourists with a stern gaze, and then it's back to world political machinations and ogling women.

The ladies in black don't discuss anything, they simply sit there. What's to discuss, right? Gave birth, cooked, did laundry, waited, loved, cried, condemned, forgave, didn't forgive, hated, harvested olives from a black mesh laid under the trees, bade farewell, buried, mourned, and then again cooked, washed dishes, and returned them to the shelf.

What's to discuss?

Official Nationality

1. The Triad of Official Nationality—a doctrine proposed by Sergey Uvarov, Russia's minister of education from 1834 to 1849—continues to amaze me with its ingenuity.

"Orthodoxy, Autocracy, Nationality." The wording is for brevity and for pleasing the tsar, but also to discourage the Illuminati, the Carbonari, and the Jacobins, with their *"Liberté, Egalité, Fraternité"*—those same who, by the basketful, used to collect their brethren's heads from under the guillotine, *fi donc!*

The Uvarov Triad, the Holy Life-Giving Trinity, assembles into a single movable structure three types of power, three kinds of force: the celestial (religion), the earthly (the tsar), and the chthonic (the lower world), whose roots spread out and creep down to God knows where, feeding off God knows what subterranean rivers, maybe even blooming with dead-white flowers, entangling themselves in underground caves impossibly hard to reach.

It is essentially the World Tree—Arbor Mundi—the heavens, the terrestrial world, and the underworld. You can only surmise what's up top, you can observe what is in the middle, and the bottom is an impenetrable and incomprehensible pit.

By comparison, *"Liberté, Egalité, Fraternité"* is nothing but gibberish smeared over a flat surface. It's not the Russian way.

Each element of the Triad, however, is a blooming garden of mystery.

First, let's take Orthodoxy. But what "Orthodoxy," pray tell? It's mostly a matter of wishful thinking, a reminder that one mustn't forget, but must pay attention. The populace has a tendency to regress, one way or the other, into the warm, damp gloom of paganism, with its obscure flickering and alarmed voices, where something hoots and hollers behind your shoulder, beckons and promises in the distance.

Jesus stubbornly grumbles and doesn't feel like performing miracles. Doesn't feel like it! That's just the way He is. Here is Lazarus for you—and that's enough. A blind man, fine. But people need miracles, they long for astonishing, lively, festive things. Abracadabra and—*bam!* Open the door—and there! Look out the window—and wow! They need Santa, on a regular basis. With presents. Otherwise, O heavenly creatures, life is empty and cold.

That Russian Orthodoxy and paganism go well together is obvious, plain to see in life's most important matters. The moment the bride and groom step away from the altar, they are showered with grain to ensure fertility, so that their progeny are as plentiful as the harvest. In fat years they shower them with wheat. And in lean years—and I remember the lean 1980s as if they were yesterday—there were two women standing around an empty Soviet grocery store, without so much as a bit of millet to be had, discussing whether they could use corn grits instead.

And the hearth? The apartment? The most important thing one can possess is his burrow, his nest, his private space. Whether a micro-studio in a tiny rural town or a penthouse on the Golden Mile—it's all shelter. Before moving in, a Russian will have a cat cross the threshold to purify the space of evil spirits; then he'll invite a priest to bless it. Sometimes the order is reversed, but only after having done both will he set foot inside. The cat and the priest go hand in hand, so to say; they protect us from evil, they chase away the darkness, exuding an inexplicable aetherial, magic fragrance.

All this despite the fact that a cat, by folk logic, is generally up to no good, and in cahoots with these very same evil spirits. But he also controls them. A cat is our ambassador to the world of evil—and thus pagan—forces; he's our protector, our Saint Tabby. (Same in Europe; see under "Puss in Boots.")

There are places where otherworldly forces swirl. In Izborsk, for instance. It's a tiny town near Pskov.

> An oak of green by curving sea bend,
> A golden chain that hugs its form;
> And day and night that chain is treaded:
> A cat walks round, he's well-informed.

> When ambling left—he tells a tale,
> When right—a song does part his lips.
> There's magic here: a wood sprite's trail,
> A mermaid hidden in the leaves.

There, in Izborsk, a powerful tree grows; it grants wishes. The top official in town is a former military man; he showed it to us. The tree stood decorated with colorful ribbons. When his wife got pregnant again, he told us, he ran to the tree and tied a ribbon to request a girl. And what do you know? A girl was born. The official's face beamed with a marvelous kind of internal light as he was telling this story—even Count Uvarov wouldn't have butted in with his "Orthodoxy," respectfully tip-toeing away instead.

A woman who sells homemade sunflower oil in the market spent forty minutes telling me about such places; she made a short, half-hour pilgrimage to the local holy spring. (I've been to those springs. One grants money, another love, a third good things in general, without specifying; take a wild guess as to which spring has more men in line, which one more women, and which one flows freely, neglected.) So this woman, with a driver named Nikolai, also sells quilted clothes; and once during a delivery they stopped by the spring. So here she is, just walking, when she finds strolling next to her a monk in black robes. He gives her some advice and warns her about a few things, what to do and what not to do; then— *zap*—he disappears, and Nikolai says, "Who were you just talking to?" She turns this way and that—the monk is nowhere to be found.

Is this Orthodoxy? A disappearing monk in black?

§

2. Autocracy is basically self-explanatory. In fact, it's hard to comprehend what to do without it. How do you live without an overlord? Whom do you ask for permission? Who would be responsible for things? Who will show you warmth and who will punish you? To whom does one complain?

Goodness me, can you imagine life without a boss? Confusion and chaos will ensue, things will fall apart. And then foreign bosses will take over, because life without an overlord cannot be.

When the Big Bad Soviet Tyrant ceased to oppress the freedom-loving Republic of Turkmenistan, the country breathed a collective sigh of relief and welcomed the one and only Beloved Serdar, His Excellency the Eternally Great Saparmurat Turkmenbashi, who immediately upped the level of what-the-fuckery.

For instance, he decreed that a zoo be built in the Karakum Desert, and that it contain penguins. (Have you ever tried those "Karakum" candies? The ones that taste like sand and rocks?) Temperatures can rise to 122 degrees Farhenheit in the Karakum, and surfaces can heat up to 176 degrees, but with a President-for-Life that's not a problem. Cost: a paltry eighteen million bucks.

He also ordered an ice palace to be built in the mountains. And a funicular to reach it. Just to have one.

Infectious diseases were declared illegal and it was now forbidden even to mention them. An ideological battle was waged against microbes. You couldn't utter the words "cholera" or "smallpox." "Herpes," too, was out. And as a fitness initiative, he ordered his ministers to participate in running a marathon. I'm guessing that a number of offices were vacated and aired out as a result of this "Walk of Health."

He also outlawed the ballet, the opera, and the circus. Outlawed gold teeth. Forbade video games, beards, smoking, and lip syncing. Sex was declared a government matter, to be engaged in only for the purposes of procreation, as "personal pleasure does not apply to the progressive culture of the Turkmen people."

He ordered his citizens to believe that the Turkmen had invented the cart and the wheel. He closed the Academy of Sciences and fired fifteen thousand health workers, taking away their pensions. (Is this beginning to sound familiar?)

He introduced a new calendar, erected fourteen thousand monuments to himself (one of them cost ten million dollars;

it was gilded and would turn toward the sun). He yearned to be called a shah, but it didn't take, so he settled for "Marshal" instead. Five times he was awarded the title of Hero of Turkmenistan, but he categorically refused to accept it the sixth time, citing modesty.

He had gray hair, but then his hair grew darker, for that was Allah's will; then he himself grew younger and died.

I'm personally an anarchist, but I dearly love autocrats and I miss Saparmurat Turkmenbashi. Who else could have concocted such a fantasy out of nothing? He made French concessionaires, holding documents for him to sign, walk on their knees from the golden doors to the golden throne. Sometimes he would refuse to sign the papers, just for shits and giggles. Let them crawl, let them polish the marble. And on their knees, in reverse, never taking their worshipful eyes off the Boss, let them take their leave of him.

If you think about it, compared to Saparmurat's, Russian autocracy, even today's, is an apple orchard in full bloom, crystal-clear waters on a July afternoon.

§

3. Nationality, however, that third component of the Triad, is incomprehensible, not subject to simple logic. Truly, who can see what is underneath the ground? Who wanders there? The Indrik-Beast, king of all animals? The one who lives on the Holy Mountain, eating and drinking from the Blue Sea, not harming a soul?

That's where, as I say, the roots of the Tree are, and the expanses of the underworld; there, something mysterious is happening, something is talking and mumbling to itself, all of it unknowable.

What is "the Russian people"? Should we decide according to blood or spirit? By face or by language? Such questions could start a brawl.

I think that "Nationality"—that approximate term cautiously chosen by Count Uvarov—as applied to the Russian people, comprises three very important features, three concepts. They are Boldness, Longanimity, and "Let's hope." If those three come together, you have "the Russian people"; if not . . . no "Russian people" for you.

All three features can be separately observed in other nations. For instance, the Poles are particularly bold. One Darwin Award went, posthumously, to a bold Polish gentleman who was drinking with his buddies. As all of them got shit-faced, one yelled out "Look what I can do!" and with a circular saw hacked off his own leg. "That's nothing," said our hero, who, grabbing the saw, cut off his own head.

Longanimity, by contrast, is not a particularly Polish quality. It does apply to the Czechs, though there aren't many stories of Czech boldness. And these nations are practically neighbors.

I'd define Boldness as a pointless rush of testosterone with no regard for the consequences. Among other peoples it might be age related, occurring mostly during puberty. But it can manifest in a Russian person well into his golden years, and in no way correlating with the calendar. For instance, getting drunk and disorderly. My Finnish editor tells me that his people, too, like falling into a drunken stupor, but only on Fridays and Saturdays and never on Sundays, Monday being a workday.

Just tell me, what Russian would be deterred in such purpose by considerations of work? "Fuck work!" they're likely to opine.

An exemplary instance of Boldness is Leskov's short story

"Chertogon." And models of longanimity are to be found in Dostoevsky's humiliated, insulted, and otherwise tortured characters, both men and women.

But, of course, the defining feature of the Russian people is "Let's hope."

This "Let's hope" is a built-in denial of causality, it's a lack of belief in the material nature of our universe and its physical laws. Remember this and carve it in stone.

"We should attach this part with screws, otherwise it might fall off along the way."

"Ah, let's hope it doesn't."

But why? Why wouldn't it fall off? Vibration, gravity, mathematical probability—all these say it will! And it always does! Always! But again and again, a Russian refuses to screw in, to attach, to prop, to fasten with rope, to hammer, to cover, to secure under lock and key. So once again the thing unscrews, comes loose, falls off, comes untied, crumbles, gets wet, gets stolen; but this does not prevent the same Russian, against all odds and with stunning stubbornness, from denying the obvious next time, too.

It must not be so obvious to him. He must be seeing something else. He must be transcending the laws of physics, mathematical probability, and other trifles, instantly focusing his inner eye upon the depths of the Absolute, the inexplicable Maelstrom, the preincarnate fifteen-dimensional vortex where the Creator, swirling inside Himself, refracting a multispectral light of His own glory, does as He pleases—juggling black holes, for instance, or on a whim bending space-time and changing laws that He Himself established.

And therefore a Russian lives every minute, every second, in expectation of a miracle. And so he doesn't expect a code of

He was toiling away on an extended opus entitled *The Animal Kingdom*—its aim was to explain, over seventeen volumes, the existence of the soul from an anatomical perspective—when, suddenly, strange things started happening to him. He began to be tormented by vivid and meaningful dreams.

Restless yellow horses, moaning women throwing themselves into the arms of men, marching soldiers; unknown forces—either spirits or God himself—that would cast him to the ground and thunder in his ears, enveloping him or seizing his arms. Crucially, he knew—yes, he absolutely knew—what all this represented. The meaning of Creation was opening up to him, both the visible and the invisible, the spiritual. The hereafter presented itself to him in his agony, convulsions, and hallucinations; a number of times, the professor could distinctly feel a dagger piercing his leg or his back. Voices dictated various passages, guiding his hand as he wrote; oftentimes he caught strong and unpleasant smells—obviously the stench of his sins. At night he was frequently tormented by evil spirits: they caused him physical pain, strangling him as they blasphemed; sometimes they'd even switch the flavors in his food—sweet for salty, say. This lasted for six months, and then something even odder happened.

It was April of 1745, London. At an inn, where he had a private room, he was eating ravenously after there'd been a delay in getting him his supper. Suddenly a dimness spread over the room; he saw the floor covered with toads, snakes, and other creepy-crawlies. When the darkness lifted, a man appeared, resplendent in imperial purple. "Don't eat so much!" he bellowed menacingly before he disappeared and the room returned to normal. The professor got scared and rushed home. That very night, in his dreams, the stranger appeared to him again. He revealed himself to be God, the Creator and the Redeemer. He had chosen Swedenborg to explain to men the interior sense of the Sacred Scripture; He would dictate to him exactly what to write. "And that same night," Swedenborg writes, "the eyes of my interior man were opened, and perfectly fitted to see into heaven, the world of spirits, and hell. . . . From that day I renounced all worldly pursuits, in order to devote myself exclusively to spiritual things, as I had been commanded."

Swedenborg began to write with inhuman speed (in Latin, with a quill) and to publish anonymously books about how the afterworld actually works. Twenty-five volumes followed, describing this new doctrine in exceedingly exhaustive and boring detail. The gist of it was that people had erred in interpreting the Word. They didn't understand that the Word had become the world, the Word was the entire world, and everything we see around us—the sun, the moon, the stars, the clouds, the horses, the donkeys, the gold, the silver, the women—everything down to the tiniest detail of existence, every little thing, is an allegory, or, as Swedenborg called it, a "correspondence." Thus, man misunderstood the words of the Apocalypse, which says that after the Day of Judgment the entire observable world will collapse, that new heavens and a new earth will emerge. How can that be? Can it really mean that our sky and the stars in it will vanish? rational Swedes and other skeptical Europeans would ask themselves. No, of course not, Swedenborg would reply, the skies and stars won't disappear, for if you truly comprehend the spiritual meaning of the Word, then you'll see that the Sun *corresponds* to the Lord in terms of love, and the moon in terms of faith; the stars *correspond* to knowledge of blessings and truth; the clouds represent the literal meaning of God's Word, and glory represents its inner meaning. "The sign of the Son of man in the heavens" is the appearance of divine truth; "all the tribes of the earth that will mourn"—that's everything that relates to truth and grace, or to faith and love; "God's appearance in the heavens with power and glory"—His revelation and presence in the Word; etc., etc. (It all makes sense now, doesn't it?)

So, in this way, the purpose of the Day of Judgment is to create a new church, since the present one is finished, it is no good, it's mired in hypocrisy—in other words, this is a spiritual Day of Judgment. Which, by the way, doesn't preclude people from living the way they had been living; they do have freedom of choice.

But what is there beyond the grave? What's there? Here's what, according to Swedenborg: When a person dies, he doesn't notice it at first, but just keeps on living as before, working from his office, riding in carriages, visiting friends. The only difference is that everything around him becomes brighter, his senses become keener. Then benevolent spirits pay him a visit (spirits, as it turns out, are simply underdeveloped angels), and they gently guide him to the realization that he's no more. Dead. That he himself is in the realm of the spirits. At first he does not believe it. Then he looks around and—Why, yes, it's true. And he keeps on living until he figures out, with the discreet aid of heavenly helpers, where to go from here.

Three kingdoms make up the afterworld: the heavens (which, in turn, are made up of three layers and a multitude of "societies"); the realm of the spirits; and the realm of the underworld (since hell is multifaceted and multitudinous). Where one goes is determined by a person's spiritual merit, but it's not so simple. For instance, sinners do not duly burn in flames, but instead rather enjoy the stench and the wretchedness that surrounds them; sinning made them happy in life and it makes them happy in the afterlife as well. The stench in hell is stupendous, but as everything is to be taken allegorically, this miasma is spiritual.

Correspondingly, the heavens are also constructed in a complex hierarchal manner. The angels, who are simply former people, are sorted by their ability to love God and to completely deny self-love—that is, to rid themselves of hubris, and not take credit for anything. They are further sorted by interests. The "celestial angels," the heavenly elite, engage in exquisite intellectual discussions; the lower angels aren't interested, nor able to participate, and should they happen to approach a VIP, so to speak, they would begin to feel suffocated by these discussions and find relief in returning to their accustomed level.

The realm of the spirits is situated between those of the heavens and the hells; its inhabitants, depending on how they stack up vis-à-vis God, grace, and divine truth, have a chance to migrate either up or down. But, once again, wherever they end up they don't suffer, each one settling where their heart desires. The heavens are insufferable and stifling to sinners— sinners don't require goodness, so they don't envy it. Similarly, the saints aren't jealous of those highest angels from the third-innermost layer of the heavens; supreme levels of love for God aren't open to them, they are simply out of their reach.

The closer to God, the more interior the heavens are. First and foremost, to achieve the highest place in the celestial hierarchy, man must believe in divine nature, and believe that all goodness and truth come from it, all wisdom and comprehension; he must desire to be ruled by it. That's when the aforementioned allegories, or correspondences, will show themselves in all their glory: a supreme angel and believer will feel himself to be living in a palace of indescribable beauty, walking among trees and flowers that are likewise indescribable. All of Sweden-borg's attempts at finding words to depict such flora resulted in jewelry clichés: "golden tree trunks," "silver leaves"—you'd expect more from a professor of mineralogy, let alone from God.

The only condition for redemption is the voluntarily man-datory, so to speak, cooperation with God, for God compels no one. He only makes an offer. But if man refuses this offer, God will turn away from him. All the heavens together constitute one man. It's clear now why the New Jerusalem is the New Heaven: obviously, feeble present-day humans are worthless, their faith is hypocritical, just for show while they wallow in sin. It's time for a change.

In general, Swedenborg's treatise is frightfully dull and righteous. Some life is breathed into it by certain not-so-incidental particulars of arrangements in the heavenly kingdom; for instance, the angels can marry, and not necessarily their earthly spouses, but lady friends who suit their tastes; love, however, exists only in matrimony and there's no funny business. For what joy is there in realizing that your faithful wife is merely an allegory, just like your desk, or a palace sparkling with precious stones, or flower beds every color of the rainbow? As far as Protestantism goes, Swedenborg's vision/treatise presents some heresy, but of the virtuous kind: Calvin, Luther, and Melanch-thon all taught justification and salvation by faith alone (*sola fide*), but Swedenborg gently insists that, no, it's not enough. You need good works, you need mercy. He was a lovely old man, kind and modest. In London, during the days of his noc-turnal visions, he'd often order meat dishes sent up to his room, only to return them untouched. He would explain to the pro-prietor of the inn that these had been ordered for the spirits visiting him to chat. They didn't eat anything, but they did inhale the pot roast aroma with great pleasure.

Out of modesty, and a fear of becoming famous, lest he find himself enjoying that fame, and thus becoming proud and arrogant, he initially published his works anonymously, as mentioned; but he was found out, and soon members of Swedish society started going on excursions to gawk at him. He had a house, and a garden with mirrors placed at the intersections of the paths in such a way that you could see all the flowers of all the allées at once—how sweet! He also played the organ and gave his guests raisins as treats.

He was adored by the nobility and by the king. (Here one should probably note—just for purposes of edification—that in Sweden, the king and the nobles traditionally belonged to different parties. The king was supported by the peasantry, while the nobles restrained any absolutist impulses of his by means of the parliament.) They viewed Swedenborg as a harmless loon. This is noteworthy: Grandpa was a heretic, he'd lost his mind—imagined himself to be a prophet, conversed with spirits—and yet no one buried him alive, no one burned him at the stake, no one chased him barefoot and in chains north of the Arctic Circle. In a letter, one distinguished gentleman, writing to another, details the heretical eccentricities of the elderly professor: allegedly the apostles visit him, and angels move his quill as he writes. And he urges: Let's stifle a smile, let's not hurt the old man's feelings. Whoa! "Stifle a smile"? Not "Let's rip his nostrils and whip him"? Yet Swedenborg still accuses the Swedes of depravity! "As a nation, the Swedes are the worst of Europe, after the Italians and the Russians," he writes.

We're biased by the familiar imagery from the Middle East: we expect a prophet to be woolly haired and dusty footed, in torn rags and with no sense of humor; the rich and famous can expect only rudeness and threats from him. Emanuel Swedenborg, on the other hand, was pleasant to all, a respected member of society despite his prophetic peculiarities. For his scientific endeavors he received a title and the surname Swedenborg (his father's name had been simply Swedberg). A rich man, he insisted, can enter God's kingdom just as easily as a pauper; the most important thing is love for God, *blah blah blah,* you know the rest. A pagan can be better than a Christian. Africans are closer to God than civilized Europeans, being more simpleminded and kind. Unbaptized infants aren't guilty of anything and so they will reach heaven with the right schooling. If ancient prophets subsisted on locusts and wild honey, occasionally afflicting themselves with hunger and thirst, our guy drank tea and supersweet coffee with pastries, and he loved almonds, raisins, and chocolate. After God had scared the bejezus out of him at that London inn, he never again touched meat, but he did not deprive himself of sweets. For social outings, he favored a lavender-hued velvet jacket, paired with a vest of black silk and shoes with gold buckles. His face was pale, his mouth wide.

All of the aforementioned eccentricities, excluding the sartorial, are of course well attested in the medical literature.

> The hallucinatory form of paranoid schizophrenia results in delusions, in isolated auditory hallucinations such as hollers and cursing addressed to the patient with the subsequent development of full-blown auditory verbal hallucinosis with "running commentary." "Sudden insight," anxiety, fear, hearing voices—commanding or

prohibiting. . . . Patients begin reporting unusual abilities to read other people's thoughts and to affect their well-being. . . . Delusions of fantastical grandeur, typical of paraphrenia, emerge, their substance absurd: patients insist that they are extraordinary beings, tasked with extraordinary missions, that they can change the fate of others and of the universe; they may experience olfactory and gustatory hallucinations. The patient is convinced that he is in two places at once . . .

Reading Swedenborg's biography as well as his own writings is akin to leafing through a psychiatry textbook. Visiting any Internet forum devoted to paranoid schizophrenia, one reads of the same feelings and experiences.

No pseudo-theories can convince me that these are my own thoughts. This was an intrusion from the outside, a possession. Call them whatever you want—demons, aliens, spirits. But I guarantee that this type of being flees from a strong concentration of grace. Two days ago I decided to get anointed, and I don't know if this is the right medical term, but right away it was as if I fell into sleep paralysis that same night. Some scum must have grabbed me by the throat. But I've already gotten the hang of chasing them away in my sleep with prayer.

Swedenborg's maidservant told this story: "One time, when I walked into his room, I noticed that his eyes were burning like a flame. I got scared and said:

" 'For God's sake, what is the matter, why are you looking like that?'

" 'What's so unusual about the way I'm looking?'

"I told him.

" 'I see, all right. Don't be frightened. God has fashioned my eyes in such a way so the spirits can see everything that is happening in this world.' "

This was the eighteenth century. In the nineteenth century, the police would beam electricity at patients; in the twentieth century, patients could feel themselves being irradiated with lasers; and now, in the twenty-first century, it's the KGB or the CIA implanting chips in their heads for the purpose of using their eyes to scan secret documents as well as sending them lecherous thoughts and compelling them to shoplift. Swedenborg felt similar urges: he noted with regret that he felt a compulsion to steal whenever inside a shop, that there was no refuge from his lecherous thoughts about "the Sirens."

All this would have been a local historical curiosity, or just another medical case, were it not for Swedenborg's remarkable visions. Angels and spirits informed him of things he couldn't otherwise have known; those incidents that could be verified are still inexplicable.

The most famous happened in 1759, during a merchant dinner party that Swedenborg attended in the company of several witnesses. It was in Göttborg, about two hundred and fifty miles from Stockholm. Swedenborg excused himself from the table and walked out into the garden, as he often did, to speak to his angel. He came back extremely agitated: "Ladies and gentlemen, there is a fire raging in Stockholm! It's moving toward the port warehouses!" The merchants became alarmed: they all had property there, but they didn't know what they could do, or whether they should even believe him. Throughout the evening, Swedenborg continued going into the garden, each time returning to announce the latest building engulfed by the fire, and which ones were still standing. Finally he returned in a calmer state: "Praise the Lord! The fire has been extinguished; it stopped three doors away from my house."

When, two days later, messengers rode in from Stockholm, they confirmed everything: it was exactly as Swedenborg had described. This inexplicable knowledge caused quite a stir in Swedish society. There couldn't have been any trickery here. Immanuel Kant, a contemporary of Swedenborg's and his near-namesake, was rather intrigued and asked around about him.

Another surprise involved Madame de Marteville, widow of the Dutch ambassador to Sweden. Shortly before his passing, the ambassador ordered a large and expensive silver service. After the ambassador's death, the goldsmith came to the widow and claimed that the bill had never been paid. The widow knew for sure that it had been settled, but she could not find the receipt. The swindler was demanding payment or the return of the silver set—forsooth, only the Italians and the Russians are worse than the Swedes!—and so Madame de Marteville came to Swedenborg with a plea: Since you can speak to the spirits, would you inquire of my deceased husband where the receipt might be?

After a few days, the medium informed the widow that he had spoken to her husband, who said he'd "take care of it personally." A week later, the deceased appeared in the widow's dreams and, by her account, said the following: "My child, I have heard of your troubles. Don't fret, go to the bureau upstairs and pull out the top drawer. You will find the receipt behind it." The widow woke up, ran to the dresser, and—miracle of miracles!—she found the receipt, as well as a hairpin set with diamonds, which she had also thought to be lost.

The third episode involved Queen Louisa Ulrika of Sweden. At a social gathering, she jokingly asked Swedenborg whether he had come across her brother, the Prussian prince, in the afterworld. No, he hadn't. Well, if you do, tell him I said hi. A week later, Swedenborg came to the queen as she was playing cards with her ladies-in-waiting and asked to speak to her privately. You may speak freely, the queen said; but the clairvoyant insisted that the matter was personal. So they repaired to an adjoining hall, a count by the name of Schwerin standing guard at the door and observing everything. Nobody knows exactly what message the deceased had conveyed to Swedenborg for the queen, but upon hearing it she "grew pale and exclaimed: Only he could have known that!" Schwerin immediately told anyone who would listen. This story was nothing to sneeze at, and, once again, it generated a lot of buzz in Swedish society, for the queen was already mistrusted and suspected of plotting for the benefit of Prussia. Specifically, while her brother was alive, she and he were believed to be exchanging letters hatching a plan to undermine the Swedish parliamentary system.

These three occurrences were well documented and confirmed, but there were countless other reports, varying in credibility, of Swedenborg's clairvoyance. For instance, somebody claimed that during a dinner they shared, the seer suddenly shuddered and said: "At this moment in Russia, Peter III has just been strangled; mark the day and time, you will be reading about it in the papers!" It's hard to know how reliable this account is, since nobody else confirmed it.

Another time, during a walk in the park, Swedenborg supposedly informed some count that the recently deceased Elizabeth Petrovna, Empress of Russia, had married the grandfather of this count in the afterworld, and that they were very happy together. How could you verify something like that? Notice, he only soothsaid about nobles, kings, tsars, and celebrities. Such was his quirk. He didn't soothsay about just anyone.

By the end of the winter of 1772, John Wesley, the founder of Methodism, had received an invitation from Swedenborg. Up in the heavens, wrote the clairvoyant, I was told that you very much want to meet me. Wesley, who indeed wished to meet Swedenborg, wrote back that he was very busy for the moment, but that he would love to pay a visit in six months' time, to which Swedenborg replied: "No, in six months' time I'll be dead. I will die on the 29th of March."

And he really did die on March 29, "with great joy," according to his household staff.

Three wishes are usually granted a hero, according to fairy-tale convention, and he foolishly wastes them. So it was with our professor of mineralogy and anatomy, philosophy and chemistry, geology and mathematics, the soothsayer and medium. He was granted a gift both extraordinary and unheard of, and how did he use his miraculous powers? Helping out a widow missing a receipt, acting as a messenger for the queen, expressing anxiety about a fire. And who should care about a fire when two years earlier the Day of Judgment had come, bringing with it new heavens and a new earth? At that point let it all burn, wouldn't you say? But no. He kept it civilized, polite, careful, bland. "I received a letter stating that in two months no more than four of my books were sold, and this was conveyed to the angels. They were surprised."

How unmysterious.

But then, what should we expect? What should we want to have happened? And how? There is a saying: "Why is it that when I speak to God, it's a prayer, and when God speaks to me, it's schizophrenia?" But what if schizophrenia is truly one of the ways God or his messengers use to communicate with us? Epileptics before a seizure can, for an instant, perceive the meaning of everything, the mystery of Creation is open to them—but then the seizure wipes out any memory of this new knowledge, leaving the epileptic with nothing but wet pants and a bitten tongue. Autistic people can see mathematical fields where giant numbers and square roots grow like beautiful flowers. Convulsions of the temporal lobe bring about visions of cities in the sky—magical four-cornered fortresses—but how do we know they are not real? What if they're actually there, but to see them one needs to have a seizure? The human body is only one side of the coin, but as we know, one-sided coins don't exist. There is always a reverse, and ours is the spirit.

Perhaps Emanuel Swedenborg, a kind, hardworking man, was privy to these otherworldly mysteries, revealed according to his abilities, his understanding, and his inquiries. Maybe they'll be opened up to another person in a different way: to an anxious one, they'll appear as fiery squares; to an innocent, as still waters; to an angry person, as ripped spirals. In the Lord's house there are many mansions; He decides, He bestows, He embraces.

The Window

Shulgin often stopped by his neighbor's apartment to play backgammon—at least once a week, sometimes twice.

It's a simple game, not as sophisticated as chess, but engrossing nonetheless. At first Shulgin was a bit embarrassed about that, as far as he was concerned only the Kebabs played backgammon—shesh-besh, lavash-shashlik—but then he got used to it. His neighbor Valery Frolov was a purebred Slav, not some fruit vendor.

They'd brew coffee nice and proper, just like the intelligentsia: in a Turkish *cezve*, letting it simmer so the foam would curl as it rose. They'd repair to the playing board. They'd chat.

"You think they'll impeach Kasyanov?"

"They might."

With each visit, Shulgin would notice yet another new item in Frolov's apartment. An electric tea kettle. Barbecue skewers, one set. A cordless phone in the shape of a woman's shoe, red. A jumbo grandfather clock, Gzhel ceramic. Beautiful but useless things. The clock, for instance, took up half the room but didn't work.

Shulgin would ask: "Is that new?"

And Frolov: "Yeah . . . I mean . . ."

Shulgin would remark: "Wasn't your TV smaller last time?"

And Frolov: "It's just a TV, nothing special."

213

Once, an entire corner of Frolov's living room was littered with cardboard boxes. While his friend was making more coffee, Shulgin peeled one of the boxes open to peek: seemed to be ladies' clothing, pleather.

And then on Tuesday he looked around and, *bam,* right where a cupboard used to be there was now an archway leading to a new room. There had never been a room there before. And there couldn't have been—the building didn't extend that far. Around the archway, a plastic ivy garland was nailed to the wall.

Shulgin couldn't take it anymore. "Now, be so kind as to explain yourself. How is there a new room there? Beyond where the building ends?"

Frolov sighed, seemingly chagrined. "Okay, fine. . . . There is this place. A window . . . That's where they hand all this out. Free of charge."

"Stop bullshitting, there is no such thing."

"No such thing, and yet they do. You know, just like on TV: 'Behind door number one' or 'A surprise giveaway!' Do people pay for the stuff that's given away? No, they don't. But the show still makes money somehow."

Frolov kept changing the subject, but Shulgin wouldn't let up. "Where is this window?" He couldn't get over that extra room. He had a studio apartment, didn't he, had to keep his skis in his bathtub. Frolov's attempts to obfuscate only resulted in Shulgin's further discontent, leading to four losses in a row—and who wants that kind of backgammon partner? The jig was up.

"Fine. First and foremost," Frolov instructed, "when they yell out, let's say, 'Coffee grinder!' you just have to yell back 'Deal!' This is of the utmost importance. Don't forget and don't mess up."

Shulgin took the bus there first thing in the morning. It was a typical Soviet building complex from the outside, the kind that usually housed auto body shops and factory offices. Right turn, left turn, another left, and into building number 5, oil and gears all over the place. Surly men in overalls running here and there. Frolov must have lied to him, Shulgin was peeved to realize. But as he was already there, he went and found the hallway anyway, and the window—nothing special, a deep casement in a wooden frame, exactly like the one where Shulgin picked up his salary. He knocked.

The shutters swung open, but there was no one there, only a wall of bureaucratic green and depressing fluorescent lighting.

"A package!" they yelled from within.

"Deal!" Shulgin yelled back.

Someone, he couldn't see who, threw him a package. Shulgin grabbed the brown bundle and ran off to the side, feeling temporarily deaf in his agitation. Finally the feeling subsided. He looked around—people walking to and fro, but not one approaching the window, not one showing any interest in it. Idiots!

He took the package home, placed it on the kitchen table, and only then did he cut the string with scissors and tear off the wax seals. He gingerly unfolded the kraft paper and discovered four hamburger patties.

Shulgin felt ill used: Frolov had pulled a fast one on him. He marched straight into their building hallway and angrily rang his neighbor's doorbell. Hard. No answer. Shulgin stood there for a bit, then went outside and reexamined the back of the building where Frolov's extra room had appeared. Everything looked exactly as it always had. So how could that room with the archway fit there?

Frolov resurfaced later that evening. They played backgammon again.

"Did you go?"

"I did."

"They give you something?"

"They gave me something."

"Nothing good?"

"Nothing good."

"You'll get more next time. Just be sure to yell 'Deal!' "

"And what if I don't?"

"Then they won't give you anything."

And so Shulgin went back, once again making his way through discarded tires, barrels, and broken containers, a right turn and then a left and another left to building number 5. And once again no one but he showed any interest in the window. He knocked, the shutters opened.

"*Valenki!*" they yelled from the window.

"Deal!" he yelled back with disappointment.

Someone threw him a pair of short gray felt boots. Shulgin examined them—"What the devil is this, what do I need these for?" He took a few steps away from the window and shoved the *valenki* in a trash can. Nobody saw him do it. He walked up to the window again and knocked, but the shutters didn't open this time.

He didn't feel like venturing to the window the next day but didn't feel like staying in, either. He went outside and examined the back of their building once more. It was already covered in scaffolding; a few dark-haired builders were hard at work.

Too many Turks, thought Shulgin.

This time there was a long line at the window, and his heart even skipped a beat: What if there wasn't enough left for him? The line moved ever so slowly; there seemed to be complications and delays, and someone, it appeared, was trying to argue and express dissatisfaction—Shulgin couldn't see above all those heads. Finally he arrived at the shutters.

"Flowers!" they yelled from inside.

"Deal!" fumed Shulgin.

He didn't throw them away despite itching to do so. He was haunted by a nebulous suspicion that today's long lines, tumult, and lost time were punishment for yesterday's uncouth behavior with the *valenki*. After all, he was getting all this stuff for free, although he wasn't sure why. Even so, others were getting big boxes wrapped in white paper. Some even came with handcarts.

Maybe I should get myself a hot dog, thought Shulgin. But his hands weren't free, and you really need both extremities to avoid getting ketchup stains on your suit. Shulgin glanced at the sausage lady—she was cute!—and handed her the flowers.

"For you, beautiful lady, in honor of your heavenly eyes."

"Oh, how wonderful!" she replied happily.

They chatted and chatted and, come evening, after work, Oksana and Shulgin were already on a date, promenading in the streets of Moscow. They talked about how beautiful their city had become, and how very expensive. Not to worry, thought Shulgin. If things go well, tomorrow morning maybe we'll have a Gzhel ceramic set, like normal, decent folk. After dusk, they made out for a long while in the Alexander Gardens by the grotto, and Shulgin returned home reluctantly: he really liked Oksana.

§

"An iron!" came from the window.

"Deal!" happily responded Shulgin.

Finally! They had moved on to appliances; all he needed now was patience. Shulgin put up a shelf at home and kept his new acquisitions there. He was already the proud owner of an enameled milk can, a pair of oven mitts, a coffee service set, a 2-in-1 shampoo, a can of Atlantic herring, two pounds of pale-pink angora wool, an adjustable wrench set, two lined notebooks, an Arabic ottoman with Nefertiti appliqués, a rubber bath mat, a book by V. Novikov entitled *Russian Parody* and another book in a foreign language, a refill of lighter fluid, a paper icon of the healer Saint Panteleimon, a set of red ballpoint pens, and some rolls of film. Life had taught Shulgin to not refuse anything, and so he didn't. They handed out wooden planks and half logs—he took them and put them in the bathtub with the skis. Maybe they'd give him a dacha and then the half logs would come in handy!

Frolov would occasionally run into Shulgin in the stairwell and ask why he hadn't been coming over for backgammon, but Shulgin would explain that he was in love and about to get married—life was good! He did stop by once out of politeness and they played a few rounds, but Shulgin was unpleasantly surprised to see a TV set in every room—one was a flat-screen, like you see in the commercials, but mounted to the ceiling. Frolov didn't invite him into the room with the archway and it was fairly obvious why: it was no longer one room but several, the enfilade stretching far and deep into a space where it couldn't possibly exist.

After the iron there truly was a qualitative leap: Shulgin started getting mixers, blenders, room fans, coffee grinders, even a charcoal grill, and then, probably by mistake, a second one, of the exact same kind. The gifts kept growing in size and he felt that it was probably time to start bringing a handcart. He was right: next he got a microwave oven. His only disappointment was that everything the window was doling out had been made in China, rarely in Japan. As the wedding drew near, Shulgin harbored secret hopes of the window people realizing that he needed a gold ring for his bride and a wedding reception at a restaurant, but they didn't, and on the day of his wedding he got an electric drill.

Shulgin didn't tell Oksana about the window, he liked being mysterious and omnipotent. At first she was delighted about the many wonderful things that they owned, but then there was simply no room left for storing the boxes. Shulgin tried skipping a few days, avoiding the window, but the next time he went he got a set of wineglasses: clearly a step backwards. Stemware was once again handed out the following day. For a week he was a bundle of nerves until, finally, they were back to things with cables—first the cables themselves, extension cords and the like, but then eventually the objects attached to the cables. Not that he could avoid punishment altogether—the window, without warning, issued an electric wok made for foreign voltage, but no transformer. Of course the wok was ruined, amid the awful burning stench, and the fuses were blown out. The window held its grudge for a few more days, slipping out one thing after another not meant for our electric grid. One item even had a triangular Australian plug. But Shulgin knowing better now, accepted everything humbly and obediently; he'd yell "Deal!" as remorsefully as he could, trying to show that he recognized his mistake and that he was willing to change. He knew what was waiting for him and the window did, too.

When Oksana went off to the maternity ward, Shulgin got a simple white envelope. He tore it open immediately, and sure enough, a handwritten note inside said in block letters: "199 square feet." After he'd rushed home in a cab, at first his heart sank: his apartment looked exactly the same. But then he noticed what seemed to be the contour of a doorway, right under the wallpaper. He picked at the plaster—indeed, there was a door, and behind it a room—199 square feet, as promised. Shulgin jumped for joy, hitting his left palm with his right fist while yelling "Yes!" and dancing around the room, as if performing the Lezginka.

If you think about it, there was no room for this wonderful addition—in that same exact spot was the neighbor's apartment, inhabited by one Naila Muhummedovna. Shulgin apprehensively stopped by for a visit—allegedly to borrow some matches. Everything was fine; Naila Muhummedovna was making dumplings, as always. He went back to his place—the room was still there, smelling of wet plaster. The wallpaper was uninspiring, but that was easy enough to change.

Oskana came home with an adorable little girl, whom they both immediately named Kira. Shulgin told Oksana that the new room was a surprise for her; that it had always been there behind the wallpaper. And Oksana said that he was simply the best, the most thoughtful man, absolutely wonderful. Also, that they now need a stroller for Kira. Shulgin zoomed off to the window, but instead of a stroller was granted a six-burner gas grill—the kind usually used at dachas, with two red gas canisters. "But I don't have a dacha," muttered Shulgin to the closed shutters. "I do have a newborn baby. . . ." The window was silent. Shulgin waited around for a bit, then waited some more, but what was there left to do? He dragged the gas grill home. "You shouldn't have done that," said Oksana. "I asked for a stroller." "Tomorrow!" promised Shulgin, but tomorrow brought something even more ludicrous—a full set of parts for a mini-boiler, complete with pipes, gaskets, and valves.

Things weren't going well for him; when he rang Frolov's doorbell, his neighbor didn't immediately open—it must have taken him that long to walk through all his endless rooms to the front door.

"Take my mini-boiler!" pleaded Shulgin.

"I won't."

"Then take one of my grills. Or both."

"No, I won't take the grills, either."

"Frolov, I'm giving it to you for free!"

"There is no such thing as 'free,'" answered Frolov, and Shulgin could see that his neighbor's eyes were dimmed with unhappiness, that behind him in the endless enfilade of rooms were TVs and more TVs—on the floor, on the ceiling, and others more still in their boxes.

"But you said that there was!"

"I didn't. I said they were handing things out 'free of charge.' There's a big difference."

"Okay, fine. . . . Can you buy this mini-boiler, then?"

"Where would I get that kind of money?" Frolov sighed.

Shulgin also didn't have any money, only things. What else could he do, he took the boiler to the Savelovsky trading complex, and there, the only buyer he could find—after much haggling and for a third of its value—was one of those gloomy Kebabs.

Can't they just stay in their sunny Shesh-besh-abad? Why do they need to come here anyway? thought Shulgin. He used the money to buy Kira a stroller, the most expensive and beautiful one there was, with pink ruffles. On the next day, the window handed him an envelope, and there, on graph paper, a hand written note: "Minus ten." Shulgin broke out in a cold sweat, terrified: What is this—this "minus" business? Once home, he grew even more alarmed: Oksana relayed to him, through her tears, how, in a corner in the new room, the plaster from the ceiling had come crashing down, scaring everybody, but thankfully not falling on the stroller with Kira in it! And wouldn't you know it, ten square feet of plaster—exactly—had fallen down, the cement peeking through. They cleaned up the mess, but that night a strange rustling was heard. Shulgin jumped up to look—but no, nothing fell. It was simply the walls closing in to make the room a little smaller.

He grew suspicious, his wheels turning.

"You didn't throw anything away yesterday, did you?" he asked Oksana.

"Just some logs from the bathtub. Why?"

"Please don't throw anything else away," said Shulgin.

"But they were crooked and useless!"

"You don't know what you're talking about, woman."

Of course, he didn't know what he was talking about, either, and he couldn't figure why his living quarters have been made smaller: Was it the mini-boiler or the half logs? What were the rules here? Maybe it's like backgammon? You make a wrong move and voilà, you can't get rid of any of your checkers? And Frolov: How did he play? Why was his apartment endlessly getting bigger and bigger, why was it packed with TV sets?

For two months following, things were boring and dull, but safe: he went to the window as if it were his job; there, random crap was meted out—baby powder, paper clips, a bland white Polar Bear waffle cake, homeopathic pellets for an unspecified illness, pots with seedlings. All of it took up space. Shulgin behaved, he kept everything, until he was finally rewarded with an envelope containing a note: "270 square feet, with balcony." It all worked the same as last time, the only difference being that Oksana herself now found the door, which was obscured by the wallpaper, and by the time Shulgin came home she had already moved the Nefertiti ottoman, along with a table and two armchairs, into their new room.

"Perhaps there are other surprises hidden beneath the wall-paper?" rejoiced Oksana.

"Perhaps . . . but not all at once," responded Shulgin, play-fully slapping her on the ass and mentally calculating that they had already swallowed up the entire expanse of Naila Muhummedovna's apartment and were now extending into the space where the Bearshagsky kitchen was. But neither Naila Muhummedovna nor the Bearshagskys were complaining.

Another week went by with Shulgin receiving things both necessary and unnecessary, and then something dreadful happened: they were invited to a birthday party at a dacha. Oksana mused and debated aloud, trying to decide which gift was best, Obsession eau de toilette or a tie; subsequently Shulgin's guard was down. Upon getting out of the cab, however, he finally noticed his wife dragging a big white box, and his heart stopped.

"What's that?"

"A charcoal grill."

"Did you buy it?"

"No, it's one of ours. We have two of them, remember?"

"What have you done?! We have to take it back right this minute!"

But it was too late: their cab, having made a U-turn, had already left, and the birthday boy had already come out from the gate to greet and joyfully thank them for such a thought-ful gift. Shulgin couldn't eat a single bite of his shashlik; he was worried sick about what the window would think about this, how it would punish him. Oksana also looked crestfallen: she must have incorrectly concluded Shulgin was just greedy, a dog in the manger. Once home later that night, Shulgin ran to check—had the walls moved, and what about the ceilings, was the balcony still there, what was going on with the fridge and the stove?—misfortune could come from anywhere. He inspected the fuse box, looked under the beds, and counted the appliances and the unopened boxes stuffed with unnecessary things imposed on him by the window. Counting was easier said than done: there were boxes up to the ceiling filling all three rooms; in the hallways you had to squeeze by sideways. But everything looked to be okay until his mother-in-law, who had taken Kira for the weekend, called to say that the child had a high fever, she was burning up.

"This, this is all your doing! That's what you get for the grill!" Shulgin yelled at Oksana.

"Are you nuts?" Oksana broke into tears.

"Don't touch my kid! You hear me? Don't you dare touch my kid!" yelled Shulgin into thin air, shaking his fists.

By morning, Kira's fever was down, and Shulgin—enraged and resolute—marched over to the window to hash this out mano a mano: What the hell is this shit? The window issued a pair of *valenki,* just as at the dawn of their liaison.

"What's this supposed to mean?" Shulgin demanded angrily, banging the closed shutters with his fist. "Hey! I'm talking to you!" The window was silent. "Answer when people are talking to you!" *Silenzio.* "Don't say I didn't warn you!" blustered Shulgin.

At home, he cooled down a bit and started contemplating his next steps. Things weren't looking good. On the one hand, the unseen evil forces behind the window were daily handing out gifts—perhaps not of the highest quality, but quite decent nonetheless. In the span of just eighteen months, Shulgin had accumulated enough to open up his own store. But on the other hand—and here was the catch—the window wouldn't allow you to sell anything. Wouldn't let you sell anything, wouldn't let you give away anything, wouldn't let you throw out anything. It was a totalitarian regime, thought Shulgin bitterly, absolute control and no free market. Then again, it wasn't totally inhumane—once the apartment became so full it was close to bursting, the window did thoughtfully expand your living quarters. In Frolov's case, they seemed to be expanding ad infinitum. Be that as it may, who needs all this square footage, even with a balcony, if you can't do with it as you please?

Maybe I should privatize it? considered Shulgin.

"What do you think about privatization?" he shouted to Frolov. His friend was silent; perhaps he couldn't hear him. It wasn't at all comfortable playing or even just sitting in Frolov's apartment anymore—there were railroad tracks everywhere, mine trolleys were zooming every which way, knocking over backgammon pieces and coffee mugs—the racket was insufferable and so was the smell. TVs now continuously covered all of the walls.

"What's all this?" shouted Shulgin over the noise, referring to the railroad traffic.

"I dunno. 'Siberia Aluminum,' they say."

"I thought Deripaska owned it."

"I think he's the majority shareholder."

Shulgin suddenly felt bad for Deripaska: if Deripaska decided to buy some more shares from Frolov for absolute happiness, he'd be shit out of luck. The window wouldn't allow it. But something was amiss, thought Shulgin—they'd started out at practically the same time, but now Frolov had an entire manufacturing plant, he was basically an oligarch. But all Shulgin had was a three-room apartment and a sausage-vendor wife. Imagine, social inequality and no free market. Take that, North Korea!

Oksana was planning to get a nanny for Kira in order to go back to work, so when the window shouted "Nanny for Kira," Shulgin hopped up—"Deal!"—and by the time he saw what was what, it was too late. The nanny came out of the window feet first, like a breech baby, and while the legs were making their way out, Shulgin began to realize the full scope of the impending disaster. She was around twenty, Playboy Bunny curves, tits from a sergeant's wet dream, dyed hair, pink lipstick, teeth playfully biting down on a blade of grass. She adjusted her miniskirt:

"Where's the kid?"

"I won't let you near her!" scowled Shulgin.

"And why not?"

"I need a stupid old hag, and not this . . . What the hell is this!"

"We'll grow old together! And I ain't that smart." She snorted with laughter.

"I have a wife at home!!"

"Oh, muffin, how sweet, he's got a wife!"

If we walk through the food market she'll get disoriented and lose her way, plotted Shulgin. But things didn't go as planned: the nanny held on tight, swayed her leather-clad hips, and loudly demanded he buy her black caviar and cherries.

Where is the Kebab mafia when you need 'em? Shulgin looked around dejectedly. Who's in charge of this market? The Azerbaijanis, I think? Or is it the Chechens? Where did they all go?!

They finally made it home, caviar and cherries in hand, passersby craning their necks—a disgrace for all to see.

"Break me off some lilacs for a bouquet, tiger," moaned the nanny.

Here's what I've got to do, he mused. Stop by Frolov's house, as if for a game of backgammon. And there, shove her into a trolley, pile on some of that aluminum he's got, and secure with a cover. And let her merrily roll along. It won't count as giving

her away—Shulgin mentally rationalized with the window—
it's simply a cruise! Yep, that's what it should count as. "Siberia,
Siberia, I'm not afraid of you, Siberia, Siberia, you're Russia
with a view," he purred softly.

Frolov's door was opened by members of indigenous peoples
of the Far North in fox-fur hats; they said the boss wasn't home.

"I'll wait." Shulgin tried to make his way inside, even though
it was rather unpleasant stepping on the snow. For that's what
everything was covered with—snow. The railroad tracks, the
backgammon table, the coffee service, all of it was a white tun-
dra, completely devoid of coziness: dim, with long rows of TVs,
icy plains with hummocks, and gas flares blazing on the horizon. A deer ran by to catch up with the herd.

"No way, José." The northern people shooed Shulgin away.

"I didn't ask you! Where did he go?"

"House of Representatives," the people answered, lying, no
doubt.

Still standing in front of the door just slammed on him, an
ordinary particleboard one with a peephole, Shulgin, of course,
didn't buy it. A faint smell of soup was emanating from the
cracks; a worn doormat lay before him. On the other hand,
anything is possible. If that was the case, he'd need to ask Frolov for a neighborly favor: maybe he could speed up the economic reforms to finally allow sale, exchange, and all that. Any
entry into the free market. It would be so convenient: whatever you don't need, you sell, and, using the money from the
transaction, you buy the stuff you do need. Don't they get it?
Look at Oksana with her hot dogs—she's free as a butterfly. But
meanwhile he's stuck with this craptastic floozy.

"Silly billy, at least I don't cost a thing!" sing-songed the
nanny.

"Drop dead!" howled Shulgin.

"Death won't separate us!"

Shulgin fumbled for his keys, pushed the nanny aside, ran in, slammed and locked the door. His heart pounding, he tried to catch his breath. He barricaded the entrance with a mattress and secured it with an unopened box of something labeled "Toshiba."

All night, the nanny pummeled the door, trying to get in. Oksana refused to listen to any explanations. Crying, she locked herself with Kira in the farthest, and, theoretically, nonexistent room. The nanny knocked on Shulgin's door, Shulgin on Oksana's, and the downstairs neighbors, angered by the noise, banged on the radiator with what sounded like a wrench. The lilac bushes swayed in the wind outside; in Frolov's universe, moss was freezing over beneath the snow and sled dogs were heard yapping in the distance. When dawn broke, Shulgin, exhausted from his sleepless night, squeezed past the boxes into the kitchen for a drink of water and saw that a new room, faint like an aspen bud in the spring, was beginning to form in the wall—it was clearly being readied for the nanny. So they wouldn't let him be, then. That was it. Do or die.

So he made a decision. Hesitated, and made it again.

Resolute, he marched off to the window—right turn, left turn, another left, and into building number 5—the nanny clinging to him and happily chirping all the way.

"One sick tricked-out ride!" swaggered the window.

"Sweeeet," egged on the nanny.

"No deal," a dignified Shulgin replied with pity.

"Oh, then it's my turn!" happily responded the window, and slammed the shutters.

They stood there, they knocked, but no answer. Shulgin turned around and walked back through the courtyard, stepping over the detritus and industrial debris.

"What the fuck? I'm in heels!" the chimera yelped like she owned him.

"Begone, strumpet!"

"How da—"

"Deal!" came a voice from somewhere, and the nanny disappeared, never having finished her sentence. Shulgin looked around—no nanny. Fantastic! A weight was lifted. On the way home he bought some carnations.

"What's this?" gloomily asked Oksana, holding Kira.

"Flowers."

"Deal!" came the answer from the faraway window and the bouquet disappeared, leaving Shulgin with a bent elbow and his fingers still angled around where the carnations had been. Something hissed in the kitchen behind Oksana's back.

"The coffee!" croaked Shulgin, his larynx contracting.

"Deal!" came from somewhere, and the coffee also disappeared, together with the *cezve* and the accompanying stain around the burner, making the stove look like new.

"Oh, the stove," whispered Shulgin.

"Deeeaal!" and the stove was no more.

Oksana got scared: "What's happening?"

"The window . . . ," Shulgin exhaled inaudibly, but *they* still heard him. The windows in his apartment vanished, dead walls appearing in their place, and all became dark, as before the beginning of time. Oksana let out a scream. Shulgin opened his mouth to comfort her with "Oksana! Oksanochka!" But having figured out the rules, he stayed silent.

He couldn't let the window have the next turn.

See the Reverse

A hot day in May in Ravenna, a small Italian town where Dante is buried. Once upon a time—in the beginning of the fifth century AD—the emperor Honorius moved the capital of the Western Roman Empire here. There used to be a port in Ravenna, but the sea has since receded greatly, its place taken by swamps, roses, dust, and grapes. Ravenna is famous for its mosaics; crowds of tourists go from church to church examining them with eyes glued to the ceiling, the faint glimmer of small multicolored tesserae up there, high, under twilit ogival arches. You can make something out, but not much. Glossy postcards give a better view, but it's too bright, too flat, too cheap-looking.

I'm feeling stuffy, dusty, and hot. There is upheaval in my soul. My father has died and I loved him so much! Way back, forty years ago, he passed this way, through Ravenna, and sent me a postcard of one of its famous mosaics. On the back there is a note, in pencil for some reason, maybe he was in a hurry: "My dear daughter! Never have I seen anything more beautiful (see the reverse)! Makes me want to cry! If only you were here! Your father!"

Every sentence is punctuated by these silly exclamation points—he was young, he was jolly, perhaps he'd had a bit of wine. I can picture him with his felt hat pushed back—

1950s style—tall, lean, handsome, cigarette between his white (and, at that point, still natural) teeth, tiny beads of sweat on his forehead, eyes shining happily behind the round spectacles. . . . The postcard—which he tossed into the mailbox, carelessly entrusting it to two unreliable postal services, the Italian and the Russian—bore an illustration of heaven. God is seated in a blindingly green, ever-vernal paradise, white sheep grazing around him. The two unreliable postal services rumpled and ruffled the postcard's edges, but no matter, it arrived, and you can still make out pretty much everything.

If heaven exists, then that's where my father is. Where else could he be? Even so, he's dead, dead and no longer writing me postcards with exclamation points, no longer sending me tidings from all corners of the earth: *I'm here, I love you, do you love me? Are you feeling happiness alongside me? Seeing the beauty that I am seeing? Hello to you! Here is a postcard! Here is a cheap, glossy photo—I was just here! It's beautiful! Oh, if only you could have joined me!*

He traveled the globe, and he liked what he saw.

And now, whenever possible, I follow in his footsteps, to the same cities that he visited, and I try to see them with his eyes, try to imagine him there, young, making a turn, walking up a staircase, leaning against an esplanade parapet with a cigarette between his lips. And here I am now, in Ravenna, that dusty, stifling town, exhausting as all tourist attractions are, crowds filling its narrow streets. It's a dead, stale, sweltering town with no place to sit. The Tomb of Dante, who was exiled from his native Florence. The Mausoleum of Theodoric. The Mausoleum of Galla Placidia, half sister of Honorius, the one who made Ravenna the capital of the Roman Empire. Fifteen centuries have passed. Everything has changed. It all got covered with dust; the mosaics crumbled. That which was important became unimportant; that which excited retreated into the sands. The sea itself retreated, and where happy green waves once splashed there is now a wasteland of dust, silence, and scorching-hot vineyards. Forty years back—a lifetime ago—my father walked here, laughing, squinting myopically, sitting down at street cafés, drinking wine, biting off a crust of pizza with his then-natural, strong teeth. A blue dimness would descend. At the edge of the table, in pencil, he'd write me hurried notes of his delight in and love of this world, punctuating indiscriminately with exclamation points.

A stifling, cloudy sky. It's hot, but you can't see the sun. It's dusty. The former seabed now surrounds the town as wide fecund fields; where crabs once swarmed, now donkeys roam; where kelp once undulated, now roses slumber. It's a graveyard, deserted; the streets of the once-magnificent capital are filled with disenchanted American ladies in pink T-shirts, dissatisfied that they have been lied to yet again by the tourist agency: everything in this Europe place is so tiny, so old! Fifteen centuries. Dante's Tomb. The Mausoleum of Galla Placidia. My father's grave. A naive green Eden on a crumpled postcard.

What amazed him so? I find the church in question, I look up—sure, something green, way up there, under the vaulted ceiling. White sheep on a green lawn. Ordinary lighting. The discordant hum of the tourist throng below. They point, they consult their guidebooks. In the such-and-such century, such-and-such school of art. It's the same everywhere. You can't even make out the particulars.

All Italian churches have a little box mounted to the wall—an additional service for those who are interested. If you deposit a coin—worth a quarter of a dollar—projectors perched high up, just below the ceiling, illuminate it for a few moments, flooding the tesserae with fresh white light. The colors get brighter.

You can make out the details. The crowd grows agitated, its murmur growing. All it takes is a quarter. After all, you did come from this far, you paid for the flight, for the train, the hotel, for the pizza and cold beverages, for the coffee. Are you really going to try to save a few cents now? But many do. They are displeased: they weren't forewarned. They expected to see heaven for free. A group of tourists lies in wait until somebody, profligate and impatient, drops a coin into the slot of this Italian rip-off machine—all Italians are swindlers, right?—so the projectors can light up, and, for a brief moment, insufficient for the human eye to register, heaven will become greener, the sheep more innocent, God more kind. The crowd's hum grows stronger . . . but the lights go out, and the murmur of disappointed tourists crescendos into rumbling protest, into greedy grumbles and frustrated whispers. And once again all is veiled in dusk.

I'm wandering from church to church with the crowds, listening to muffled multilingual voices that sound like breaking waves, swirling in the whirlpool of people; meaningless tired faces—just as meaningless as mine—flash by, eyeglasses glisten, guide pages rustle. I squeeze my way through the narrow doors of the churches, trying to push away those near me, trying, just as everyone else is, to find the best spot, trying not to get annoyed. If heaven exists, I say to myself, then I'll be entering it with a crowd just like this one, a crowd of sheeple—old, dimwitted, and a little bit greedy. For if heaven is not for us, then for whom? pray tell. Who are those others, the more exceptional and the noticeably better than us statistically average folks?

There aren't any; it's entirely possible that I'll have to wander the green pastures of heaven in a herd of American tourists unhappy about everything being so ancient and low. And if that is so, it means heaven is boring and awful—something that shouldn't be true. Heaven can only be fantastically splendid.

"Never have I seen anything more beautiful (see the reverse)!" Father wrote to me. I flip to the other side. A garden-variety paradise. What did he see that I can't see?

Together with the crowd I squeeze into a small building, about which the Russian traveler Pavel Muratov, living at the turn of the twentieth century, wrote this in his famous book *Images of Italy:*

The dark blue color of the ceiling at the Mausoleum of Galla Placidia is surprisingly and impossibly profound. Depending on how the light hits it, as it passes through the small windows, the blue, beautifully and unexpectedly, glistens with green, lilac, or crimson hues. And onto this background is superimposed the famous depiction of the Good Shepherd, sitting amongst a flock of snow-white sheep. Semicircles surrounding the windows are decorated with large ornaments of deer drinking from a spring. Garlands of leaves and berries spiral down low arches. The sight of their splendor makes you think that humanity has never been able to create a more artistic way of decorating church walls. And here, thanks to the tininess of the mausoleum chapel, the mosaic doesn't appear a thing of vanity and icy grandeur. The air blazing with a blue light, which surrounds the sarcophagus that used to hold the embalmed remains of the empress, is worthy of the dreams of those with an ardent religious imagination. Wasn't this also the aim, though by different means, of the artisans staining the glass of Gothic cathedrals?

fully navigating the wheelchair through the crowd, turns him around to roll him out of the mausoleum. People are gawking at them; it doesn't matter to him, and she must be used to it. The chair bounces on the cobblestones of the square, causing the man minor additional torment. It starts to rain, but immediately stops.

"See the reverse!" But there is nothing on the other side, only darkness, stuffiness, silence, irritation, doubt, gloom. On the other side is a time-worn depiction of something that was important a long time ago, but not for me. "Makes me want to cry!" wrote Father forty years ago about beauty (or perhaps about something bigger) that astounded him then; and now I feel like crying because he is no longer here, and I don't know where he went, all that's left of him is a mountain of papers. And this postcard of a green paradise, which I moved from novel to novel as a bookmark.

But what if that's not it at all, what if everything was predestined a long time ago, it all went according to plan, and came full circle only today? An unknown Byzantine artisan, inspired by his faith, imagined the beauty of God's garden. He depicted it to the best of his ability using his language, perhaps annoyed that he couldn't do it better. Centuries passed, my father came to Ravenna, looked up and saw that picture of Eden, bought a cheap replica, and sent it to me with love, fortifying it with exclamation marks—everyone chooses their own language. And had he never sent this to me, I would never have come here, would have never made my way to the dark chapel, would have never seen that blind man, never witnessed how, with a wave of his hand, wielding the blazing blue light on the reverse side of darkness, he illuminated the heavenly vestibule.

For we are just as blind—no, a thousand times blinder—as that old man in the wheelchair. The truth is whispered to us but we cover our ears, we are shown the truth but we turn away. We lack faith: we are afraid to believe because we are scared of being fooled. We are certain that we are in a crypt. We know for sure that there is nothing in the darkness. There couldn't be anything in the darkness.

I can see them disappearing down the narrow streets of this small, dead town, the woman pushing the wheelchair and telling him something, bringing herself close to the blind man's ear, faltering, probably, while trying to find the words that I'd never be able to find. He is laughing at something; she fixes his collar, pours some more coins into the box in his lap, and, walking into a café, she brings him a slice of pizza, which he consumes with gratitude, diligently and messily, fumbling in the dark for that invisible and magnificent sustenance.

Acknowledgments

My deepest gratitude to my lifelong agent, Andrew Wylie, and to Jacqueline Ko.

To my thoughtful and erudite editor George Andreou and his tireless editorial assistant Brenna McDuffie for their attention to every word.

To my dear translator Anya Migdal for re-creating my world in English, and to Alice and Anton for letting me borrow her.

To my beloved sons, Artemy and Alexei, for making me who I am today.

And last but certainly not least, to my eternal friend and sole advisor, Alexander Timofeevsky, for round-the-clock literary support.

The story "Aetherial Worlds" is dedicated to my friend John Shemyakin, with love.

A Note About the Author

Tatyana Tolstaya lives in Moscow. For twelve years, she was the co-host of *The School for Scandal,* a popular talk show on Russian television covering culture and politics. She is also a co-founder of a creative writing academy in Moscow. She has written for *The New York Review of Books* and *The New Yorker.* Five of her books, including her novel *The Slynx,* have been translated into English.

A Note on the Type

This book was set in Adobe Garamond. Designed for the Adobe Corporation by Robert Slimbach, the fonts are based on types first cut by Claude Garamond (ca. 1480–1561).

Typeset by Scribe, Philadelphia, Pennsylvania

*Printed and bound by Berryville Graphics,
Berryville, Virginia*

Designed by Michael Collica